Robert G. Barrett was raised in Sydney's Bondi where he worked mainly as a butcher. After thirty years he moved to Terrigal on the Central Coast of New South Wales. Robert has appeared in a number of films and TV commercials but prefers to concentrate on a career as a writer. He is the author of fifteen books, including *So What Do You Reckon?*, a collection of his columns for *People* magazine, *Mud Crab Boogie*, *Goodoo Goodoo*, and *Leaving Bondi*, his latest novel published by HarperCollins.

Visit Bob's official web site
and the home of Team Norton at:
www.robertgbarrett.com.au

THE WIND AND THE MONKEY

ROBERT G. BARRETT

HarperCollins*Publishers*

HarperCollins*Publishers*

First published in Australia in 1999
Reprinted in 2001, 2002
by HarperCollins*Publishers* Pty Limited
ABN 36 009 913 517
A member of the HarperCollins*Publishers* (Australia) Pty Limited Group
www.harpercollins.com.au

HarperCollins*Publishers*
25 Ryde Road, Pymble, Sydney, NSW 2073, Australia
31 View Road, Glenfield, Auckland 10, New Zealand
77–85 Fulham Palace Road, London, W6 8JB, United Kingdom
Hazelton Lanes, 55 Avenue Road, Suite 2900, Toronto, Ontario M5R 3L2
and 1995 Markham Road, Scarborough, Ontario M1B 5M8, Canada
10 East 53rd Street, New York NY 10022, USA

National Library of Australia Cataloguing-in-Publication data:

Barrett, Robert G.
    The wind and the monkey.
    ISBN 0 7322 6707 2
    I.Title
A823.3

Cover illustration by Brad Quinn
Cover design by Darian Causby, HarperCollins Design Studio
Printed and bound in Australia by Griffin Press on 50gsm Bulky News

7 6 5 4 3   02 03 04

ACKNOWLEDGMENTS

The author would like to thank the following people for their help in getting this book together:

Bob, Mick and Tina, Pro Dive, The Entrance, NSW.

Shannon White Commercial Dive Service.

Steve Sharpe, Newcastle and Port Stephens Game Fishing Club, Shoal Bay.

The management and staff, Marlin Hotel, Shoal Bay.

Jim and Gino, Kunara Charters, Nelson Bay.

The police at Nelson Bay.

Dale Berry — aka 'Issac'.

And all the good people I met while I was in Port Stephens. I only hope the descriptions in my book do justice to what has to be one of the most beautiful places in NSW.

DEDICATION

This book is dedicated to Don and Lois Linklater. Undersee Products Bondi. And to The White Water Wanderers.

A percentage of the royalties from this book is being donated to:

The Wombat Rescue and Research Project
Lot 4, Will-O-Wynn Valley
Murrays Run NSW 2325

Whether it was the offhand way Eddie Salita asked the question or just the casual way the question seemed to come out of nowhere, Norton wasn't quite sure. But there was just something about the question, that if it didn't quite make Les overly suspicious, it somehow managed to get the big, red-headed Queenslander's antenna up.

It was the Monday night of an ANZAC Day long weekend and the boys were all seated in Price Galese's office at the Kelly Club, having an after-work drink. Price was sitting at his desk, a vision of sartorial elegance in a grey suit and blue tie, sipping a Scotch and soda. Eddie was on his right in a black leather jacket and black jeans drinking Mount Franklin and ice, and on Price's left George Brennan was in a slightly crumpled blue suit and matching tie sipping Vodka with lemon and Hepburn Spa. Facing the others were Les Norton and Billy Dunne dressed in leather jackets and dark trousers, guzzling heartily on cold bottles of Eumundi Lager. They'd been there about an hour or so, talking and joking about different things, mainly funny incidents that had occurred in the

1

club, when the conversation seemed to momentarily lapse. That was when Eddie slipped the question in.

'Hey Les. Did you ever get your PADI?'

Norton shook his head. 'No.'

'How come?' asked Eddie.

'I don't know. I just lost interest,' replied Les.

Norton's attempt at getting his PADI, or scuba diving ticket, was a bit of a sore point with him actually. Being a keen snorkeller, he joined a dive class at Clovelly one summer with getting his PADI in mind. He ticked off all the questions and answers getting about sixty per cent of them right, then it was time to gear up for their first dive; five in the class plus the instructor. They got to Clovelly pool, where it was drizzling rain, unbearably humid and the water absolutely filthy. Les clambered into a two-piece, full-length, 5mm wetsuit with what seemed like enough equipment to land on the moon. A scuba tank, a BCD jacket with tubes and gauges hanging off it everywhere, his mask and snorkel, a lead belt big enough to anchor the HMAS *Parramatta* and a pair of flippers you could waterski on. His lead belt kept slipping to one side, along with his scuba tank. His mask and wetsuit were full of sweat and Les felt like he was suffocating. And even though he was only standing up to his waist in water he still couldn't see the bottom. So Norton, more or less politely, told the instructor to stick his dive class up his arse, got out of his gear, dumped it in the back of the dive truck and drove home happy to remain a common, or garden type snorkel sucker.

'Oh well,' nodded Eddie. 'It don't really matter that much, I suppose.'

'No. I don't suppose it does,' replied Les slowly, his antenna still up and rotating a little.

There was silence in the office for a moment or two, then Price spoke. 'Okay, now what's this about you wanting to take a week off from work? Just piss off and leave us all in the shit when we're busy.' The silvery-haired casino owner shook his head from over his glass of Scotch. 'God strike me, you're good. As if life isn't just one big holiday for you as it is.'

'Yeah, pig's arse,' replied Les. 'In fact I wouldn't mind a month off to tell you the truth. But a week'll do. I just want to get away for a while. Recharge my batteries.'

'Fair enough,' conceded Price. 'In fact you've been looking a bit ocean liner ever since you got back from Cooktown.' Price smiled round the room. 'I reckon the big bludger got up to something up there and he's not letting on. A bit of heavy tooling or something.'

Les shook his head. 'No. It was just the heat and all that driving. It's caught up on me.'

'Driving?' exclaimed George Brennan. 'What are you talking about, you cunt. You flew up and back — business class.'

'Yeah. But I had to drive to Cooktown. In the wet season.'

'Wet season?' George shook his head. 'I don't believe it.'

3

'So?' said Price, when George had finished. 'I suppose you've got plenty of money to blow on a holiday?'

'No.' Les shook his head emphatically. 'In fact I'm shorter than Toulouse-Lautrec's little brother at the moment.'

Price shook his head sadly. 'Shit! That's no good.' The casino boss looked at Les for a moment. 'I'll tell you what I'll do. How would you like a week at Shoal Bay?'

'Shoal Bay?' Norton's eyebrows knitted. 'Isn't that up in Port Stephens? The other side of Newcastle?'

'That's it,' nodded Price. 'My darling wife owns a block of units up there. There's one vacant at the moment, and it's all yours for a week if you want it. Twenty seconds from the beach. Two minutes from the pub. Fully self-contained and rent free. What do you reckon?'

Les looked at Price for a second or two. Norton had heard a few good things about Port Stephens and he'd always wanted to check the place out. He'd be a complete mug not to take up an offer like this. 'Okay Price,' he said. 'You've got me. Thanks a lot.'

'For you, Les, me old china plate, it's a pleasure.' Price smiled benevolently around the office. 'Fair dinkum. Am I a good boss or what?'

Les raised his bottle. 'You'll get no argument from me on that. Thanks again.'

'You'll like it up there,' said Eddie. 'It's the grouse. Good fishing. Beautiful beaches.'

4

'Yeah, I've heard a bit about it. Warren goes up there now and again.'

'I've just been up there for a few days myself,' said Eddie.

'You have?'

Eddie nodded. 'Yeah. In fact I might even go back and join you for a couple of days.'

'You what?' Norton's antenna started to rotate. 'Listen, hang on a second. When you go back somewhere and join people for a couple of days, certain citizens around that certain somewhere have a tendency to disappear. Never to be seen again.' Les turned to Price. 'Righto. What's going on? I should have known this was too bloody good to be true.'

'Bloody hell,' said Price. 'Talk about a suspicious, ungrateful bastard. I don't believe it.'

'Yeah, well I didn't quite come down on the back of a turnip truck from Dirranbandi last week,' said Les. 'Though I'm sure certain people in this room think I did.'

'Okay Eddie,' sighed Price. 'You tell him what's going on.'

'Thanks,' grunted Norton.

'Allright,' said Eddie. 'I'm going up there to get rid of a crooked cop. A detective.'

'Oh is that all.' Les gestured round the room with his beer. 'I mean, doesn't everybody go for a holiday and put a few bullets in a cop while they're doing nothing else? Go on, Eddie.'

'It's not quite like that, Les,' said the little hitman. 'In fact, what I got lined up is pretty cool. And anyway,

5

you don't have to put your head in if you don't want to. You're having a holiday.'

'Yeah, terrific.' Les went to the bar for another beer and got everybody else who wanted a drink one while he was there, then sat down again. 'So who's the lucky member of NSW's finest that's going ta-ta's? Am I allowed to know?'

George Brennan spoke. 'A low, dirty, miserable arse called Fishcake Fishbyrne.'

'That's right,' said Price. 'You know the prick.'

'Jack Fishbyrne. Yeah I know him,' nodded Les. 'I seen his rotten melon on TV a couple of times through the week.'

Through his job and whatever, Les had had the occasional run in with Detective Fishbyrne. The last time he saw Fishcake however was on the six o'clock news. The black and white video camera was hidden in the dashboard of the car and there was Fishbyrne receiving a nice fat roll of notes from another cop driving, who'd turned supergrass.

'That's him allright,' said Price.

'So what's Detective Fishbyrne done to deserve a couple of bullets in his fat, ugly scone?' asked Les.

George swallowed some more Vodka. 'He's off work on stress leave at the moment before he gets dragged in front of ICAC. The thing is he's got a bit of shit on Price and the rest of us that could go down rather nastily if it came to the pinch.'

'So he wants some money to keep his mouth shut?' said Les.

'That'd be our boy Fishcake,' said Billy Dunne, over his fresh bottle of Eumundi Lager.

'And I refuse to give the sour-faced, fat prick another zac,' said Price.

Les pointed with his bottle. 'Which, I imagine, is where young Edward comes in.'

'That's right,' said Eddie. 'But it's not like you think.' Eddie smiled a completely villainous smile. 'What I've got lined up is a ripper. It's foolproof. And you might even get to meet an old mate of ours again.'

'Terrific,' said Les. 'I can't wait.'

'Yeah, but like I said, you don't have to put your head in if you don't want to. I can handle it on my own allright.' Eddie gave Les a brief once up and down. 'In fact I'd probably be better off without you getting your big, fat arse in the road all the time.'

'Thanks.' Les swallowed some more beer. 'No Eddie. Seeing as I'm going to be up there I may as well hang around and make sure you don't fuck everything up.'

'Exactly mate,' smiled Eddie. 'And don't think for one moment I don't appreciate it.'

'That's the spirit,' said Price. 'What a guy.'

'Yeah, that's me,' said Les. 'Everybody's mate.'

George winked up from his Vodka. 'Hey. This'll be a good chance for you to flash up the freeway in that grouse new car of yours.'

'Yeah,' laughed Billy. 'The deceased estate.'

'Deceased estate.' Price had to laugh too. 'I love it when he tells people that's how he got it.'

'Well it was,' pleaded Les.

The car had belonged to a Lebanese drug dealer from the western suburbs. He was sitting in the back seat at Surry Hills counting some money, when two young gentlemen came up with automatic shotguns and fired twelve shots through each window spreading the drug dealer, his money and his heroin all over the back seat. Norton got onto the car through a young uniform cop who owed him a favour. The immediate family didn't want the car because it was considered unlucky, the police didn't need it any more for evidence and after sitting in the pound for some time with congealed blood and pieces of brain matter splattered all over the back seat it stank to high heaven and nobody in their right mind wanted it. Les was able to get it registered in his name then had it towed to Chicka's Garage where they went over it with a gurney and plenty of disinfectant and put new windows and a seat in the back. For not all that much money, Norton had a late-model, metallic green Holden Berlina that went like a shower of shit with the late owner's four-speaker stereo and amplifier in the boot.

Les was rather pleased with himself and apart from a small whiff of brain matter now and again on a hot day it was a bargain; and compared to the mighty Datsun it was like driving a Porsche Boxster. If anybody asked him how he got it so cheap Les told them it was from a deceased estate.

'And yes George,' said Les, finishing his beer, 'it will be a chance to go for a burble up the freeway to

Shoal Bay. Where, even though I look like being involved in murder most foul, once that's out of the road, it could be a nice relaxing holiday.'

'Good luck to you, Les,' said Price, raising his glass.

They talked and joked a bit longer. George gave Les an envelope with a brief letter for the estate agent at Shoal Bay plus a couple of weeks' wages and Eddie said he'd fill Les in on all the details of what was about to go down when he got up there on Thursday morning. But not to worry, it would all be sweet. A few more drinks went down and before long the night wasn't getting any younger. They locked up then George got a taxi to Balmain and the rest left in Price's Rolls with Eddie at the wheel. Billy got dropped off first then it was Norton's turn. He said goodnight to Price and told him he'd see him when he got back. Price wished him all the best. Eddie said he'd see Les on Thursday morning. Then Les waved them off as the Rolls did a sweeping U-turn before disappearing up Cox Avenue as he stepped inside his front door.

It wasn't a cold night and Les stripped straight off down to his jox and a clean T-shirt before making his way from the bathroom to the kitchen where a mug of warm Ovaltine had soon pinged out of the microwave into his hand. Warren was in Adelaide shooting a TV commercial for Beenleigh White Rum, so Les had the house to himself. He also had access to a case of Beenleigh Rum Warren had brought home from the advertising agency. But Les didn't feel like any more booze. It had been a fairly busy night at work, he was dog-tired and all Norton wanted to do was put his head down, mull a few things over that were on his mind for a minute or two then go to sleep. Before long Les was in bed with the light off staring up through the darkness at some shadows on the ceiling.

What should have been a quiet holiday on his own somewhere was now a week in Port Stephens helping Eddie with a murder. And a cop at that. It would have been nice to just have a quiet break. But knowing Eddie, everything would probably run smooth as a Swiss watch and once Eddie was gone he could relax and enjoy himself. From what Les could gather, Port Stephens was the place to do it. Funny him asking me if I had my PADI though. I wonder what that was all about. Oh well. There were other things on his mind, but it wasn't long before Norton's eyes were starting to flicker. About the last thing he remembered thinking was he'd take six bottles of Warren's rum with him which wasn't a bad drop mixed with pineapple juice; and maybe some of Warren's pot. A few short minutes later the big red-headed Queenslander was snoring peacefully.

It was almost nine the next morning when Les walked into the kitchen wearing his training gear and put the kettle on. Outside it wasn't a bad day — sunny with a few clouds around and warm enough to go down the beach and maybe hang around the surf club or the north corner and have a mag to whoever might be there. But Les figured seeing he was going to be involved in a bit of shifty business over the next few days, the less people he met for the time being, the better. So after a cup of tea and some toast, Les did a few stretches then jogged off the back way up past the Royal Hotel to tackle the steps at the bottom of Birrell Street. It was an ideal day for a run and while the exercise opened up his arteries and cleared his head, Les was able to think a few things over.

Since his return from Cooktown Norton didn't say much to anybody about what had happened. He left a message on Beryl's answering service, left her with the bills and didn't return her call. He also didn't bother to ring the Rainbow Princess and she didn't ring him. It was either in the stars or in the Runes. So let sleeping space cadets lie. He was talking to Taekwondo Kate, but that was about all. Her rah-rah brothers still hated him with a vengeance because Les was definitely 'NOOU'. Not one of us. And he actually came to a bit of push and shove with Steve at the Clovelly Hotel one Saturday. Luckily some people got between them or it would have been on for young and old. Blood being thicker than water, Kate naturally sided in with her brother and after that it was a bit of a drag going round to her place never knowing whether Steve would be there and they'd finish up at each other's throats. So the relationship with Kate was definitely on the slide going down. With what was about to go down with Eddie, Kate's brothers were probably right anyway.

For all his good points, Les was still a gangster of sorts. Solid citizens certainly didn't go around shooting cops. Even if the ones getting shot weren't much better than gangsters themselves. His other squeeze, Evelyn, had gone back to the country to run a nursing home, so Norton's love life was just about batting zero. Warren was in the same boat. What Warren said over a few drinks before he flew off to Adelaide was fairly true — a pair of eunuchs guarding an empty brothel would get more roots than what they were at the moment. Norton laughed to himself as he jogged along and winked up at the sky. Whenever things got a bit down he always thought of that old joke:

What's got two hundred legs and eats rotten cabbages?

A meat queue in Russia.

Les went up and down the Tamarama steps six times. After the last effort, his legs were bursting along with his lungs and he wondered for the life of him how Major Lewis used to do it so casually. He wiped the sweat from his eyes, caught his breath and headed back home.

He had a shower, changed into his blue tracksuit pants and a clean T-shirt then made a stack of sandwiches for lunch and washed them down with a pot of tea while he read the paper. After that he did some washing, hung it out the back on the Hills hoist and pottered round the house cleaning this and moving that. When he'd finished Les started packing everything he thought he'd need for a week in Shoal

Bay into two bags plus his backpack. He packed everything from his snorkelling gear to some books to read, his training gear and six bottles of Warren's rum plus some of Warren's home-grown pot the dynamite advertising executive kept hidden in a shoe box under his bed. He rang Billy Dunne and had a mag for a while. There was no point in ringing Kate. She was in Darwin at a convention, more than likely having a better time without him anyway. Before long the day was almost over and Les felt it was time for an early dinner. He strolled down to the Hakoah Club, joined God's chosen people and had two bottles of Carlton long neck and a delicious schnitzel with horseradish sauce, veges and the Hakoah Club's beautiful creamed spinach. This got washed down with a cappuccino then Les decided to stroll back home and zone out in front of the TV.

Warren had brought home a video called *Mouse Hunt* — two stooges wreck an old mansion trying to kill a little mouse from hell and it completely cracked the big Queenslander up. Especially after the two stooges finally obliterated the mansion then left with the little mouse clinging to the diff under their car like Robert De Niro in *Cape Fear*. After that Les watched a couple of episodes of *South Park* that Warren had taped and then it was time to hit the sack. About the last thing Les was thinking as he lay in bed staring up at ceiling was, this time tomorrow night he'd be in Shoal Bay. And if only he could have spoken to his mother like Cartman. Except he'd have no front teeth and probably be walking with a limp.

Les was up reasonably early the next day and he would have left for the North Coast by eight, except Billy just happened to lob on his doorstep. It was a peach of a day — blue skies, mild and a light sou'wester blowing. Did he fancy going for a paddle around Sydney Harbour seeing there were such ideal conditions? Les had figured earlier it would be about a four-hour drive to Shoal Bay, so no matter what time he left the day would more or less be half over when he got there. Yeah, why not. So they piled into Billy's station wagon, got the skis from the surf club and drove over to Rose Bay. It was that nice on the harbour they ended up paddling around Clark Island and all the marinas and houses around the water's edge for over an hour and a half. Not a great deal was said during the paddle because Les was pushing to keep up with Billy; and Billy was not only horribly fit, but going for it on the day. When they'd finished and put the skis away Les had a shower, another coffee then finally climbed into his black 99FM T-shirt and jeans and tossed his bags in the boot of the Berlina. Dear old Mrs Curtin was out the front watering her flowers. Les tooted the horn and gave her a wave as he did a slow turn around Cox Avenue then drove off towards the Harbour Bridge.

Les tuned the radio to some yadda-yadda, talkback station mainly for the news and traffic reports while he ground along with the late morning traffic through the northern suburbs. He felt good after the paddle and was concentrating mostly on the cars in front of him not thinking about much; just his quick holiday combined with an even quicker murder. The minute he reached the F3 turnoff at Hornsby, Les brushed the talkback waffle and slipped in a cassette. *Running Up And Down The Stairs* by The Michael Hills Blue Mob faded easily into *Mystery To Me* by John Gorka. Les kicked the Berlina past a line of trucks and headed for Port Stephens.

Compared to the mighty Datsun, Norton's Holden felt like the Queen's Rolls with a howling stereo and it seemed to simply eat up the kilometres. Les kept a steady eye on the speedo yet in no time at all he was past the Gosford turnoff and heading for the Wyong River. As the river neared Les couldn't help but think of the night he and Jimmy Rosewater got lost when they tried to find Avondale Airport. Les shook his head. Poor, bloody, good-looking Jimmy. Whatever his faults, he didn't deserve the horrible thing that finally happened to him. A sign loomed up — Charlestown Newcastle — as *Chicken Shack Boogie* by Willie And The Poor Boys started thumping through the speakers, so Les knew he was heading in the right direction. Now what am I looking for? The Hexham turnoff. Yep. There it is. Les angled his way around the back of Newcastle, crossed the Hunter, took another right turn and he was on Nelson Bay Road heading for Port Stephens. Blue Water Wonderland.

Now it was flat plains dotted with trees, houses and farm buildings set amongst signs saying Williamtown, Salt Ash, Bob's Farm. A sign alongside some trees on the right said One Mile Beach and a bit further on Les took a right at a roundabout with a police station on the corner and got a glimpse of a huge bay in the background. He eased the Berlina down a hill and Nelson Bay shopping centre was tucked behind a hotel on his right with a park, the marina full of boats and the marina's shops on his left. He drove under a concrete walkway, rounded a bay then went up another rise. Past that, a large grey building with smoked windows appeared amongst the trees and houses on the left. Port Stephens War Memorial Club. That could be worth a look, mused Les as he followed the bay on his left shimmering through the trees in the afternoon sunlight. A long, flat caravan park fenced off with cyclone wire loomed up on his right, then Les pulled up at the stop sign for the Fingal Bay turnoff marking the start of sleepy Shoal Bay, its shops and holiday units. The ABC Real Estate Agency, where Les had to go, was on the corner; Les stared at it through the windscreen for a moment then decided he might as well cruise down main street, do a scorching, tyre smoking donut at the other end then come back with a house music track pumping through the speakers loud enough to make everyone in the vicinity's ears bleed and their dogs start barking their heads off.

Shoal Bay village was about a kilometre long, the shops and units facing a beautiful, wide, blue expanse of water that swept towards a towering pair of rugged, green mountains, forming a narrow entrance to the bay. Amidst the strip of holiday homes was a plaza, a small shopping mall, an Italian restaurant called Luigi's, and the local big game fishing club. There was a chemist, another real estate agency and a long, white, stucco hotel with a red tile roof and palm trees out the front that reminded Les a little of a Mexican villa. The Dolphin. Opposite the hotel was a small wood and concrete jetty that pushed out from the sparkling white sand into the sparkling water of the bay. Les drove on past the remaining homes and holiday flats till he came to a locked-up swimming pool on the left and a metal gate set in a low, brick wall that said Restricted Entry. Tomaree Lodge. Department Of Community Services. Near this a sign said Tomaree National Park and another sign, in front of a pathway in the sand, pointed to Zenith Beach. There were a couple of park rangers in brown uniforms and apart from them hardly anyone else around. Les gave it all a quick once over then did a quiet U-turn, switched off the stereo and drove back up Shoal Bay Road parking the car between the real estate agency and a motel. The office was set down a couple of steps below the street; Les locked the car, stretched his legs for a moment then walked down.

Inside was all chrome and light with blue furnishings and photos of houses and units all over the walls. There was a small lounge on the right, the counter in front, then offices spread around to the left and in front. About six women in blue dresses and matching shirts hovered around their computers and phones while a couple of men in suits seemed to hover around them. There was a man standing at the counter and two men in jackets talking to another suit further on the left who had to be cops. Even with their backs turned, their mannerisms and the way the suit was looking at them told Les they were cops; a brief glimpse of folded handcuffs and the bulge of a holstered gun verified it. I wonder what they're doing here? mused Les. Probably been a break-in at one of the units. Crime. There's just no escape from it, is there? Les approached the counter to wait his turn, giving the other man standing there a quick, sideways up and down. He was about as tall as Les, with a flat nose and a grainy, freckled face, possibly in his mid-twenties. A tight mop of reddish-brown hair with a pair of sunglasses jammed in it spread across his head and two arms covered in more freckles stuck out of a black Beastie Boys T-shirt tucked into a pair of yellow jeans. He seemed to be having a mild beef with the woman behind the counter who had given him the wrong key to the automatic garage door.

'I'm very sorry about that, Mr Hakin,' apologised the dark-haired woman behind the counter as she squeezed the key onto his key-ring for him. 'It's just that sometimes these keys all start to look the same.'

'That's okay,' replied the customer, with a deep resonant voice that seemed to carry effortlessly around the office. 'I understand. But you can assure me of complete privacy from now on, can't you?'

'Oh certainly, Mr Hakin,' assured the woman. 'Complete privacy.'

'That's good.' Mr Hakin stared directly at the woman. 'Because I'm up here doing a big drug deal.'

The woman gave him a clunking, double blink. 'I'm sorry. You're what ...?'

'I'm a drug dealer,' asserted the customer with the freckles. 'I'm bringing in two hundred kilograms of cocaine and fifty thousand ecstasy tablets tomorrow night. Plus a great big pile of marijuana.'

'Oh,' the woman blinked again.

'That's why I want complete privacy.'

'Of course.'

'And if I don't get it ...' Freckles made out he was holding a gun in his right hand, pulled an imaginary trigger in front of the woman's face then abruptly turned and left the office.

The two cops at the end of the office turned as one, looked at each other for a second then let their eyes follow Mr Hakin out the door and around the corner. Face on, they were both about thirty, with brown hair, fairly fit looking with a hard edge. They watched Hakin disappear then their eyes momentarily settled on Les. Les avoided them and turned to the woman behind the counter.

'Hello,' he smiled, handing the woman his envelope. 'I'm Mr Norton. I think you've got a unit here for me. Till next Wednesday.'

The woman looked blankly at Les as she took the envelope. 'Yes ... yes,' she said. 'Mr Norton. Yes ... I'll, fix that up for you. No ... problem.' Between the mix up with the garage keys and finding out Pablo Escobel was in town, it had been a big morning.

While the woman flustered around getting Norton's key, Les picked up a free map of Port Stephens the agency provided and tried not to make eye contact with the two cops, although for some reason he could feel they were looking at him. Finally the woman handed Les his keys and a receipt to sign, told him he was in unit two upstairs and explained about the parking. Les thanked her then walked back to his car. As he got behind the wheel he knew one of the detectives had watched him through the window and memorised his number plate. The entrance to the parking bay was round the corner past a bike hire shop and next to the main entrance to the units. Les decided to check out round the back of the flats first. There was another parking area and on the opposite corner was a bakery that had once been the local squash court; the street was a dead end that finished in another parking area behind the hotel. The next street on the left ran up a hill into another street. Down to the left was the hotel and the beach front and further up the hill were more houses then bush. Les did a U-turn and drove back to the flats. The roller door to the parking area was open, Les nosed the Berlina down and pulled up in his car space next to an open door into the units. He switched off the engine then in the ensuing silence stared through the windscreen at the concrete wall in front of him.

Well, who was that fuckin idiot in the real estate agency? Les wondered. What a goose. He must have known those two blokes down the end were cops. Either that, or Freckles has got a pumpkin for a bloody head. Les shook his own red head. Maybe he did know and it was intended as a joke. Very funny. It went over like a dose of the pox. Now if anything goes wrong, the local constabulary know I've been in town. Thanks a lot, you red-headed dill. Remind me, if I get the opportunity, to boot you fair up the arse before I leave. Les shook his head then got his bags from the boot and went upstairs.

Unit two was roomy, bright and rather nice — a dining area with a round table and bamboo chairs as you walked in, a modern kitchen on the right with a bench table and cupboards built over it and a small laundry at the rear. Cream walls and two exposed brick walls in the lounge gave it a casual feel while blue-grey carpet, a matching blue floral lounge and several framed prints of dolphins on the wall gave the unit a kind of holiday feel. There was a TV in the corner, coffee tables and table lamps and a closed strip of white, vertical blinds led to the balcony. Left of the dining area was the toilet, the spare bedroom then the bathroom and the main bedroom; complete with a double bed, blankets, pillows and built-in wardrobes with mirrored doors. Les put his bags in the spare bedroom for the time being then walked back to the loungeroom, pulled back the vertical blinds, opened the sliding glass doors and stepped out onto a large, triangular-shaped balcony covered in green astro turf with a set of brown, plastic, outdoor furniture in the middle. Very nice, Mrs Galese, mused Les. Very nice indeed. Though I'll bet Myra's block of units belongs to Price and he's got it in her name. I wouldn't mind owning one of them though. Les moved over to the edge of the balcony to check out the view.

Directly across the road, a long strip of green parkland dotted with trees and picnic tables was separated from the sandy bay by a low wire fence and smatterings of scrub. On the left was a small toilet block near a circular blue sign saying Port Stephens Blue Water Wonderland and to the right of this was a pile of aluminium dinghies for hire. From the balcony Les got a better view of the two mountains at the entrance to the bay and across the bay in the distance was a long strip of white, sandy spit leading up to the furthermost headland that Les surmised from his roadmap was Hawks Nest and Tea Gardens. There was hardly a cloud in the sky, the light sou'wester gently rippled the water and the unit got the sun all afternoon. Yes, I think this might do me just nicely for the next few days, thought Les. He glanced at his watch. Anyway, time to unpack my swag. Les closed the flyscreen behind him then went into the spare bedroom and unzipped one of his travel bags.

Before long, Norton had his clothes and whatever unpacked and either hanging in the wardrobe or arranged above the sink in the bathroom. He found a place for Warren's six bottles of rum in the kitchen and placed the small bag of Woz's ganja in the fridge. That done, Les was sitting back on the lounge with a glass of water — his ghetto blaster placed on a coffee table tuned to some FM station in Newcastle — wondering what he should do. A couple of mellow pop songs went by and it was very relaxing on the lounge. Too relaxing actually, and after almost being rocked to sleep driving up in the air-conditioned comfort of the Berlina, Les could have dozed off quite easily. However, Les knew if he did that, he'd probably wake up about eight then wouldn't be able to get back to sleep. And there were dirty deeds to be done dirt cheap with young Edward on the morrow. Les glanced out the window then at his watch. There was still plenty of sun around. Why not go for a walk? Check out Zenith Beach and the local pub. Especially the local pub. It looked pretty good and Les had a feeling he might be spending a bit of time there. Norton locked the flat and walked down the front.

It took Les about a fifteen-minute stroll to reach the pathway leading to Zenith Beach. On the way he found Shoal Bay had a plaster painting shop in a small arcade, reeking of acetone and full of paint splattered tables and plaster models of indians, birds, clowns and such. In a landscaped plaza there was a butcher, a newsagency and a mini-market, along with some other shops and a small coffee shop on the corner that seemed interesting. There were a number of punters in the hotel and it looked and sounded inviting, but Les thought he might leave it for the time being and put his head in on the way back.

Zenith Beach was a brisk stroll down the pathway and was a little bigger than Bronte; the sou'wester was ruffling the blue water and flicking at the white sand while the late afternoon sun threw lengthening shadows into the rugged headlands at either end. According to Les's free map, there were two other beaches to the south — Wreck and Box — then a narrow spit of sand ran out to a kind of island in the distance. Zenith Beach looked quite pretty and gave Les the impression it could be a good surfing spot with the right conditions. Also the mountain at the north end that formed Tomaree Point looked like it would be an exhilarating climb and he imagined the view from the top would be quite spectacular. Les let a handful of pure white sand run through his fingers while he had another look around then walked back to the local hotel.

The Dolphin was bright and roomy and split into sections with a square of bar surrounded by old fishing photos just out from the wall on the left as you walked in. There was a video gaming room plus a TAB with a bank of TV screens showing the prices, a SKY channel TV hanging down from the ceiling and no shortage of punters drinking, smoking and gambling their money away. On the far right was another TV gaming area with two more Sky channel TV sets and facing that a beer garden. Behind a small bandstand in a corner was a large, sepia photo of a past Australian Rugby League team. Les stepped up for a closer look and recognised Bob McCarthy, Mark Harris and Graeme Langlands amongst the players jogging along in their battered old training gear. I wonder if I'd've made the Kangaroos had I kept playing football, mused Les. I think the answer would be — highly unlikely.

Les gave the beer garden a glance then walked back around some pool tables to check out the hotel's bistro. The bistro looked very inviting with comfortable chairs and tables and plenty of space. A fairly extensive menu on the wall featured mainly woodfired pizzas from the kitchen in the corner along with meat and fish dishes. Les gave it all an approving nod, noticed another smaller bar against one wall then walked out to the beer garden and over to a cocktail bar opposite. Inside it was blue walls, bamboo stools and tables with a bar on the left as you walked in and a mural of two parrots on the wall next to it. In the corner near the street was a tiny bandstand with a couple of old speakers sitting on it; another door led to the hotel foyer and what appeared to be the guests dining room. Les figured he'd seen all he needed to see for the time being, so he didn't bother to check it out. He also thought he might leave it till later for a beer as well. He left the hotel happy with what he'd found and headed for the flat, stopping to get some chops, sausages, milk, eggs, tomatoes and whatever on the way home.

It didn't take Les long to put everything away while he found out where things were in the kitchen and about half an hour later Norton was standing on the balcony with a mug of tea in one hand and a handful of Arrowroot biscuits in the other, deep in thought. Should he cook a feed at home, or go down the pub? The chops he bought looked quite delectable, but the fare on offer in the bistro didn't look too bad either. It was a momentous decision.

Les was deep in decision when he noticed movement on the balcony next door. It was Mr Hakin from the estate agency. The drug baron was his next door neighbour; and of all things, he'd just walked out on the balcony smoking a skinny joint. Silently Les watched him smoke it down to the tip then stub the roach out and bury it in the soil round a mini-palm tree on the balcony.

Les nodded to the palm tree with his mug of tea. 'Well if that wasn't a potted palm before, it sure fuckin is now,' he said.

Hakin spun around, a little out of it and a little paranoid at the same time. 'What was that?'

Les shook his head. 'Don't worry about it, mate.'

'Yeah, sure.' Hakin stared at Les then seemed to regain his composure. 'Hey. How are you man? What's happening?'

'What's happening?' echoed Les. 'Not much ... man. Just having a cup of tea and minding my own business. What about you ... man? What's your story? When you're not doing multi-million dollar drug deals and waving imaginary guns in women's faces?'

Hakin looked at Les for a moment then started to laugh. 'Ohh yeah. You were in the estate agency. Hey, did you see the look on the faces of those two cops?'

'Yes I did,' nodded Les. 'And I didn't think it was a real bright thing to say.'

Hakin made a dismissive gesture with one hand. 'Ohh what else could you do with those two oinkers standing there? I had to stir the pricks up.'

'Yeah. Well you sure did a good job. It went over like a turd in a punch bowl.'

Hakin made another gesture. 'Hey. It's all part of my scene anyway man.'

'Part of your scene?'

'Yeah. I'm a writer.'

'A writer?' Les moved the mug from his lips. 'Well I read the odd book now and again. Who the fuck are you?'

Hakin cocked his chin just a little. 'Emmett Hakin.'

'Yeah? Never heard of you.' Les thought for a second. 'Oh hang on a minute.'

Billy had brought one of Hakin's books to work one night. It was some kind of grunge crime writing written in the first person. Billy read twenty pages, said it was pretty fuckin ordinary and offered it to Les. Les took Billy's word for it and read something else. But he'd glimpsed Hakin being interviewed on SBS one night.

'Yeah, I've heard of you,' said Les. 'I saw you being interviewed on TV. I still haven't read any of your books though. But they reckon they're absolutely sensational.'

'They are,' preened the writer. 'You should get into them.'

'Okay,' said Les. 'I will. How about a freebee? You can sign it for me. To my mate Les.'

'I . . . haven't got a spare copy at the moment.'

'Oh well, don't worry. I'll get one off the hoisters.'

'The who?'

Les looked at Hakin for a moment. And you're writing crime? 'Forget it. I'll see if they got one at the library.'

Hakin gave Norton a bit of a once up and down. 'So your name's Les?'

'That's right.'

'I'm Emmett. Nice to meet you Les.' He offered Les his hand.

Norton took it. 'Yes. You too Emmett.'

Hakin seemed to study Les. 'So what do you do, Les?'

'Me? I work for BHP in Newcastle. I'm foreman in charge of all the forklift trucks.'

'Yeah. And is that a good job Les?' The way Hakin spoke, it was hard to tell if he was interested in Norton's job or deriding it.

Les nodded his head enthusiastically. 'Yeah. My work can be very uplifting at times.'

'Well. That's pretty cool Les.'

'Thanks.' Les sipped some more tea. 'Anyway Emmett, don't tell me, let me guess. You're up here on some kind of arts council grant writing a book.'

'Not quite,' replied Hakin slowly. 'I did get a grant. And I won a prize. But I'm up here with Kastrine Kreen. You've heard of her, surely?'

Had Les what. Kastrine Kreen was a screaming, howling, feminist werewolf. She hated blokes with a vengeance. Especially their poor little Mr Wobblys. If Kastrine had her way, she'd rally the sisters, get done up as Herod then run out and slaughter every newborn male for the next hundred years. She was tall and gaunt-looking with long brown hair and good legs and could have been half a good sort in her day. But the word was she got chopped up by a young swimming team at an Adelaide university, and she'd been dirty on men in general since. Les and Warren reckoned she was just plain frustrated and under all the feminist bullshit she'd kill for a root. Unfortunately no bloke would leave a poisoned mine shaft to get to her.

'Yeah. I've heard of her,' said Les.

'I thought you might have.'

Les took Emmett in over his mug of tea. 'So what's the rest of your story, Emmett? If you'll pardon the pun. Are you Ms Kreen's handbag, or her toyboy? Or something?'

'No,' smiled Emmett. 'We're,' Hakin raised his fingers and made quote signs. 'Friends. Through our publisher. She's paying for the flat. I do the driving and sort out the details.'

'Fair enough,' replied Les. 'So where is the lovely Kastrine right now? Inside going for it with her vibrator? Or down on the pier shoving fish hooks in bloke's nuts? Before she castrates them with a rusty bread knife.'

Emmett managed to conceal a smile. 'No. Kastrine's out walking.'

'Madam's taking her evening constitutional is she? How perfectly delightful.'

Emmett was about to say something, when a mobile phone rang from inside. 'I'd better get that, man.'

Les nodded as Hakin turned away. 'It's probably your agent.' Norton watched Hakin disappear, finished the last of his tea and biscuits and went inside.

Well can I find them or can they find me? Fancy cracking it for those two living next door. It could only happen to me. Les squinted an eye towards the sky. Are you sure you're not dirty on me for something boss?

The sun was streaming down on the balcony outside and you got the noise of any traffic or people going past, plus Ernest Hemmingway might come back, and bring his mentor with him this time. The loungeroom seemed quite mild and the blue lounge more than comfortable. So the kid, I say the kid, thinks he's a writer does he? Righto. Les went to the spare room and dug out the book he was currently reading — *Hollywood* by Charles Bukowski. He opened it at his bookmark then settled back on the lounge. Chinaski, with the help of Sarah, was still trying to get his movie together and stay sober at the same time when Les looked up to find the sun was well and truly over the yardarm. A horrible rumbling noise told Les something else. It was time for vittles. And plenty of them. Stuff making a great mess then having to clean it up. The bistro at the Dolphin Hotel had just started red hot favourite. Les had a quick shave, threw a blue, cotton bomber jacket over what he already had on and hid his wallet and credit cards. Then armed with nothing more than some cash and his *Daily Telegraph*, he headed for the local.

There was a good crowd at the hotel, drinking, talking and smoking. Les got a sparkling schooner of

VB, glanced up at some of the fishing photos while he was waiting then walked over to the bistro. It took him about five seconds to decide. T-bone steak with Diane sauce, chips and salad. Medium thankyou. The chef gave Les a thick strip of plastic with a number and a pager on the end; Les found a table and sipped his schooner while he read the paper. Les was at the sporting pages when the pager on his piece of plastic went off to say his meal was ready. Come and get it.

Norton couldn't fault his meal — the steak was tender, the sauce tangy, the chips were crisp and the salad fresh. All washed down with a delightful schooner. Les was rubbing his stomach and thinking a coffee would go well. But not there. Back at the flat. Then watch a special two-hour *NYPD Blue* they were showing that night, have an early one and see what Murder Incorporated had lined up for him when he arrived in the morning. He folded his paper and left the hotel.

Les was walking past the local Shoal Bay Game Fisherman's Club and was about to go straight up to the flat when he thought of something. He'd left a cassette that had some good tracks on it in the car. He decided to get it and maybe play it before he hit the sack. Maybe even roll up a little hot one. Les walked in the entrance and out to the parking bay. There wasn't a great deal of light in there. Les had his keys out and had just placed his newspaper on the roof ready to open the door, when he felt something hard and cold pressed behind his ear.

'You're under arrest,' said a voice, equally as hard and cold. 'Move and I'll blow your fuckin head all over the garage.' Les felt another gun barrel being jammed into his ribs. 'You heard him. Now put your fuckin hands on the car and spread 'em.' Les did what he was told and felt himself being patted down. 'Now put your hands behind your back. Slowly.' Les did that too and a pair of handcuffs snapped round his wrists. The guns were removed, then Les got shoved in the back towards the door he'd just walked through. 'Righto. This way.'

Before Les had time to think, let alone say anything, he was marched round to the back of the units and bundled into the back of a dark blue Ford Falcon. The Falcon did a U-turn then turned left at the Fingal Bay turnoff. As they went past the caravan park, Les got a better look at the two cops. They weren't the ones in the estate agency. They were both wearing drab suits and drab ties and ponged a bit of BO. The one behind the wheel had thick, black hair, big ears and a square jaw. The one next to Les had a blonde buzzcut, a long nose and heavy bags under his eyes and was looking indifferently out the window as if he was trying to act cool. He was the one who'd handcuffed Les. The Memorial Club went past on the right and Les thought it might be an idea if he knew what was going on. Even half an idea would do.

'Look. I don't want to sound like a nark or something,' said Les, 'but do you think one of you could tell me what the fuck's going on?'

Buzzcut pulled out a wallet with a badge on it and flashed it in front of Norton as if it was a ten-inch dick. 'I'm agent Corris. Federal police. We'll tell you all you need to know at the station.'

'Thanks.'

They were federal cops. Australia's version of the FBI. Les knew a few from a bar in the city and they weren't bad blokes. But some of them were complete morons. Would be G-men, out for the glory and the elusive, multi-million dollar drug bust. Les had a feeling that's what he was dealing with now. He also had a feeling this was all because of his next door neighbour. Why didn't I throw the cunt off the balcony earlier when he was stoned? fumed Norton. He stared out the window cursing his rotten luck and hoped this didn't stuff things up with Eddie. So far it wasn't looking too good.

Nelson Bay Marina went past, they turned left then circled a roundabout and Les got a glimpse of a cyclone wire fence as they drove in the back of the police station he'd noticed earlier. The Falcon pulled up outside two black garage doors on the left then Les was bundled out and shoved through a brown wooden door into the station. After that Les just kept being shoved left down some corridors. He got a glimpse of an older, fair-haired, uniformed cop standing at the front desk as he went past, brick walls, a shower and bathroom, more rooms. Then Les was shoved left for the last time into another room with bare, brick walls. There was a desk with a computer on it, a brown filing cabinet against one wall and a window with venetian blinds and a security grill opposite. There was a whiteboard on a different wall and another cabinet stood in a corner with a TV sitting on top. A swivel chair sat in front of the desk, Les got pushed down into it backwards while Buzzcut dragged another swivel chair across the scuffed, grey-brown carpet and his mate dragged another chair in from somewhere else. The two federal police sat down and stared at Les, while he stared back at them — Buzzcut on Norton's left, the other cop facing him to the right. No one was saying anything so Les thought he might as well get the ball rolling.

'Like I said before, I hate to come across as a vexatious complainer. But would one of you two fine gentlemen mind telling me just what the fuck's going on.'

'Okay smartarse,' said Buzzcut. 'I'm agent Corris, and this is agent Pope.'

'Wonderful. Well I'm Les Norton. And I'm up here on holidays. Or I was. Until you pair of clowns trussed me up like a Peking fuckin duck.'

Agent Pope smiled at Norton. 'So you're up here on holidays, are you Les?'

'That's exactly right,' answered Les.

'And bringing in a nice big shipment while you're at it.'

'What?'

'You fuckin smarties are all the same,' said Corris. 'You get a nose full of whoof and everybody in the world's a mug except you. You couldn't get in that real estate office and shoot your big mouth off quick enough, could you?'

'That wasn't fuckin me,' protested Les.

'Of course it wasn't,' said agent Pope. 'Tall guy, red hair, black T-shirt. It was a clone.'

'And the clone was driving Embett Hakeem's car too,' smirked Corris. 'Send in the clones.'

'Are you fair dinkum?' said Les. 'I bought that car fair and square. He's dead.'

'We know he's fuckin dead,' said Corris, almost in Norton's face. 'And now you've taken over. You're the new kingpin.'

'That's right,' smiled Pope. 'Yo de man Les. Yo de fuckin man.'

Norton shook his head. 'I don't fuckin believe this.'

'Of course you fuckin don't,' said agent Pope. 'But we'll have a search warrant by the morning. Then we'll go through your car and all over your flat. You'll fuckin believe it then. Smartarse.'

Agent Corris smiled at his partner. 'How's the clown's form. You can bet he helped murder Hakeem. Now he's driving round in his car just to show the world how cool he is.'

Agent Pope smiled right in Norton's face and patted him on the shoulder. 'Yo de man Les. You sho' enuff is de man. And we love you.'

Les stared at the two federal police in disbelief. How could two people get anything so wrong. Even these two mules. It would all work itself out eventually, because apart from owning a car that once belonged to a drug dealer, he hadn't done a thing. But what a bloody inconvenience. In the meantime, thought Norton, what have I got to lose with these two woodenheads?

'Okay,' shouted Les, squirming about in his chair. 'You've got me. It's true. I am masterminding a massive drug shipment. I can't handle it no more.' The two federal cops looked at each other then back at Les. 'But I ain't goin' down for those fuckin Arabs. I'll confess.'

'You will?' said agent Pope.

Les nodded to a mini-cassette on the table. 'Turn that on boys.' Corris switched on the mini-cassette and placed it closer to Les. 'I'll go state witness. I'll be your new supergrass. Then I want to enter the witness protection programme.'

'Witness protection is a big ask,' said Corris. 'What have you got that's worth it?'

'What have I got? Hah! The deal's got a street value of at least a billion dollars, boys.'

'A billion dollars?' Agent Pope gave Les a massive double blink. 'Start talking, Les.'

'Okay. We're bringing in half a tonne of cocaine from Colombia. Five hundred kilograms of heroin from Afghanistan. Five tonne of Bhuddha sticks from Thailand. And two hundred thousand tabs of LSD from San Francisco. Is that worth witness protection?'

The two federal cops gave each other a double blink. 'You got it,' said agent Pope.

'Ohh boys. You've got the big one here,' said Les. 'I also know where there's twenty kilograms of heroin. Pure China white, buried under a synagogue in Rose Bay. And two hundred AK–47s in a mosque at Lakemba. I'll give you the names of all the principals going right back to Tibet and the Golden Triangle.'

'Keep talking, Les,' said Corris. 'You're beautiful.'

'That's nothing fellas. I'm also the syndicate's accountant. I know where there's millions of dollars hidden in banks on islands all over the world. We've even got a bank account on Clark Island in Sydney Harbour.'

'Keep talking, Les,' said Pope. 'This is fantastic.'

'Ohh let me tell you,' said Les. 'It's a fuckin relief to get it off my chest.'

'I'm sure it must be,' said Corris.

'And we're going to look after you Les,' agent Pope winked at his partner, over Norton's head.

'That's good,' said Les. 'It's nice to know I've met two cops I can trust.'

'You can trust us mate,' smiled agent Pope.

'Good.' Les wiggled a bit in his seat. 'So seeing how I've done the right thing by everyone, how about getting rid of these handcuffs? I want to scratch my nuts.'

Corris looked at his partner for a second. 'Okay. We'll move them round the front.' While his partner watched, Corris moved the handcuffs so Norton's hands were now sitting on his lap.

'Thanks,' said Les. He wiped his eyes, had a good scratch then smiled up at the two federal police. 'What about one more little favour?'

'What now?'

'How about a phone call?'

'Turn it up.'

'One lousy phone call?' said Les. 'Come on. I've done the right thing by you. You've got to give me one anyway. Christ! You can listen on the other end. You got that thing going there. You can tape it.'

The two federal cops exchanged glances. 'Okay,' said Pope. 'One call.' Corris placed a phone in front of Les and held the receiver next to Norton's ear while Les dialled. Pope noted the number and listened on another phone.

Les heard a familiar voice at the other end. 'Hello Billy. It's Les.'

'Les. How are you mate? What's doing?'

'Not much. I'm in Nelson Bay police station.'

'You're what!?'

'It's no big deal. I'll probably ring you back before long. In the meantime, can you do me a favour?'

'Sure. What is it?'

'You've got tonight off from work. Are you watching *NYPD Blue*?'

'Reckon.'

'Will you tape it for me?'

'Sure mate. No worries.'

'Good on you Billy. I'll ring you ...'

Les was about to say more only Corris snatched the phone away. 'Righto you fuckin smartarse. What was all that about?'

'What was all what about?' replied Les.

'Tape *NYPD Blue*. That was some sort of fuckin code wasn't it? You cunt,' cursed agent Pope.

'Code?' said Les. 'It's a fuckin show on TV you peanut. Sipowicz, Martinez, Kirkendall. Surely you two galahs watch it.'

'You just made cunts of us.' Corris's face reddened and he jabbed a finger into Norton's chest. 'But don't worry. We'll trace that. We'll get the lot of you. And you can forget witness protection.'

'Good,' said Les. 'You can shove your witness protection up your fat arse, for all I care.'

By now Les had had enough of Corris and Pope. At least the night wasn't a complete disaster. Billy was going to tape the *NYPD Blue* special for him and the two federal cops could get stuffed. Les was going to tell them that too. And if they tried anything heavy, he'd kick them both in the nuts while he could still move his feet. They could sort the 'assault police' thing out later on. Les was about to get into it, when who should walk into the room, but the two cops who were in the real estate office.

'What the fuck's going on?' said the taller one.

'Okay,' replied Pope, getting to his feet. 'We jumped the gun on you a bit. But you're too slow. This prick's the top gun in the old Hakeem syndicate. We got him to confess everything.'

'It's all here on tape,' said Corris.

'That's not the bloke in the real estate agency,' said the tall cop's mate.

Agent Pope looked at Les then back at the state cop. 'It's not?'

'No it's not. You pair of fuckin hillbillies,' said Norton. Les was about to say more, when a violent argument broke out between the four detectives. By keeping quiet and listening to what was going on, plus a little detective work of his own, Les was able to more or less figure out what happened.

The first two cops had seen and heard Hakin in the real estate office shooting his mouth and took note of what he'd said. Back at the station, they'd briefly mentioned it to the two federal cops, who actually were in Port Stephens trying to trace a major drug operation. They'd both got giant hard ons, jumped the gun and raced down to the real estate agency where they questioned the flustered woman behind the counter. She gave them Hakin's description, which more or less fitted Les. They saw the name Emmett Hakin on the agency's books. Saw Norton's car. Ran the number plate which came up Embett Hakeem. Thought Les was trying to be smart and had tripped himself up. So they decided to swoop, arrest Les and squeeze the information out of him after they'd searched the car and the flat. And get themselves a nice big collar at the same time right under the noses of the two local cops. Les always knew that at times there was a bit of underlying hostility between state police and the feds. He could see why. Besides doing a bit of a dump on their colleagues Corris and Pope wouldn't know shit from shaving cream. The argument in the room was just about getting into top gear, when Les started whistling and waving his handcuffed arms around.

'Hey! Yoohoo! Remember me,' he yelled. 'Hello.'

The cops stopped their arguing for the moment and turned to Les. 'Would you like to hear my version of the story? Like ... the truth?'

'Yeah. Go on,' said the tall, brown-haired NSW cop.

'That bloke you saw in the real estate office is a writer named Emmett Hakin. He was just being a smartarse.' Les told them he how bumped Hakin on the balcony and it was all just a gee-up. 'So that's the story boys. I'm up here for a holiday. Hakin's up here writing a book with Kastrine Kreen. A mate of mine read one of his books, and reckons he couldn't write a shopping list. But there's no dope deal going down. He's just a bit of a mug. That's all. And yes, my car did belong to Hakeem. But I bought it all legally and I've got the receipts and registration papers to prove it.' Les smiled icily at Pope and Corris. 'Which I would gladly have got from the glove box if the two other Marx brothers here — Stretch and Skid — hadn't pistol whipped me into the back of their car, then flung me in the nick and tried to force a confession out of me. Bastards.'

Agent Pope and agent Corris gave Les a dirty look and shuffled their feet. The two NSW cops exchanged glances and tried not to laugh. 'Sorry mate,' said one. 'What can we say?'

'Not much, I don't suppose,' replied Les. He held up his manacled wrists. 'What about ...?'

'Hang on,' said agent Pope. 'What about all that stuff you just told us?'

'Are you fair dinkum?' said Norton. He nodded to the mini-cassette still winding round on the desk. 'If you believe any of that, you're even sillier than you look. Come on. Get these fuckin things off.'

Corris clenched his jaw. 'Allright,' he grunted, and unlocked the handcuffs.

'Thanks.' Les rubbed his wrists then smiled round the room. 'Right. Now, after I see my lawyer, who do I sue for malicious arrest, indecent language and police brutality? You? Or you?'

The shorter of the two NSW detectives held his hands up in front of his chest. 'Sorry. Leave us out.'

'Then it must be you.'

'I don't know what you're talking about,' said Corris. 'We were just doing our job.'

'Playing with your dicks'd be more like it,' retorted Les.

'Hey. Don't get too smart,' said Pope.

'You're right,' said Les. 'I won't use words with more than one syllable again. Sorry.' He turned to the two NSW cops. 'Okay then. Instead of pressing charges I'll settle for a lift back to Shoal Bay. How about it?' The two NSW cops looked at each other for a second. 'Well come on,' said Les. 'You're not going to leave me here with Duckman and Cornfed — are you?'

'No. Come on.'

'Thanks.' Les turned to Corris and Pope. 'Well good luck with your investigations gentlemen. But could you do me one small favour before I leave town?'

'What?'

Les nodded to the mini-cassette still whirling happily away. 'Can I get a copy of that tape? Just pop it under the door. You know where I live.'

This time Les was led out the back to a beige Holden Commodore where he was able to get in the back on his own this time. The two cops introduced themselves; the taller one was Stewart, the other was Grant. Les told them who he was and that he was in Shoal Bay for a quick holiday.

'Did you notice me looking at you in the real estate office earlier Les?' said Stewart.

'Yeah. Sort of,' answered Les.

'You used to play for Easts, didn't you?'

'Yeah. Second row.'

'You'd know my cousin then. Carrotts.'

'George McCarthy. Shit! I haven't seen him in ages,' said Les. 'How's he going? Still up the North Coast?'

'Yeah. Got three kids now.'

'Fair dinkum? Good on him. Say hello for me next time you see him.'

'I will.' Stewart turned round and gave Norton a grin. 'Christ, he told me a funny story about you and him and some young pommy bloke.'

'Peregrine,' said Les. 'Sir Peregrine Normanhurst the third.'

'That's him.'

The short drive home was infinitely more pleasant than the one going in, and when they pulled up outside the flat, if Grant and Stewart hadn't been on their way out to Raymond Terrace, Les would have been almost tempted to invite them up for a drink or a cup of coffee.

'Hey Les,' said Grant, as Norton was about to get out of the car. 'Did you say that dillbrain author was smoking a joint out on his sundeck?'

'Well ... yeah,' replied Les, a little hesitantly.

Grant turned to his partner. 'That means he's got some stash in there. We may as well bust him.'

'Yeah. That'll teach him to be clever,' agreed Stewart.

'What — now?' said Les.

'No, not now,' said Grant. 'Probably tomorrow. We'll just put a little rocket up his arse. For fucking us all around.'

'And maybe his girlfriend Kreen too,' said Stewart.

'Yeah righto,' said Les, trying to sound like he meant it. 'Good idea. Anyway, I'll see you later fellas. Thanks for the lift.' Les got out of the police car, waved the two cops off as they did a U-turn back towards Nelson Bay, then went upstairs.

Once inside, Les hit the lights then went straight to the kitchen, opened a bottle of Beenleigh, poured some in a glass with ice, hit it with a bit of pineapple juice and downed it. Then before his eyes stopped spinning, poured another one and attacked that as well. Getting arrested and dragged off to the nick first night in town was punishing enough; even if he knew it would all work itself out. But it was the bloody ramifications. Eddie and he still had to do a murder the next day. Now they'd have two cops hanging around for a piddly, square-up pot bust. They needed that like the proverbial hole in each of their heads. Plus, Les had given Pope and Corris a reasonable gobful on the night. They might decide to come back just to show their authority and make pests of themselves. If anything went wrong, Eddie and he were first cabs off the rank to be taken in for questioning. Les stared into his drink and shook his head. Isn't it amazing how things can stuff up. Just because of one flip. He stared into the loungeroom. There wasn't much worth watching on TV now. Then his eyes drifted across to the ghetto blaster. I'll turn the radio on. No I won't. I'll shove some music on. That might take my mind off things. Les found a cassette and slipped it into the ghetto blaster and faced it towards the sundeck. As Etcetera Theatre Company set the conga drums thumping into *Stairway To Heaven*, Les topped his pineapple juice with more rum, opened the sliding glass door and stepped out onto the balcony.

There was a yellow street lamp on the corner right outside the unit, throwing a thick wash of soft, shadowy light across the sundeck and the one next door. Les went over to the edge of the balcony and stared across the bay at a tiny sprinkle of lights on the far shore. It was still a pleasant night with a little dew falling and a slight nip in the air. The first track went into another and Les steadily sipped on his rum. Another track started, the rum spread through Les and he was now getting to the 'who gives a stuff', stage of drinking. An ironic smile creaked across his face and he shook his head. Well. What happened, happened. And nothing was going to change it. If the shit hit the fan, too bad. That's the way it goes. But Eddie always knew what he was doing. The little hitman was always on the money a thousand per cent. Les had another sip of rum. Well he had been so far. Yeah. So far. The Wheel were harmonising nicely into *Good Noise* when out the side of his eye Les sensed movement on the balcony next door. He didn't bother to turn round. 'You can bet it'll be that dopey bloody writer sucking on another yabba,' Les muttered to himself. 'I'd like to give him a gobful. Bugger him, I'll just ignore the goose. If he says hello, I'll say hello back, and that's about it.'

Les sipped his drink and continued to stare out at the inky waters of the bay. From the angle of the sundeck, however, it was difficult not to look at whoever was next door. Les felt himself glancing to the right. It wasn't Emmett Hakin. It was a tall woman, with long, brown hair combed down either side of her face, wearing a loose, white hemp dress with a split up the front and a matching, white hemp sailor's top. She had a long, angular face and in the wash of the streetlight looked around forty. Les had a feeling she'd seen him standing there and a sudden glow near her face told Les she too was smoking a skinny joint. She smoked it down to the tip then stubbed it out in the soil round the same mini-palm tree Hakin buried his in earlier. As Les half watched her she started boogieing around a little to the music coming from Norton's ghetto blaster inside. Suddenly she turned and caught Norton's eye.

'That's a nice track,' she said, in a deep, well-spoken kind of voice. 'Who is it?'

'I'm not sure,' replied Les honestly and a little taken aback. 'Some Australian band. It's just a tape of various tracks. I forget who they are half the time.' Despite the few rums, Les couldn't help feel a little intimidated. It had to be Kastrine Kreen and it wasn't everyday you came face to face with a world famous author who hated men.

The woman moved over a little. 'You like music, do you?'

'Yeah,' nodded Les. 'There's nothing better than kicking back with a nice hot one and getting into a bit of boogie.'

'You smoke dope?' The woman sounded surprised.

Les shook his head. 'I don't smoke dope. I smoke pot. Ganja. Junkies use dope.'

'Fair enough,' agreed the woman. 'Emmett brought some with him. But it's not all that good.'

'Yeah. I was talking to him earlier.' Les looked at the woman for a second. 'I got some that isn't too bad. You can have a bit, if you want it.'

'Really?'

'Yeah. I bought a bag before I left Newcastle. It's all Queensland heads.'

'That's very nice of you. Thanks.'

'My pleasure,' replied Les.

The woman stepped up to the low, metal railing separating the two balconies and offered her hand. 'I'm Kastrine,' she said.

'Les. Nice to meet you, Kastrine.' Les gave her hand a squeeze. It was firm and a little leathery, almost manly. 'Anyway. You wait here Kastrine, and I'll get you something decent to smoke.'

Les went inside, opened the fridge and got out the bag of ganja he'd got from Warren's stash. Les had inadvertently brought a few seeds back from Jamaica in his clothes, which he gave to Warren. Warren might have been a bit of a fusspot round the house at times, but he knew how to grow good pot. So between the Jamaican seeds and Warren's expertise, the end result was pure, stepping dynamite. Les had a few cones or a yabba now and again and it could be the best, most relaxing get-into-the-music stone imaginable. Other times however, it could slam dunk you straight into paranoid valley. Les pulled out a couple of juicy little purple heads that looked and felt like liquorice allsorts and folded them in a piece of brown paper. So you like, I say you like a little puff now and again, do you gal, chuckled Les. See what happens when you wrap your miserable, man-hating lips around this. Yet Les had to admit, he was a bit surprised by Kastrine's manner so far. She was quite pleasant. Though it would have to be a bit hard to hate some bloke who's only crime was playing a bit of decent music then laying a smoke on you.

He walked out and handed Kastrine the pot. 'There you are. Go roll yourself a nice hot one.'

'Thankyou,' she smiled. 'I'll be right back.'

Les resumed sipping his drink and staring out at the bay. The odd car drove past below, another track cut in and before long Kastrine was back at the railing holding a neat joint with a tip rolled into the end.

'How's that look?' she said.

'Pretty good,' answered Les. 'I've aways reckoned women roll better joints than men. They seem to give them that soft, woman's touch.'

Kastrine nodded thoughtfully. 'I'll accept that,' she said. 'In fact, how about I come over there and smoke it with you?'

'Be my guest.' Les watched Kastrine clamber over the railing. He didn't get a flash of knickers. But for an auntie, she had a pretty good pair of shapely legs with a trim ankle. 'Can I offer you a drink?' he asked, as she dusted her hands and straightened her dress.

'Yes. I'd appreciate that. Thanks.'

Les went to the kitchen and returned with a delicious. 'There you go.'

'Thankyou.' Kastrine took a healthy swallow. 'Mmhh. This is nice. What is it?'

'Beenleigh and pineapple juice.'

'Kastrine took another sip. 'It's very ... more-ish.'

'There's plenty there. Help yourself if you feel like another one.'

Kastrine put down her drink and fired up the joint with a Bic lighter. She took about three healthy tokes then handed it to Les. Les shook his head.

'No thanks,' he said. 'I'm right for the time being.'

'Are you stoned?'

'Off me head,' smiled Norton.

Kastrine gave Les a double blink and took another toke. 'Hey, this is a lovely smoke Les.'

'It'd want to be,' replied Les. 'Three hundred and fifty bucks a bag.'

'Where did you get it?'

'Some hippie sheila from up the North Coast sold it to me in a pub in Newcastle. She looked like a cross between Miss Piggy and a Mayan princess.'

Kastrine fell back laughing. 'God! What a description,' she giggled. Eventually she got herself together, finished the joint and stubbed it into the nearest palm tree on Norton's deck. She stared at Les for a moment then gave him a slow, double blink. 'Les. This dope ... ganja, is absolutely sensational. How do you handle it so cool?'

'I don't know,' replied Les. 'Guess I've just built up a tolerance over the years.'

'Fuck!'

'Whatever,' replied Les, smiling to himself. Just give it a few more minutes to creep up Kastrine baby. See what you've got to say then.

Kastrine picked up her drink, took a sip and looked at Norton. 'Les. Do you think you could turn the music up?'

'How do you mean Kastrine?' said Les. 'Turn it up all together? Or turn up the volume?'

'No. No. Turn up the volume.' Kastrine rubbed her arms. 'In fact, why don't we go inside. It's getting cold out here.'

'Okay. If you want to.'

Les opened the flyscreen door and followed Kastrine inside. She had a quick look around then eased herself onto one of the lounge chairs while Les spread himself along the lounge to her left.

'This place is much like showers,' she said slowly.

'Showers?' said Les. 'What kind of showers? Those April showers that come in May. They bring the sunshine, that lights the day?'

Kastrine looked quizzically at Les. 'What are you talking about?'

'You said this place reminds you of showers. So I started singing *April Showers*. Sorry if I offended you.'

'I meant — *ours*,' deliberated Kastrine. 'This place reminds me of *ours*.'

'Oh.'

'God you're mad.' Kastrine started giggling again and spilt some of her drink down her sleeve.

Les handed her a tissue. 'Do you still want to turn the music up?'

'No,' Kastrine shook her head. 'No. This is fine.'

'Righto.'

Les sat back and watched Kastrine. She closed her eyes and started boogieing around on the lounge. She did a kind of light head bang and her long hair swept from side to side in time with the music. It looked good. Les sipped his drink and after a while she opened her eyes. Or at least managed to creak the lids half open.

'Les. This pot. It is so good.'

'Yeah,' agreed Les. 'It sure kicks out the jams, don't it.'

'But I just can't believe how you're so cool. I mean, I've left the asteroid belt and I'm heading for hyper space. I'm spinning. Yet you're like a cucumber. How?'

Les shrugged. 'I just sit back, relax. And if it gets too heavy, I kind've do a slow boogie.' Les pointed his index fingers out and started poking them around half in time with the beat. Kastrine started laughing again, then she got up and sat down on the lounge on Norton's left. 'You're not going to start psychoanalysing me now or something, are you?' he asked her.

Kastrine got a strange look in her eyes. 'How about I just kiss you?'

'On the first date?' said Les. 'I don't know. What would the vicar say?'

'Fuck the vicar.'

Before Les got a chance to reply, Kastrine pounced. She put a headlock on Les and clamped her mouth over his. She was good to kiss. Wide, sensuous lips, a sweet breath and when she slipped the tongue in, both Les and Mr Wobbly started getting interested. Their kissing and groping started getting heavier. Kastrine got a choker hold on Les and shoved her tongue halfway down his throat. In the melee on the lounge, Les got his hand up under her top and got hold of two, big, droopy boobs strapped into a wire-framed bra; Les gave them a bit of a squeeze and thought he might leave them where they were. He slipped his hand up under her dress, ran it over her stomach then started massaging her backside; which was fairly broad, but had so far managed to defy the law of gravity to a certain degree. Les rubbed away for a while then slipped his hand onto her ted. Ah-ha, thought Les. Now we're in business. It was hairy, hot and meaty beneath his hand like a big, steaming haggis. Les gave it a few strokes, Kastrine kicked up a gear and started pig rooting all over the lounge then tore open Norton's fly and uncoiled Mr Wobbly. This is allright, Les smiled to himself. This auntie, for all her feminist faults, is probably an unreal root. And even though it's considered unsporting I got to tell the boys back at the Kelly Club about this. Les hooked a thumb into Kastrine's matching white knickers and started easing them off. Kastrine's retro rockets fired up and it was all systems go.

'Do you want to go into the bedroom?' said Les.

'What's wrong with right here on the lounge?' she panted. 'Next to the music.'

'Fair enough.'

Les moved the pillows around and propped one under Kastrine's behind then pushed his jeans down round his knees, got between her wide open legs and went to ease Mr Wobbly in.

If Mr Wobbly hadn't been attached to Norton's thighs, he would have lost him along with his scrotum and all it contained. Kastrine Kreen's ted was a monster. Les didn't have a porno star's dick, but it was no stack of buttons either. And it had a grouse bowyang to the left, that made it feel twice as thick as it was when it skidded off a few erogenous zones. But this was beyond Les. He pushed and shoved and tongue kissed Kastrine, who wiggled her backside around seething with frustration.

'Come on. Give it to me,' she hissed.

'I am,' said Les, putting in a few big ones. 'I'm giving it everything I've got.'

But it was no good. It had all the firmness of a box of fairy floss. Les may as well have stuck his dick out the flyscreen and tried to root Shoal Bay. In desperation he got a towel from the lounge, gave it a wipe and jumped on again. Still nothing. Les pounded it a few more times then literally threw the towel in. So did Mr Wobbly.

'What's the matter with you?' gasped Kastrine.

'Sorry Kastrine,' said Les, pulling his jeans back up and zippering them. 'But when they say size is everything, that doesn't just apply to blokes.'

'What are you talking about?'

'Allright Kastrine,' said Les, pointing to Kastrine's business, sitting between her legs on the lounge like a pair of worn out, harachi sandals. 'I'll give it to you straight. You've got the mother of all teds. That's the biggest one I've ever come across. Truly.'

'It's not that big,' said Kastrine.

'Not that big? Mate. You could hide a boat load of illegal immigrants in there.'

'Oh bullshit!'

'Bullshit? Listen. At one stage, when we were having sex, I fell in, and saw a bloke wandering round with a horse and cart, carrying a hurricane lamp. He called me over and said, "Hey mate have you got a match? Mine are wet."'

'You bastard.'

Les moved his face a bit closer to Kastrine's fanny and looked at it. 'It's big allright. It's big. It's big.'

'Allright. You've made your point. There's no need to keep repeating yourself.'

Les shook his head. 'I wasn't.'

'Oh!' Kastrine slipped her knickers on and sat back on the lounge with her arms folded.

'Would you like another drink?' asked Les.

'No thankyou,' she humphed.

'Fair enough.' Les walked over to the kitchen and made himself one. 'Well, sorry the night turned out a bit of a disaster,' he said, standing at the bar beneath the cupboards. 'But there's certain things in this world best left alone.' Les pointed with his drink. 'And that's one of them.'

'Huh,' snorted Kastrine. 'What about you? Super stud. Pah!'

'Yes,' admitted Les. 'I agree, I have let the side down badly in the sexual stakes. But I'm willing to give it another try. How about we take a run down to Old Sydney Town tomorrow. I'll see if I can borrow one of those primers they use to jam the big, steel balls into those old cannons. I'll pour a jug of olive oil over the end and give you a serve with one of those. We'll give you an orgasm, Kastrine baby. I'll get you blowing like an Oklahoma tornado, only louder. If you'll just give me one more chance darling.'

Kastrine got to her feet, giving Norton a withering look as she did. 'You absolutely disgust me. No wonder men are such cunts,' she seethed.

'I agree with you there too,' said Les. 'But we're just cunts in general. Not particularly big ones.' Kastrine moved to the flyscreen door. 'I'll walk you home,' smiled Les.

'You needn't bother.' Nevertheless, Les followed her across the balcony and stood by as she clambered back over the railing.

'Well you can't complain too much about the night Kastrine,' he said. 'You might've cracked it for a dud root. But you finished up with a bit of good mull. And you got to hear some nice music.'

'Wonderful,' replied Kastrine. 'I'm always thankful for small mercies.'

'That's a good attitude to have Kastrine,' said Les. 'I rather like them myself.'

'Get fucked.'

Les didn't bother to reply. He went inside closing the sliding glass door behind him. The cassette had stopped playing so Les put the radio on, finished his last drink and had a think. The night had certainly finished up a joke; except Les wasn't laughing. If anything, between Kastrine and the cops, he was left feeling grubby. He peeled his clothes off and got in the shower. After a good scrub, he got into a clean T-shirt and jox, walked back into the kitchen and made a mug of Ovaltine. Les sipped it while he listened to the radio and shook his head. You know, nothing changes, he thought to himself. All that shit went down tonight. And here I am, back in some kitchen drinking Ovaltine. Same as last night and the night before. I'm like that bloke in *Groundhog Day*. What did John Lennon say? Strange days. Les raised his Ovaltine towards the sky. Strange days indeed John. He finished his Ovaltine, turned off the radio and the lights then climbed into bed, absolutely delighted to find it was as comfortable as his own: maybe even more so. He scrunched his head into the pillows and in no time flat was snoring peacefully.

Les tumbled out of bed around eight the next morning and the memory of last night's events flittered across his mind for a moment or two. He shook his head, climbed into a pair of Levi's shorts then cleaned his teeth and stepped out onto the sundeck to check out the day. The sky was blue again and it was quite mild with just a light sou'wester rippling the blue waters of Shoal Bay. Beautiful, nodded Les. A perfect day for a murder. There was no sign of life next door, one or two people were walking around below and a couple of cars drove past. Les wasn't sure when Eddie would arrive. But it would be no good him getting there and Norton was nowhere to be found. Les decided to get the paper and have breakfast at home. He left the same white T-shirt on he'd slept in, got some money and his *South Park* cap with Cartman on the front, then walked round to the paper shop.

The streets were quiet and there was only one person in the newsagents — a girl wearing an olive-green, Thomas Cook vest with pockets all over it, khaki fatigues and a grey *South Park* T-shirt with Chef on the front. Much like Wednesday afternoon in the estate agency, the girl was having a mild altercation with the woman behind the counter. She was two dollars short for the price of a map. What did I say last night, Les smiled to himself. *Groundhog Day*. That's what it is. I'm trapped in a time warp. While she was talking to the woman behind the counter, the girl half-turned to Les for a moment and Les checked her out some more. She looked to be in her late twenties with lustrous, shoulder-length black hair, brushed down either side of her face then cut in a fringe. A pretty, petite mouth sat daintily beneath a small nose and a pair of chubby little cheeks and in her white trainers, she came up to around Norton's chin. She reminded him a lot of Cher Bono.

'Yes, I'm sorry,' said the woman behind the counter brushing absently at her blue dress. 'But they're nine ninety-five now. They went up.'

'Oh crumbs,' the girl fumbled through her pockets. 'I must have left my purse at home. I wasn't thinking.'

'Mmmhh,' smiled the woman behind the counter. She'd more than likely heard the same story a hundred times before.

Les looked at his handful of change then caught the dark-haired girl's eye. 'How much short are you Miss Crabtree? Two bucks? There you go.' Les put two dollars in the girl's hand.

'I ... Oh. Thankyou very much,' smiled the girl. She had perfect white teeth when she smiled and deep, emerald-green eyes. She wasn't stunningly beautiful. But she was quite attractive, with a strange, dark allure about her, especially in her eyes.

'That's okay,' said Les, returning her smile. 'Give it back to me next time you see me.' Les then paid the other woman the correct money for his paper, tucked it under his arm and walked briskly back to the unit.

A couple of hours later, Les had finished a huge plate of chops and scrambled eggs with all the trimmings. He'd cleaned up and was sitting in the loungeroom, reading the paper with the radio playing, when there was a knock on the door. Les put the paper down and opened it. Someone had deposited a tourist on his doorstep. He came up to Norton's chin and was wearing a loose-fitting blue Hawaiian shirt over a pair of baggy check shorts, a baseball cap with a dolphin on the front and a pair of expensive, Italian sunglasses. The tourist had also brought a large suitcase on rollers with him.

'You know what you look like, Eddie?' said Les.

'No. What?' replied the little hitman.

'The tourist from hell.'

'That's exactly what I want to look like. Now are you going to let me in, or what?'

Les didn't have to show Eddie his way around. He threw the suitcase straight up on the lounge and drew the blinds a little as Les closed the door behind them.

'How was the drive up?' asked Norton.

'Pretty good,' replied Eddie. 'I gave myself plenty of time.'

'You want a coffee or something?'

Eddie shook his head. 'How about getting us a glass of water while I have a quick snakes.' Les poured a tumbler of water and handed it to Eddie when he came back from the bathroom. He took a couple of swallows and looked at Les. 'So what's been happening? I got a funny phone call from Billy last night.'

'What's been happening?' Les gave his shoulders an indifferent shrug. 'The federal police pinched me on drug charges last night. Then I came home and porked Kastrine Kreen. Or at least she tried to pork me. That's about all.'

'You what?'

Sticking mainly to what happened with the police, Les gave Eddie a fairly detailed account of the previous night's events. Eddie pulled up a chair at the dining room table while he listened. The expression on Eddie's face didn't change all that much, but he finished his first glass of water fairly smartly and got into another.

Les shrugged his broad shoulders again. 'Anyway Eddie. That's what happened last night. All because of that fuckin dill next door.'

Eddie sort of nodded and shook his head at the same time. 'Well,' he said slowly. 'I can't see it making that much difference. Better if it hadn't happened. But ... nothing we can do now.' He

60

looked at Les from over his glass of water. 'So what happened with Kastrine Kreen? Are you fair dinkum about her?'

'Fuckin oath. She's an old wobbegong.' Les gave Eddie pretty much a blow by blow description of his quick romp on the lounge with the renowned feminist author.

Eddie shook his head and chuckled into his second glass of water. 'So you've plied this poor woman with drugs. Took advantage of her, and it turns out she's got the giant, enormous tomato. A bit of vaginal trauma Les.'

Les gave his head a quick shake. 'Vaginal traumas? Vaginal tremors? I don't know. I think this thing had been hit by an earthquake.'

'So you don't think you'll be getting back there again, big fellah?'

'I doubt it very much Eddie,' replied Les. 'Of course, you can always be my stunt double, if you so desire.'

Eddie seemed to think for a second. 'Is it really that big?'

'I wouldn't mind it full of second-hand Harley-Davidsons.' Les looked directly at Eddie. 'Anyway. What's happening Eddie? When are we going to start putting holes in people?'

'We're not.' Eddie finished his glass of water and stood up. 'Come on out on the sundeck.'

Les followed Eddie out onto the balcony. A radio was playing next door. But there was still no sign of life. The odd car went past and the sun still sparkled on the blue waters of Port Stephens. Eddie pointed across the water. 'You see the other side of the bay over there, where there's a few houses and that?'

'Yeah,' nodded Les.

'Well that's called Tea Gardens — Hawks Nest.'

'Right.'

'You see that long stretch of white sand leading up to those rocks?'

Les gazed across Shoal Bay guessing it to be about five kilometres to the other side. There was a handful of houses in the distance then nothing but scrub and pure white sandhills surrounding a long strip of equally white beach. The beach ended where some rocks formed the start of another towering, green headland. 'Yeah,' Les nodded again.

'That's Jimmy's Beach. Those rocks are called The Boulders and after that is Yacaba Head.'

'I'm with you,' said Les.

'Well. We're going over to Jimmy's Beach where a bloke'll be waiting for us with a mini-submarine. Then we're going to take the mini-sub out between Jimmy's Beach and The Boulders. And we're going to drown two blokes fishing in an old aluminium dinghy.'

Les looked impassively at the little hitman. 'Eddie. That's got to be the most ridiculous thing I ever heard of in my life.'

Eddie gave Les a pat on the shoulder. 'I knew you'd say that. Now come inside, and I'll show you exactly how we're going to do it.'

Les sat on one of the lounge chairs with his feet under the coffee table. Eddie eased into the lounge chair opposite. The still unopened suitcase sat on the lounge between them. Eddie removed his cap and sunglasses and placed them on the coffee table.

'Okay,' he said. 'Fishcake goes out fishing with a mate of his called Forbes Zaccariah in this old, tin runabout. They always go out at high tide after bream and whiting and they take gallons of piss with them so they can get completely shitfaced while they're at it. I've been watching them for the last week. And I've had someone else watching them for me too. So I know their every fuckin move.'

Les looked a little concerned. 'You never mentioned anything about this other bloke Zaccariah, Eddie. He's not some poor bastard with eight kids or something — is he?'

Eddie shook his head. 'He's got no family that I know of. And he's a complete dropkick from what I can gather. He used to be the manager of the Port Stephens Memorial Club. But at the moment he's out on bail for knocking off a hundred grand. Plus he's a good mate of Fishcake's. So that'll give you an idea of his form.'

Les nodded. 'Righto. It's just that I like to know who it is I'm going to murder. That's all.'

'Fair enough,' smiled Eddie. 'Anyway. I'll be going round to a place called Fly Point to pick up a boat. It belongs to an old mate of mine from Vietnam. He's in the local game fishing club.'

'Does he know what's going on?' asked Les.

Eddie nodded. 'Yeah. He's allright. He's in on the rort.'

63

'Okey doke,' said Les.

'Then I'll come back and collect you from that jetty in front of the Dolphin Hotel. We'll zip over to Jimmy's Beach. Pick up the mini-sub, lash it under the boat, then take the boat out and anchor about two hundred metres from Fishcake and his mate. We get into the mini-sub. Sneak across and hover just under their boat. Then get out of the mini-sub and swim up. You pull down on one side. I'll push up on the other. And we'll tip them both out and drown them. They'll both be that pissed, they'll be dead before they even know what's happened. Then we jump back in the mini-sub. Sneak back to the boat and lash it underneath again. Then get in the boat and head back to Jimmy's Beach where the same bloke'll be waiting for us. He'll piss off with the mini-sub. And we piss off back here.' Eddie picked at his chin. 'I reckon, counting the time we're in the water, getting over there and back and all the other fartarsing around. We should have it all wrapped up in …?' Eddie gestured with one hand. 'Two hours tops.'

Norton stared at Eddie for a moment. 'Two hours? Just like that?'

'Yeah. Just like that,' replied Eddie confidently. 'Someone'll see the bodies floating around eventually. And the post mortem will read: DEATH BY ACCIDENTAL DROWNING. DUE TO INTOXICATION. The only thing you have to watch Les, is make sure you grab your bloke by his clothes. Don't leave any scratch marks or bruises.'

'Is that why you asked me if I had my PADI the other night?' said Les. 'We'll be using scuba tanks.'

Eddie's eyes seemed to light up a little. 'Sort of Les. But not quite. Have a look at this.'

Eddie opened the suitcase. There was some diving gear and a couple of overnight bags at one end. Packed neatly at the other end were six, small, black scuba tanks. He took them out and placed them on the lounge. Two were about half the size of a normal scuba tank, with regulator valves and hoses attached. The other four were a little bigger than a shampoo bottle, with a white, silicone rubber mouth piece at the top.

'The two big ones,' said Eddie, 'are Pony Bottles. They're good for about half an hour and they'll be clamped to the mini-sub. The other two are Spare Airs. They're good for about five minutes. We'll put them on when we leave the mini-sub to drown our two mates.'

'Five minutes?' said Les.

'Yeah. Christ. You could drown a hippopotamus in five minutes.' Les picked up one of the tiny scuba tanks. Near the mouth piece it said: SSI. Submersible Systems Inc. H.B. California. Round the bottom was a yellow sticker saying: Instructor. Not For Resale. 'Don't bother telling me where you got these Eddie. But how come you got four?'

'There's a couple extra for backup.'

'In other words, in case something fucks up.'

'Les,' smiled Eddie. 'You always allow for contingencies and situations. How do you think I managed to stay alive in that fuckin jungle for so long? Just shove them down the front of your wetsuit. Or in your lead belt.'

'Yeah righto.' Les stared at the tiny scuba tank in his hand. 'Just one small thing, Eddie?'

'Yes Les. What's that, old mate?'

'While we're out roaming around underwater, what happens if someone comes past, sees an empty boat and decides to stick their head in?'

Eddie held up a finger. 'I knew you'd say that. Have a look at this.' Eddie opened up a small overnight bag and pulled out two blow-up dolls. 'I stick a bit of air in these. Shove a hat on them, stick a fishing rod under their wings. And what have we got? Two instant fishermen.'

Les placed the tiny scuba tank back with the others. 'You think of everything Eddie, don't you?'

'Like I said, Les,' winked Eddie. 'Contingencies. And situations.'

'I must remember that. Okay. When are we going to start getting ready to take Fishcake and his mate synchronised swimming?'

Eddie looked at his watch. 'Within the hour. So we might as well start getting our shit together. You brought all your snorkelling gear with you, didn't you?'

'Yeah. My short-sleeved wetsuit. Lead belt. The lot.'

'Good.'

Les started getting to his feet. 'Righto. Well, while I'm sorting out all my junk, you can run me through this mad rattle again. Just in case I'm imagining things.'

Eddie got up too. 'Don't worry mate. It's all sweet,' he said. 'And when we're finished. If you want to come into Newcastle and give me a hand with something tonight. Something easy. There could even be a nice Jules Verne in it for you.'

'An earn?' said Les. 'Now that's something I haven't had for a while.'

'I'll tell you about it when we get back.'

Taking their time and discussing a few things, with Norton's radio playing softly in the background, it took them about thirty minutes to pack everything. They'd leave their clothes on and get changed into their wetsuits at Hawks Nest, then put their clothes back on over the top. Les packed all his stuff into one of his overnight bags and Eddie crammed everything else, including the assorted scuba tanks, into one he'd brought with him. He zipped it shut, placed the suitcase in the spare room then put his cap and sunglasses back on.

'Okay,' he said, taking a quick glance at his watch as he picked up his overnight bag. 'I'll meet you at that jetty in twenty ... twenty-five minutes.'

'Allright. See you then.' Les opened the door, closed it again and Eddie was gone.

Les checked his things once more then walked out onto the balcony and gazed across Port Stephens shaking his head. How do I get myself into this shit? He looked up at the sky, where a small, white cloud had drifted across the sun. This is half your fault you know. It is too. The sun came out and almost as if it was in reply to his question *Send The Divers Down* by Australian Crawl started playing on the radio. Les looked back up at the sky. Don't do it to me boss. No omens. Please. Les had time for a quick cup of coffee and figuring he was going to get wet one way or another, put his trainers on without any socks and a maroon and blue GAP anorak he had folded up in a small, matching bag. He finished his coffee, switched off the radio and picked up his overnight bag. Ten minutes later he'd left the flat, and was standing next to a landscaped circle of bricks with a few small trees in the middle, just back from the jetty.

For such a mild day Les was surprised that there weren't more people around. There was hardly anyone. I guess that's what it must be like up here when the season finishes, he thought. It's certainly nice though. The jetty was about twenty metres long, built of concrete and wood, with chipped, white railings and faded, white poles, some starting to split with age, running down either side. A pipe jutted out across the sand from some rocks underneath and on the left-hand side a set of concrete steps ran down to the water. Several boats bobbed gently at their moorings out in the bay and about the same number of seagulls hovered above the sand. One kid, a boy about twelve in an old straw hat, probably wagging school, was fishing off the right-hand side. While Les stood there absently watching him, a couple of thoughts crossed his mind. Les knew he was a little on edge about what was going down. But Eddie definitely wasn't being fair dinkum. The way he went on when they were packing their gear, he seemed to be foxing about something. Les could always tell when he was being conned, or something wasn't quite kosher. It was just a sixth sense he had. And Eddie was definitely holding something back. He hadn't told him about this Zaccariah bloke being in the boat. Now there was something else. Les could feel it in his bones. Les nodded to himself. I think I might have a word with young Edward when we get to Hawks Nest. Or wherever it is we're going. Les was still mildly brooding, when an object approaching on the left caught his eye.

It was a fairly new, five-metre aluminium runabout with the console in the middle and a squat, black outboard motor throbbing quietly at the stern. The bow was partly enclosed with a railing either side and an aerial wobbled in the air above the console, where the flash of an Hawaiian shirt told Les Eddie was at the controls. Les walked down to the concrete landing as the boat drew nearer. A few moments later Eddie swung the boat alongside and Les dropped his bag in the back and stepped aboard. Apart from where Eddie was sitting there were no other seats, just a white, fibreglass storage compartment in front of the console.

Eddie nodded to it. 'Plonk your arse down there,' he said.

'Righto.' Les did as Eddie directed and they drew away from the jetty.

There was a life jacket under the bow and an anchor tied to one of the railings. Les held onto the

69

rope and made himself as comfortable as he could while Eddie expertly gunned the runabout past the boats moored out from the jetty. The light sou'wester coming across the bay had managed to stir up a few whitecaps plus a slight swell, yet Les was surprised at the lack of noise and vibration coming from the motor as they skimmed quietly over the waves.

'Shit! That motor's quiet Eddie.'

'Yeah. Instead of a two-stroke, it's a four-stroke diesel. They're allright, aren't they?'

'Reckon,' replied Les. They skimmed over a few more small swells leaving a couple of the boats behind them rocking at their moorings. Les had a good look around and couldn't believe how big Port Stephens was. It was immense. 'How come you wanted to pick me up at the jetty?' he asked Eddie. 'I could have come with you.'

Eddie stared straight ahead. 'How many people were on the jetty?'

Les shrugged. 'One kid fishing. That's all.'

'There were twenty golfers having a barbecue at Fly Point, just for starters.'

'Oh.'

The patches of sea grass on the bottom began to disappear and the water started turning jade green as it deepened. Although the wind had chopped the surface and stirred things up a little the water still looked reasonably clear. Eddie wasn't saying much and Les was still mulling over what he'd been thinking about at the jetty. Les kept hold of the rope, as the odd spray from the boat's bow slapped him across the face and before long Jimmy's Beach drew closer, along with The Boulders and the looming green rise of Yacaba Head. There weren't many fishing boats around. A ferry full of dolphin spotters chugged through the whitecaps way off to their left then a reflection of sunlight on something out from The Boulders caught Norton's eye and he felt Eddie tap him on the shoulder.

'Did you see that?' asked Eddie.

'Yeah.'

'That's them.'

Les peered towards The Boulders, then the water started getting shallow again and the shoreline began approaching rapidly. It looked totally deserted. Just a long strip of white sand with a thick band of seaweed at the water's edge and after that nothing but scrub-covered sand dunes rising and falling into the distance. Eddie slowed down then nosed the boat straight up onto the beach. Les didn't have to be told. He jumped out, waited for a small swell and dragged the boat up a little further onto the sand as Eddie cut the motor. With the boat almost completely out of the water, Les noticed two thick fibreglass tubes, two metres apart, sticking out just below the waterline. Pushed through the centre were two stainless steel pins attached to a short length of chain and it appeared the two tubes were sitting on a fibreglass base, stuck to the hull of the boat with epoxy resin.

'We're a few minutes ahead of time,' said Eddie. 'But we may as well start getting changed now.'

'Righto,' replied Les.

Parallel with the beach, Les noticed a trail cutting through the scrub and sand dunes; he would have liked to have had a good look around, it all looked so quiet and beautiful. Instead, he kicked off his trainers, had a quick pee then got his bag from the back of the boat and began changing into his wetsuit. Eddie did the same. While they were changing, Eddie still seemed to adopt this strange attitude; not talking and somehow managing to avoid eye contact with Les. Before long they were both in their wetsuits; Eddie with his Hawaiian shirt over the top and Les in his maroon and blue anorak. By now however, Norton had had enough. Something was going on. He was about to put it straight on Eddie when a sound approaching on the right caught his attention.

'Hey Les,' said Eddie. 'Have a look. It's the Bush Tucker Man.'

'What?' A few moments later a battered, brown Land Rover with a canopy on the back came bumping along the trail. As it drew closer, the driver swung the vehicle around and reversed it down to the beach level with the boat. Sticking a metre or so out the back was an oblong shape tied with black sheeting. The driver cut the motor and got out. He was wearing an old army hat, wraparound sunglasses, an old pair of blue shorts and a khaki shirt with the sleeves hacked off. His right arm was heavily bandaged and there were a few patches of Elastoplast on the other. Despite the sunglasses, Les had no trouble recognising him. It was Major Garrick Lewis. The Gecko.

'Don't tell me Major. Let me guess,' smiled Norton, pointing to the Major's bandaged arm. 'You've got a couple of plutonium rods or something shoved in there.'

'No Les,' replied the Major. 'All I've got in there is about thirty stitches, lad. From an altercation fitting a sliding glass door. But my word,' smiled the Major, offering his hand, 'it's certainly good to catch up with you again, young fellah.'

'You too, Major,' said Les. 'You too.' Les shook hands with him as carefully as he could.

'I was meaning to tell you the Major would be here Les,' said Eddie. 'But I just know how much you love surprises.'

Les felt a bit awkward at first. He was right in his suspicions. But now he realised what Eddie had been up to he could have kissed him. It was a surprise allright catching up with the Major again. An exceptionally pleasant one.

'And how's Bondi Baths these days Les?' asked the Major.

'Pretty much the same as when you left it Major,' replied Les.

'Excellent,' said the Major. 'Excellent.' He clapped his hands together and gave them a brisk rub. 'Anyway. I imagine Eddie's told you what's going on Les?'

'Major,' replied Les snapping a salute. 'I've been briefed, rebriefed and debriefed. I'm ready to jump.'

'Good lad.' The Major looked at both Les and Eddie. 'Then let's get fully operational.' The Major went to the back of the Land Rover and pulled away the canopy. 'Will you let the tray down, Eddie?'

'Sure.'

Eddie let the back tray down and the Major removed the black sheeting. Then they carefully slid the mini-sub out from the back of the Land Rover and laid it on the beach. It was dark-blue, fibreglass, and about four metres long with dark green streaks. There was a small propeller and two flukes at the rear, and another two steering flukes towards the front. The mini-sub had an open seating compartment with a small perspex shield in front, a joy stick, two pedals and a couple of gauges and buttons on a small fibreglass dashboard. A small seat was bolted in front of the joy stick and behind that was a flat, metal tank with another seat on top. Sticking out, a little up from the bottom, were two thick fibreglass tubes that Les imagined slotted into the two on the boat. Sitting on the sand, with the tail at the back and the flukes on the side, it reminded Les of a lean dugong. Whatever it reminded him of, they'd both be packed in pretty tight and Les was glad he was wearing his small jet fins. They moved the mini-sub down to the boat and clamped it onto the side. For a battery-powered vessel, Les was surprised how light it was. He stood back as Eddie clamped the pony bottles into two, stainless steel brackets near the seats, then attached the regulators and tested them.

'Did you make this, Major?' asked Les.

'Yes. It's another one of my little knick-knacks,' replied the Major.

'Shit, it's light. What sort of batteries do you use?'

'I don't. It runs on compressed air. Same as a dentist's drill.'

'Compressed air?' said Les. 'What about all the bubbles?'

The Major shook his head. 'It's got a built-in rebreather system. Including one for your pony bottles.'

Les took another look at the tank beneath the back seat. 'Very ingenious, Major.'

'Yes. It's not too bad. Needs a little refinement. Anyway,' the Major clapped his hands together, 'we can't stay here talking all day. I'll move the car back amongst the bushes.'

'Allright.' Eddie snapped the Major another salute. 'I'll see you when we get back.'

'Good luck, Les.'

'Yeah. Thanks Major.' Les was going to snap him a salute as well. But somehow it didn't quite seem appropriate. With the Major's help he pushed the boat out then jumped in the back next to their bags. Eddie fired up the engine and they were off once more.

Again they slipped quietly and smoothly over the water. The sandy bottom began to disappear and as they got closer to The Boulders and the heads the water seemed to get a little murky. Eddie was going at a fair pace, but the mini-sub never moved at the side of the boat and even though it was just under the surface, its dark blue and green colouring made the tiny craft almost invisible. Eventually Eddie found a good enough spot about five hundred metres out from The Boulders and slowed down. Off to their right Les could now make out the two figures sitting at their fishing rods in the old runabout. Eddie cut the engine as Les went to the bow and dropped the anchor over; the rope went out a little over ten metres. The only sound now was the breeze and the gentle slapping of water against the hull. In the comparative silence, Les caught a burst of boozy, wheezy laughter drift across from the old runabout. Eddie took a small pair of binoculars from his bag, focused them on the other runabout for a few moments then handed the binoculars to Les.

'Fishcake's sitting on the right. I'll grab him. You get the other bloke.'

Les adjusted the binoculars as the boats slewed round with the wind. Both men were wearing T-shirts, sunglasses and terry-towelling hats, but there was no mistaking Fishbyrne's fat, ugly head. Zaccariah wasn't much better looking; he had slick black hair, a hooked nose and a florid, jowly face that said it loved beer and beef. Les looked at the man he was about to murder for a few moments then ran the binoculars over the foreshore. There was one bloke fishing further up The Boulders, a brief glint of light reflected from a bottle or tin can amongst the scrubby sandhills and a few seagulls and pelicans hung in the breeze along the water's edge. Les looked at Zaccariah again then handed the binoculars back to Eddie.

'Yeah. I got him,' said Les. 'He's just as ugly as Fishcake.'

Eddie put the binoculars back in his bag. 'All you got to do, is go up Zaccariah's side of the boat and pull down. I'll hit the other side. Just watch out for their fishing lines.'

Les still had his eyes on the old runabout. 'No worries.'

Eddie gestured with both hands. 'Okay. Let's blow up the two dolls and we'll start getting ready.'

Eddie got the two blow-up dolls from his bag and handed one to Les telling him not to fully inflate it. This didn't take long and when he handed it to Eddie, Eddie jammed a couple of hats on them, shoved them between the boat rail and the console and pushed the two fishing rods under their arms. Les wasn't quite sure how Eddie managed it, but from where Les stood the two dolls looked quite convincing. Absolutely stupid close up. But convincing. Eddie then took the four Spare Air bottles from his bag, handed two to Les and removed his Hawaiian shirt. Les pulled his anorak over his head and jammed one Spare Air in his lead belt and the other in the arm of his short-sleeved wetsuit. His flippers went on next then he leant over the side of the boat, cleaned his face mask and pushed it down over his eyes and nose. Eddie did the same.

'Okay,' said Eddie, as he pushed his snorkel into his mouth. 'Let's go for a dip.'

'Yeah, why not.' Les put his snorkel in also and they both slipped quietly over the side.

The water was a little cool at first, but it was reasonably clear. Les pushed down off the runabout and squashed himself into the back seat of the mini-sub while Eddie got behind the controls. The Pony Bottle was sitting snugly in its bracket just a little to the left. Les exhaled a stream of bubbles, took his snorkel out then put the regulator in his mouth and took a breath. It made a rasping, hollow sound and the air felt cold and a little unnatural. It was certainly different to plain old snorkel sucking and when he exhaled there were no bubbles. The rear pin holding the mini-sub was just behind Les. He pulled it out while Eddie did the same. Eddie shoved the mini-sub away from the runabout and started the engine. Les could scarcely believe his ears; the noise coming from the propellor had the same horrible whine as a dentist's drill. Eddie moved the joystick taking the mini-sub down a few metres, banked to the right in front of their boat, then straightened up and headed directly towards the old runabout.

Being squashed up behind Eddie, Les could feel the surge of water going around and behind him, but apart from Eddie's hair drifting about in the slipstream Les couldn't see a great deal. He noticed the rippling, silver canopy of the surface above but he couldn't make out the bottom and on either side the water faded off into a green, purply gloom then an inky nothingness. A scattering of shiny silver pilchards, catching the rays of sunlight coming down from the surface, flashed in the gloom. Some smaller fish glinted in the sun rays and a school of pink jellyfish parted round the mini-sub as they went through them. A movement over Norton's left shoulder made him gasp and suck hard on his regulator. Two big kingfish came in for a look, stayed with them for a few seconds then with a flick of their powerful tails disappeared into the gloom. Les peered after them and a burst of adrenalin squirted into his stomach. It was probably his imagination, but now Les was certain he could see shadows and movement all round them. Then the realisation of where he was and what they were up to sank in and Les started to feel a little apprehensive. This wasn't a pleasant day's snorkel sucking down North Bondi. This was spooky. It was too late to turn back. But Les would be glad when the whole thing was over and they were back on dry land.

The dentist-drill whine of the engine changed pace as Eddie began slowing the mini-sub down. Ahead of them something caught Norton's eye. Two fishing lines and an anchor rope arrowed down towards the bottom and above, the dark hull of a boat was rocking gently from side to side against the mirrored surface of the ocean. Eddie brought the mini-sub up a little positioning it about five metres beneath the old runabout. The dentist drill stopped and Eddie turned around and pointed his thumb towards the surface. Oddly enough, the adrenalin squirting around in Norton's stomach seemed to settle down now that the job was at hand. Eddie eased himself out of the mini-sub and Les unfolded from the back seat as well. He sucked one more mouthful of air from the Pony Bottle then took the Spare Air from his lead belt and put it in his mouth, clamping his teeth hard on the silicone mouthpiece; he had to suck a little harder than on the regulator for air, but there wasn't that much difference. They were both out of the mini-sub now kicking gently with their flippers, while it hovered in position, moving very slightly with the current. A swarm of bubbles came from Eddie's Spare Air. He motioned to the surface with his thumb again then closed his fist and started poking his fingers out. One-two.

Right on three they both kicked like crazy and sprinted for the surface. Les was going that fast when he got there, he burst out of the water, waist level with the side of the old runabout. He just had time to see Forbes Zaccariah's jaw drop and get a glimpse of Fishcake's back, as the fat cop pissed over the side, when Eddie hit the bottom of the boat like a human torpedo. Les slammed down on the rail at the same time and the old boat nearly capsized. Zaccariah yelped and pitched head first into the water while Fishcake did a quick pirouette and went over the side backwards. Through the bubbles, Les took Zaccariah's T-shirt by the scruff of the neck and started swimming him down face first towards the bottom. Zaccariah tried vainly to put up a struggle. But the more he struggled, the harder Les squeezed, till it was almost as if Norton was choking him to death instead of drowning him. Les sucked on the Spare Air and held Zaccariah down. Fishbyrne's mate gave a few more kicks, his arms flailed around then his movements got slower till they finally stopped altogether. Les held him away at arm's length as a few bubbles came from his nose and mouth; and then for Forbes Zaccariah it was all over. Suddenly, several flashes of silver in the water above Norton caught his attention.

For a couple of drunks, Forbes and Fishcake hadn't put in a bad morning's fishing. Les and Eddie had hit the boat that hard they'd knocked over the day's catch. Drifting languidly around them in the current were ten good sized bream, about the same number of whiting, a trevally and two flathead at least two kilograms each, plus some fish guts and a bit of burley. Les looked at the fish for a moment then loosened his grip on Zaccariah's old T-shirt before finally letting go. Zaccariah's hair floated above his head as he drifted beneath the ocean with his back to Les. He began to slowly turn around. When he did, Norton groaned inwardly. Zaccariah's skin looked light blue under the water and right across the side of his neck a thick, red welt stood out like a neon sign. Eddie had warned Les to be careful. But in his excitement, Les had just held on and squeezed. Now there was evidence something had happened. Norton had stuffed up. Fuck it! Les cursed to himself. Finally Forbes Zaccariah faced Les. His eyes were open and there was a strange, half smile on his face almost as if in his death he was getting the last laugh on Norton. Shit! Les cursed again. Zaccariah's right arm floated up as if he was pointing at Les or at something behind him. It was uncanny. In his anger and confusion, Les was almost tempted to turn around and see what Zaccariah was pointing at. When from out of nowhere, a grey shape went past Norton's right flipper and with one quick snap of its jaws, took the two-kilogram flathead floating near Zaccariah like it was a cocktail frankfurt, then shot off into the gloom.

Les turned towards Eddie just in time to see another grey shape take one of the bream floating near Fishcake. Another shape swam between Eddie's flippers and snapped its jaws round the remaining flathead. Les looked around them as all the shadows began coming to life. Somehow they'd managed to swim into a school of sharks. Les was no expert. But he'd read enough diving magazines to know what bronze whalers looked like, and there were at least a dozen, the smallest over two metres long. However, they weren't all bronze whalers. Drifting at the edge of the inky gloom was a three-metre hammerhead. And if the bronze whalers and the hammerhead weren't bad enough, circling them was a monstrous tiger shark; at least five metres long and as thick as a car body. Norton's blood froze in his veins. A bronze whaler swam in and took another bream, then another came in behind Les and hit Zaccariah in the side. Its powerful jaws crunched easily through his rib cage, then it shook its head from side to side and wrenched off a huge slab of flesh, leaving a cloud of blood, shards of bone and fluttering entrails in its wake. Through the blood, Les turned to Eddie again as the hammerhead came in and snapped Fishcake's leg off, just above the knee. Another bronze whaler hit Zaccariah shaking him like a rag doll as it tore off his arm and part of his shoulder. What had Les fascinated and slightly mesmerised however, was that the expression on Forbes Zaccariah's face never changed. Through the clouds of blood, he still had that half smile on his face as the sharks tore him to pieces.

Then an expression began to form on Norton's face — eyes bulging, blood curdling horror. With his heart pounding, Les sprinted back to the mini-sub in a flurry of terrified kicks and breast strokes and tried to squash himself into the back seat just as Eddie shoved himself behind the controls and started the engine. Les stashed the Spare Air back in his lead belt and started sucking on the Pony Bottle as if it was the last air left in the world. Eddie banked the mini-sub around as the tiger shark came up from the bottom with its massive jaws open, ready to take a bite. It missed the mini-sub by less than a metre and kept going through the other sharks up to the dingy, hitting it that hard it ripped a piece out of the back and flipped the old aluminium boat completely over. Les looked up and got a quick glimpse of a radio, some fishing equipment and an esky full of VB fluttering down beneath the upturned dinghy, then Eddie gunned the mini-sub back to their boat. Too terrified to look behind him, Les held on for grim death, and prayed. He was still saying Hail Marys, and anything else he could think of when Eddie slowed the mini-sub down and nestled it alongside the two tubes sticking out from the bottom of the runabout. He cut the motor and in a nanosecond they had the mini-sub secured and were back on board ripping off their diving gear.

'Jesus fuckin Christ!' howled Les, tossing his mask and snorkel on the deck. 'Did you see that?'

Eddie's eyes were wide open and almost sparkling. Les couldn't tell if he was frightened or having some kind of crazy adrenalin rush. 'Yeah. Wasn't that a turn up for the books.'

'A turn up for the books!' yelled Les. 'Fuckin hell! I'm lucky I'm still in one bloody piece.'

'Shit happens. Don't it.' Eddie grabbed his knife and slashed the two blow-up dolls. 'Come on,' he said, kicking them to one side as he gathered up the two fishing rods. 'Let's get out of here.'

'Yeah,' answered Les, trying to control his shaking. 'Let's.'

Les didn't bother getting into his anorak. He just pushed his eyeballs back in his head, sat on the storage compartment and held on to the rope again as Eddie flattened it towards the shoreline. By the time they got back to Jimmy's Beach, the Major was waiting by the water's edge with the Land Rover. Eddie gunned the runabout up onto the sand and cut the engine as Les jumped over the side grateful and absolutely ecstatic to be back on dry land again.

'How did everything go?' inquired the Major. 'You look a bit green round the gills, Les.'

'Green round the fuckin gills?' answered Les. 'You tell him what happened, Eddie. Just in case that might have been my imagination.'

Eddie seemed to give the Major an indifferent shrug. 'We landed in a school of sharks.'

'Sharks?'

'Yeah,' nodded Eddie. 'Plenty of 'em too.'

While they unfastened the mini-sub and stowed it back in the Land Rover, Eddie told the Major how everything went according to plan except for the unexpected arrival of a dozen or more sharks. Including the tiger and the hammerhead.

'Yeah,' said Eddie, as the Major tied the canopy on the Land Rover. 'It got a bit hairy there for a while.'

'Bronze whalers, eh,' said the Major. 'You know, it's funny. I was going to tell you the mullet are running at the moment and to keep your eyes open. But somehow it slipped my mind.'

'The mullet are running,' snorted Les. 'I got something running down the leg of my fuckin wetsuit at the moment. I can tell you that.'

'Like I said, Les,' smiled Eddie. 'Shit happens.'

'Indeed,' said the Major. 'The main thing is — mission accomplished. And you both returned safe and well. So why don't you get changed and we'll skedaddle.'

'Good idea,' agreed Norton. 'Let's get to the shithouse out of here.'

Les almost tore off his wetsuit. He threw it in his overnight bag along with anything else he could find, and changed back into his shorts and trainers with his anorak over the top. Eddie did the same.

'Actually,' said the Major, 'this could work to our advantage. I'll ring 000 from a phone box on the way home and report seeing a shark attack.'

'That's a thought,' agreed Eddie.

Les threw his bag in the back of the runabout next to Eddie's and got ready to shove off.

'Well goodbye, Les,' said the Major, shaking Norton's hand. 'I'll see you again some time. You too, Eddie.'

'See you Garrick.' Eddie jumped up and got behind the console.

Les climbed aboard, sat back on the storage compartment and took hold of the anchor rope. 'Yeah. Don't hold your breath.'

The Major got behind the wheel and drove back up the beach towards the trail. Eddie hit the starter, spun the boat around and headed back towards Shoal Bay. Not a great deal was said on the return journey. Eddie kept staring ahead, concentrating on handling the boat. Les could only see pictures in his mind of the sharks tearing Forbes Zaccariah's body to pieces and just considered himself lucky to be alive. However, if he wasn't saying much now, he'd certainly have something to say back at the flat. Soon the boats appeared at the moorings with the jetty not far behind them. Eddie brought the runabout alongside the landing. Les picked up his bag and jumped off.

'I'll see you back at the flat, in about twenty minutes,' said Eddie.

'Yeah. See you then,' grunted Norton.

Eddie swung the boat around and headed back to Fly Point. Les trudged off up the stairs at the side of the jetty. He was just about to get into his stride when he heard a voice call out on his left. It was the same kid with the old straw hat he'd seen earlier.

'How'dja go?'

Les stopped and glared at the kid. He almost had to bite his tongue to stop from letting go a string of expletives. 'How did we go. How do you think we ... went. We went by boat. You ... inbred, hillbilly ... moron.'

'Gee, sorry mister,' said the kid. 'I was only asking.' A grin lit up the kid's face. 'I went allright. Look at these.' Proud as punch, the kid held up five good-sized bream on a piece of cord, all scaled and gutted.

Les half-expected the kid to tell him to go pull his head in for being so rude. Instead, the kid's friendly, young exuberance still shone through and Norton felt like a proper mug.

'Yeah ... They're the grouse,' said Les. 'Good on you matey. Keep up the good work.'

'Thanks mister.'

Les was about to get going again, but he stopped. 'Hey, do you want to sell them?'

The kid thought for a bit. 'Allright. Ten dollars.'

'I haven't got any money on me at the moment. But I'll tell you what.' Les pointed to where he was staying. 'Bring them over to those flats down there. Number two. And I'll give you twenty dollars.'

'Allright mister. You're on. Give me about another half an hour.'

'Okay me old. See you then.'

The first thing Les did after he walked inside the unit and kicked off his wet trainers was throw his overnight bag full of diving gear in the spare room. And it would stay there exactly as it was till he left.

Snorkelling in Shoal Bay was definitely off the menu. And he'd be leaving sooner than he intended also. Sunday. Probably Saturday. Maybe Friday. They could stick Port Stephens. Blue Water Wonderland. Right where the monkey stuck the penny. Les put the radio on and walked around in circles muttering to himself for a while. The fact that he'd just murdered some bloke in cold blood never entered his head. All Norton could see was man-eating sharks.

Eventually, he took off his clothes and got under the shower. After finishing with a shave, Les changed into a pair of jeans and his blue, Eric Clapton T-shirt then walked out to the kitchen. The opened bottle of white rum looked inviting. But he'd get into that later, and plenty of it. A cup of tea would do for the time being. He went to put the kettle on when there was a knock on the door. Les opened it to find the tourist from hell was back. The tourist gave Les a brief glance, took his cap and sunglasses off and walked into the kitchen.

Eddie poured himself a glass of water. 'You want one?' he asked Les.

Norton shook his head. 'I was just about to make a cup of tea.'

Eddie swallowed the glass of water and poured another one. 'Well. What about that, Les?'

'Well Eddie. What about it?'

'What about it? Fuck! Did you see that hammerhead take Fishcake's leg off?'

'No. I was having too much fun watching a bronze whaler rip Zaccariah's ribcage to bits.'

Eddie sat down at the dining room table and sipped his glass of water. Les spread himself into a lounge chair with the sun on his back and they compared notes. Les couldn't believe Eddie's nonchalant, almost flippant attitude towards what they'd just been through. Although Les was doing his best to act cool and not show his true emotions, underneath, he felt like running out onto the sundeck and screaming his head off.

'Anyway Les,' Eddie raised his glass of water and smiled, 'you know what we've just done, don't you? We've committed the perfect crime.'

'Yeah. Isn't that wonderful,' replied Les, sarcastically, then thought of the predicament he was in earlier when he saw the welt on Zaccariah's neck and he started to calm down.

Eddie looked directly at Norton. 'I'll be honest with you Les. In a way, I'm glad that happened.'

'You are? How do you work that out?'

'When I grabbed Fishcake, I know the cunt recognised me. And pissed and all as he was. He started putting up one hell of a fight. I finished up grabbing the fat bastard by the throat. And I think I choked him before he got a chance to drown.'

'Yeah? Well, I suppose Eddie,' conceded Les, 'sometimes things do have a tendency to happen for the best.'

'I think they do.' Eddie gave a little chuckle. 'Tell you what though, I think I might be turned off fish for a while.'

'Really?' said Les. 'It's funny you should say that.

Cause that's just what I feel like right now. A big feed of fresh fish.'

Eddie screwed his face up. 'Christ! You're kidding aren't you?'

Les shrugged. 'No.' There was a soft tap at the door. Eddie spun around nervously. 'Will you get that Eddie? You're closest. It'll only be the paper boy.'

Eddie got up and answered the door. 'FISH! Why the fuck would I want any fish? What is this? Some sort of gee-up. You cheeky little prick. Piss off.'

'Gee. Sorry mister. I was only doing what that big red-headed bloke asked me to.'

'Fish? You little bastard.' Eddie brought his hand back. 'I ought to put me boot right up your ... '

Les appeared at the door with the twenty dollars. 'There you go, mate. Don't take any notice of him. He's always like that.'

The kid smiled up from under his straw hat and took the money. 'Gee. Thanks mister.'

'You're right, mate.' The kid had put the fish in a plastic bag. Les shut the door and handed them to Eddie.

'What am I gonna fuckin do with these?' snorted Eddie.

'Cook them. Italian style. You know how to do it.'

'Get fucked.' Eddie threw the bag of fish in the sink. 'You want them cooked. You fuckin do it.'

'Okay.'

Eddie took another look at the fresh fish. 'Hey, they're not bad sized bream. Did you get all those for twenty dollars?'

'I could have got them for ten.'

'How? What the fuck's going on? Am I missing something here?'

Les told Eddie how he came across the kid and how he was impressed by the kid still being so polite after the way he had spoken to him.

Eddie looked at the fish again. 'So what are you going to do with them?'

Les gave a slight shrug. 'Probably cook them. I dunno.'

'Give them to me. I'll take them back to Sydney with me tonight. Lyndy'll cook those up a treat.'

'I thought you were off fish.'

Eddie gave a slight shrug also. 'I've changed my mind.'

'Okay. But they cost me twenty bucks you know.'

Eddie slipped an arm around Norton's shoulders. 'Didn't I say I had a nice earn for you tonight? If you're interested.'

'You did mention something earlier.'

'Okay. Well make that two cups of tea. And I'll tell you about it out on the sundeck.'

Eddie started taking his clothes off and got under the shower. A short while later he walked back into the kitchen dressed in a plain white T-shirt and a pair of jeans.

Les had made the tea. He poured himself a cup and was just about to pour Eddie one, when there was another knock on the door. Only this time it wasn't a gentle tap. This was a knock. One that said, 'We know you're fuckin in there. So open the fuckin door.' Les pointed to the spare room. Eddie tip-toed quietly across and went inside leaving the door slightly ajar behind him. Les picked up his mug of tea and opened the front door.

'Well, well, well,' said Les breezily. 'If it isn't two of Canberra's finest. Agents Pope and Corris. Good afternoon gentlemen. Can I be of any assistance?' Norton's greeting was certainly polite enough; even if it dripped with enough sarcasm to almost flood the stairwell.

'G'day Les,' said agent Corris. 'We just thought we'd call in for a minute.'

'That's extremely decent of you,' replied Les.

'Yeah. We just wanted to apologise for last night,' said agent Pope.

'Are you fair dinkum?' said Les.

Corris nodded. 'Yeah. We were a bit heavy-handed last night.'

'Yeah. Well nobody likes getting guns shoved in their ear,' said Les. 'Especially when they ain't done nothin'. They do have a tendency to go off,' he added.

'Fair enough,' conceded agent Pope. 'Anyway. We phoned around. And we both know some cops you've done favours for.'

Les gave a bit of a shrug. 'Just doing my part, as a concerned citizen.'

'So we brought you this.' Agent Corris handed Les a tape. 'We got that put onto a cassette this morning. You're right,' he said, trying to hide a smile. 'It is bloody hilarious.'

Les looked at the tape and put it in his pocket. 'Well, I'm glad somebody got a laugh.'

'Whatever,' replied agent Corris.

'No. I appreciate it. Thanks.' Les offered his hand. 'Anyway. No hard feelings.'

'Yeah. No hard feelings,' said agent Pope.

Les shook both their hands then held up his cup of tea. 'I just made a pot of tea. Would you like a cup?' The only reason Les asked the two cops that, was because he was pretty certain what the answer would be.

Agent Corris shook his head. 'We'd love to. But we are on a case.'

'Okay,' said Les. 'Maybe some other time.'

'Yeah. Some other time,' said agent Pope.

'Allright. Well thanks again fellas. And good luck with whatever it is you're doing.'

'Yeah. Same to you Les. See you again.'

Les closed the door then leant his back against it and took a deep breath. He went back into the kitchen and put down his cup of tea. A minute or two later, Eddie came out of the spare bedroom and joined him.

'Who was that?' he asked.

'Those two federal cops from last night. Duckman and Cornfed.'

'Shit! What did they want?'

Les took the cassette from his pocket and told Eddie what happened. Even how he invited them in for a cup of tea.

'You're a fuckin cool hombre Les. Good shit.'

Eddie rubbed his hands together. 'Righto. Where's my cup of tea?' Five minutes later, they were seated comfortably on the sundeck sipping tea and munching biscuits while they watched a flurry of activity in the distance. There appeared to be a police launch and a small ferry amongst one or two spectator boats. A few minutes later a police helicopter clattered overhead, followed by a news helicopter with NBN.3. on the side.

'Well. I'd say the shit's certainly starting to hit the fan Eddie,' commented Les.

'Yes,' agreed Eddie. 'It's not often a crooked cop and a shonky club manager get eaten by sharks.'

'It's not that often anybody gets eaten by sharks Eddie,' said Les.

A movement on the right caught their eye. Kastrine Kreen came out of her flat wearing a loose-fitting yellow dress, held a hand above her eyes and stared out over the balcony.

'Good afternoon, Ms Kreen,' Les called out.

She spun around and looked at Les like he was a six hundred dollar phone bill. Then walked straight back inside. Emmett Hakin came out about a second later in an old white shirt and jeans and took up her position. After a few moments he noticed Les and Eddie.

'Hey. Did you hear the news?' he called out.

'I heard something,' replied Les. 'What happened?'

'Four people got taken by a white pointer shark off Jimmy's Beach.'

'A white pointer,' said Les. 'I didn't think they came this far north.'

'Yeah. They migrate up with the currents.'

Les seemed to think for a moment. 'But wouldn't the change in sea temperature give them migrate headaches?'

Hakin stared at Norton. 'I'm not sure,' he said seriously.

Les managed to ignore Hakin and returned to Eddie. Hakin continued to stare out across Port Stephens.

'Is that the award-winning writer?' asked Eddie.

'That's him allright,' answered Les.

'He sounds like he couldn't write his name on a shithouse door.'

'Probably not.'

'And the auntie in the yellow dress. That's the lovely Kastrine Kreen?'

'That's her.'

Eddie winked. 'She might make someone a good wife.'

'She'd make a better female impersonator,' replied Les. 'Now. What's this about an earn, Eddie?'

'Okay.' Eddie chewed up a piece of biscuit and washed it down with tea. 'There's a bloke in Newcastle. A white shoe car dealer named Maurie Maxwell. Owes me thirty-five grand.'

'What for?' asked Les.

'A racehorse. Me and Price sold him a yearling. Price got his end. But I still haven't got mine.'

'The rotter,' said Les.

'That's what I reckon,' said Eddie. 'All I've got is, "The cheque's in the mail. Mr Maxwell's in a meeting." And the old, high hat.'

'I see,' replied Les, taking a sip of tea.

'Anyway. Maurie likes to bet SP. Thursday night is settling night. And through sources close to Price I found out Maurie just had a big win.'

'Lucky Maurie.'

'Yeah,' said Eddie, contemptuously. 'Maurie's also a shocking big-noter. So he's going to be running around Newcastle somewhere tonight flashing his chops.'

'And you'd like to meet him somewhere in the course of his travels and politely ask him for what belongs to you.'

'Very politely,' smiled Eddie. 'I know thirty-five grand isn't all that much.'

'All that much?' said Les. 'There's blokes work all year in a pickle factory for less than that.'

'Yeah,' agreed Eddie. 'What I meant was, it's not worth me shooting the prick and whoever's with him for thirty-five grand. Then having to clean up all the mess afterwards. Which is probably what I'll have to do, if I go by myself.'

'Which is where I come in?'

Eddie nodded. 'If he's with a couple of mugs and there's two of us, we can just grab the money and adios muchachos.'

'A couple of mugs,' said Les. 'Probably a team of coal miners from Kurri or somewhere. All built like brick shithouses.'

'Don't worry. If it's too heavy we'll piss off. I can always come back.'

'See what happens,' shrugged Les.

'I'm pretty sure I know where to find him,' said Eddie. 'If I can't, I know where his daughter is. She'll tell me. If I haven't found him by about half past ten though, I'll brush it for now. But if I do find him, and I get my money, I'll give you five grand.' Eddie winked. 'Not bad for a couple of hours work. And I'll shout you an Italian meal while we're at it.'

'Sounds good to me,' said Les. 'So how do you want to work this?'

'You follow me to Newcastle in your car. And we'll do all the running around in mine. When we're finished I'll split for Sydney. And you can come back here.'

'Righto. What time do you want to leave?'

Eddie looked at his watch. 'About six o'clock. Casual dress.'

'Okay.'

'In the meantime, we may as well stay in the flat. I might have a nap. What'll you do?'

'Probably have a read,' replied Les. 'I won't be going for a swim. I know that.'

They took their empty mugs inside and Les turned the radio off. Eddie went inside and had a snooze on Norton's bed. Les settled back in the loungeroom with Charles Bukowski and the sun coming through the vertical blinds. Before Les knew it, Chinaski was no closer to getting his film deal together, the afternoon was shot and they were standing in the loungeroom ready to get going. Eddie had his black leather bomber jacket on and Les was wearing his blue gaberdine one.

Eddie nodded to the big suitcase he'd left near the front door. 'All the rest of my junk's in the boot of the car. I'll sort it out when I get home.'

'I might pop the TV on for a minute before we go,' said Les. 'See what's on the news.'

'Okay. Any more plastic bags in the kitchen?' said Eddie. 'I don't want those fish leaking all over the boot of the car.'

'There should be some in the laundry.'

While Eddie was wrapping the five bream up Les switched the TV on and stood in front of it. They'd made the lead bulletin on the local TV station. Along with a po faced woman newsreader, there were helicopter shots of Port Stephens, shots of the old runabout with a piece out of the stern and a police diver standing beside two terry-towelling hats, a ripped T-shirt and two pairs of cheap thongs.

'The missing men are believed to be,' continued the newsreader, 'suspended detective Jack Fyshbyrne. And sacked club manager Forbes Zaccariah.' As she said that the two men's photos flashed up on the screen.

'Believed to be?' scoffed Eddie. 'What the fuck are they talking about? That was Fishcake for sure. He might have been drunk the last time I saw him. In fact he was almost legless. But it was definitely him.'

Les nodded to the TV screen. 'And I'm positive that was Forbes. I never forget a face. Especially that ugly and that close. I don't remember seeing any white pointer sharks though Eddie. Plenty of everything else. But no great whites.'

Eddie made a dismissive gesture. 'They'd've only had to have been gummed by a Port Jackson and they'd say it was a great white.' The little hitman shook his head. 'Come on, turn the fuckin thing off and let's go.'

Eddie got the fish and picked up his suitcase; Les switched off the TV along with the lights and followed him down to the garage.

Eddie was driving a white Commodore hire car. He put the suitcase in the boot and got behind the wheel. Les slipped his key in the lock and the garage door rolled open. He walked over to the Berlina and half smiled when he noticed his newspaper still folded neatly on the roof where he'd left it the night before. He tossed it on the back seat, started the engine and followed Eddie out of the garage, stopping to close the door behind him. A few minutes later, they were past Nelson Bay heading for Newcastle.

Les wasn't thinking about much during the drive, just the lazy five thousand that might fall in later and hoping he didn't get pummelled too much earning it. Mainly he was concentrating on keeping Eddie's white Commodore in his headlights. Somewhere between Bob's Farm and the Williamtown turnoff Les turned on the cassette still sitting in the stereo from when he'd arrived in Shoal Bay and Troy Cassar-Daley started twanging out *Lay Down and Dance*, which slipped neatly into Carl Perkins bopping out *Matchbox*. Before long Les saw a sign saying Fern Bay. They crossed a couple of bridges, Dave Hole was pumping out *More Love Less Attitude* and they were cruising along the darkened streets of Newcastle.

Les didn't have the foggiest idea where he was and hoped Eddie did. He also hoped the restaurant Eddie had in mind was okay and put plenty on your plate because by now he was past starving and approaching ravenous. They drove down Hunter Street with its shops and hotels and Les noticed a railway station, then some building sticking up in the air like a watch tower. Next thing Eddie turned up into Bolton, did a U-turn at King and parked facing back downhill. Les pulled up behind him and got out of the car. He noticed what looked like a courthouse at the top of the hill as Eddie pointed to a restaurant nestled under an office block.

'This is it,' he said. 'Cafe Nicole. You hungry?'

'Are you kidding?' replied Les. 'What about tossing me one of those fish out of the boot.'

The cafe was spacious with soft ceiling lights, posters, black tables and black directors chairs. Dean Martin was crooning in Italian from a pair of speakers near a fairly extensive blackboard menu. Norton wasn't that fussed about variety and surroundings. All he wanted was food, and plenty of it. A smiling man in a blue shirt and white apron came over to take their order. Les went for Garlic Prawn Risotto, Veal Parmigiano, a salad and garlic bread. Make that two garlic breads. Eddie ordered a salad and Veal Fettuccine. They both decided to stay off the booze, so Eddie asked for two bottles of Santa Vittoria mineral water.

The garlic bread arrived almost immediately. Eddie took one piece and just managed to get his arm away in time as Les gobbled down two slices quicker than the bronze whalers took the two flathead. The rest of the meal arrived and Les was more than happy. The food was excellent and they gave you heaps. The rice in the risotto was perfect with heaps of prawns and the Veal Parmigiano was spicy and tender with wedges and crispy vegetables. The salad was about perfect. Les washed down the last piece of garlic bread with mineral water and belched lightly into the back of his hand.

'Well that wasn't real bad, Eddie,' he said. 'Thanks mate.'

'I'm glad you liked it,' replied Eddie. 'I notice you haven't lost your appetite,' he added.

'What are you talking about? All I've had all day is a couple of lousy chops. And you knocked off my fish. Give me a break.'

'That's right. I owe you twenty bucks too.'

'You were hoping I might have forgotten. Weren't you?'

'Come on.' Eddie paid the bill then they walked outside and got in the Commodore.

'So where's our first port of call?' asked Les, doing up his seatbelt.

'The Kendall Hotel. About ten minutes from here,' replied Eddie, as they headed back towards Hunter Street.

'What's this Maxwell rooster look like?' asked Les.

'Pretty ugly,' said Eddie, stopping for a set of lights. 'Grey hair, a real pisshead's face. Got a nose looks like a dog sleeps in it.'

'Sounds like George Brennan.'

They drove off. Les saw the Newcastle Workers Club go past and Eddie pointed out the notorious Star Hotel. A few minutes later Eddie pulled up outside a Turkish kebab shop next to an open air restaurant ringed with small palm trees. When they got out, Les noticed an old, colonial-looking hotel on the next corner with a blue, neon sign on a black background saying Kendall Hotel. With his hands in the pockets of his bomber jacket Les followed Eddie through the front door.

The hotel was fairly roomy inside. Coloured leadlights sat above the bar, a pendulum swung lazily in a grandfather clock on a wall above the door as you walked in and the smoke from about fifty cigarettes hung in the soft light coming from the ceiling. There were stools and tables spread around the bar area, old black and white jazz posters looked down at you from the walls, along with the usual TV sets showing rock clips, while music played quietly from a brace of speakers. A solitary bouncer in a blue denim shirt barely gave them a second look as Les followed Eddie past a raised pool table and a bank of video poker machines, out to a beer garden. There was a green staircase in the middle, a wrought iron fence at the back and another room full of poker machines. Eddie had a good look around and shook his head.

'No. He's not here,' he said.

'You sure?' said Les. 'This doesn't look like a bad pub.'

Eddie shook his head again. 'Positive. We'll have a look at the Pirate Flag.'

'You're the boss,' shrugged Les. They walked back outside and got in the car.

This time Les got a glimpse of some car yards, a Harley-Davidson dealership and more shops and houses before Eddie did a U-turn at a set of lights on some wide, flat road. He then pulled up outside a long, flat hotel with a black front and a pirate's face above the entrance. There were two bouncers in black, zip-front jackets having a conversation just inside the door. After getting a desultory once up and down, Les followed Eddie up a set of stairs on the right.

The Pirate Flag was just one big room. A band had been playing on a stage at the far end, the bar was on the right and opposite the bar was a mirrored DJ's stand. Behind the DJ, a sign said Better Music And More Of It and another sign behind the bar said NEW.FM Rocks The Flag. In the dim lights Les could make out about six ordinary-looking girls smoking cigarettes and drinking booze and about thirty ordinary-looking blokes shuffling about with cans of beer in their hands, trying to look tough. Eddie had a quick look around as the DJ belted out *Blue Monday* by New Order loud enough to make your ears bleed.

'Fuck it,' said Eddie. 'He's not here either.'

'Thank Christ for that,' shouted Norton.

Eddie nodded. 'Come on. Let's get back to the car. Before we both finish up with industrial deafness.'

'So where to now, bwana?' asked Les, putting his seatbelt back on.

Eddie drummed his fingers on the steering wheel, a disgruntled look on his face. 'At the rate we're going, we'll be here all night. I'm going to have to see his daughter.'

'Where's she live?'

'Adamstown. But she's a mad, fuckin headbanger. So she'll be out at the uni.'

'Newcastle University?'

Eddie looked at Les. 'You reckon that was loud in there. Wait till you hear Reaper And Binder.'

'Who?'

'They're a thrash-grunge band from up here. They'll be playing out there tonight. They make silverchair sound like the David Jones Christmas Choir.'

'Yeah? I can't wait.'

They drove off again. This time Les got a glimpse of Marathon Stadium, wide roads and signs saying Georgetown, Nth Lambton, then they were entering the sprawling, tree-covered grounds of Newcastle University. Signposts pointing to the various facilities said Chemistry, Physics, Geology, Medical Sciences and other studies. Eddie swung the Commodore this way and that till they came to a rambling, timber building set amongst the trees, walled with plate glass windows and long verandahs. Eddie pulled up alongside some other cars parked away from the building.

'Not a bad uni they got here,' said Les, as he got out of the car.

'Yeah. It's a pretty good,' agreed Eddie.

Then Norton's ears pricked up. 'What the fuck's that?' he said.

Although they were at least two hundred metres from the building, this heavy, pulsating thump-thump-thump pounded out through the trees. It had the same sound and rhythm as a building being demolished.

'That's Reaper And Binder, Les,' smiled Eddie. 'Good, aren't they?'

'Good? Eddie, you're talking to an old bootscootin', blues, rock'n'roll man. What are you trying to do to me?'

'Come on you big sheila,' said Eddie, walking off. 'They're waiting for you in the mosh pit.'

'Mosh pit? I'll tell you what. How about I give you five grand and you let me stay here in the car with the windows up.'

'Stop being such a fuckin square.'

'I think the expression Eddie, is: "A come down or a blank slate".'

'Whatever. Come on.'

The entrance was on the nearest verandah. They walked across to the front desk where a blonde girl, surrounded by bouncers in black zip-front jackets, told them it was eight dollars in for non-members. Eddie paid her, then along with a curious look from the bouncers, they got their wrists stamped and walked along a wide hallway into a large room with a bar on the left and a wall full of posters on the right showing some of the bands that had played there. The Porkers, Frenzal Rhomb, Renegade Funk Train and of course silverchair. In the auditorium opposite, about three hundred students had crammed themselves into a screaming, howling mosh pit at the front of the stage, where they banged their heads around while they jumped up and down like Zulus. The band was young, with hair of varying lengths and were outfitted exclusively by op-shop and army disposals. The song they were currently singing had four chords and three words getting screamed repeatedly into the microphone. 'Eat my lunch.' Behind a metal rail in front of the stage, a wall of bouncers wearing earplugs kept the baying mob from the band.

Eddie pointed to a door leading onto the nearest verandah. 'Come outside,' he said.

'Okay,' nodded Les.

They stepped out onto the verandah and mingled amongst some other students. As Les went past a door opening into the auditorium a single bar from the bass whomped out through a speaker and shook him from head to toe.

'You may as well stay here,' said Eddie. 'I'll see if I can find her.'

'Thanks,' replied Les.

Eddie strolled off amongst the kids milling around the maze of verandahs, leaving Les to check out the punters. They were all plainly or poorly dressed. The blokes in old jeans, baggy shorts and firemen's jackets. The girls were dressed much the same with the odd, cotton dress here and there and a few battered Doc Martens; a lot of girls wore glasses. The T-shirt collection was Smashing Pumpkins, Sepultura, Foo Fighters, Fat Boy Slim etc. One thing Les did notice — although the students couldn't afford clothes, they all seemed able to afford plenty of cigarettes and booze. The band clanged into another song with one less chord and even less lyrics than the previous number. However, any lack of talent was made up for in volume. Another bass chord hit Les like a force field. He shook his head and moved across to the edge of the verandah. He wasn't there long and Eddie came walking back with a straggly-haired, dumpy-faced girl wearing razored jeans and a pink T-shirt with Nobody Knows I'm A Lesbian printed on the front. They stood talking away from Les then Eddie gave the girl fifty bucks and she walked back to wherever her friends were.

'He's at the Sand Box,' said Eddie.

'Where's that?'

'About twenty minutes from here.'

'Can't we stay here a bit longer?' asked Les. 'That band's the grouse. I'm just starting to get into them.'

Eddie ignored Les and headed back towards the car.

Norton didn't say a great deal as he watched the houses go past on the way back into town. In a few minutes it could be action stations one way or the other. He just hoped there weren't too many on the opposing team and they didn't carry knives. It wasn't long and Les thought he recognised the long, flat road they drove along earlier. Eddie took a right at another set of lights and parked outside a McDonald's built back from the road. Across the median strip on the opposite side of the road, Les noticed a two-storey, wedge-shaped hotel sitting on the corner. It was painted silver and black with streaks of pastel colours and a red neon sign above the frosted glass door at the foyer said The Sand Box.

'So this be it,' said Les, looking through the windscreen.

'Yep. This be it.' Eddie pulled a Heckler and Koch VP.70 from a shoulder holster under his left arm, checked it and put it back. 'And that be that,' he said. 'Come on. Let's go say hello to Maurie.'

It was one flight of stairs up into the foyer. There was another bouncer in a black, zip-front jacket as you walked in and a girl in a red, polo-neck jumper behind a desk. The foyer was dim with black carpet and everything had a metallic or bronze look about it. This time it was five dollars entry. Eddie paid again, they got another stamp, along with more curious looks and went inside.

Entry to the nightclub was behind the front desk and to the left. It was one big, sunken room with a tiny bar in one corner and another near the dance floor at the far end. Up on stage a four-piece band with a spunky brunette singer were belting out some unknown song as if their lives depended on it, while about thirty or so punters hovered between the bars and the dance floor or sat around smoking cigarettes and drinking booze. Everywhere from the ceiling to the roof were metal girders painted in various colours, metal seats and tables, metal statues and fittings and painted metal sheets along the walls.

'You know what this place reminds me of, Eddie?' said Les.

'No. What?'

'The spaceship in *Red Dwarf*.'

Eddie nodded. 'Whatever it is, he ain't down here. Let's have a look upstairs.'

A set of black, carpeted stairs angled up past the foyer. Halfway up, a couple of young girls wearing pyjamas and carrying teddy bears were sprawled across an old lounge smoking cigarettes. They didn't give Les or Eddie a second look as they went past. At the top of the stairs were the toilets then an archway led into another, smaller disco. There was a bar and bartender on the left, a pool table further down near a small, deserted dance floor, with a DJ's stand next to two empty cages. Against the wall on the right, as you entered, were half a dozen poker machines and above these a couple of TV sets showing re-runs of *Minder*. The music was soft and it was smoky, dim and almost empty except for four men standing at the end of the bar as you walked in. Three were big, lumpy, dark-haired blokes wearing jackets and corduroy jeans. The other was an older man with grey hair and a bulbous red nose wearing a grey suit. He looked like W.C. Fields. Sitting on the bar behind him was a brown leather briefcase. The older man saw Eddie and a look of surprise flashed across his face for an instant that was quickly replaced by a look of smug, boozy confidence.

Eddie smiled thinly. 'Hello Maurie,' he said. 'Fancy bumping into you here.'

'Yeah,' replied Maurie. 'Nice to see you too, Eddie. Can I get you a drink?'

Eddie shook his head. 'No thanks, Maurie. I'm just on my way back to Sydney.'

'Oh,' smiled Maurie. 'Well, that's too bad.'

'Yeah. Isn't it,' replied Eddie. 'Anyway. While I'm here Maurie. What about that thirty-five thousand you owe me?'

'Yeah? What about it, Eddie?' Maurie glanced at his heavies, who looked at each other, then looked at Les and Eddie and started coming to life.

'Well I'd like it Maurie. If that's okay with you?'

Maurie shook his head. 'Gee. I'd love to help you, Eddie. But I just don't have it at the moment. Things are a bit tight.'

'Like Dick Tracy's hat band,' said Eddie.

'Yes,' laughed Maurie. 'That's one way of putting it.'

'Oh well,' said Eddie. 'It's not worth worrying about that much I suppose. Nevertheless, Maurie, how about I take that briefcase on the bar behind you in lieu of payments. What do ya reckon?'

Maurie smiled around at his three heavies. 'Pull up, Eddie. You're not in Sydney now, son.'

While Eddie was having his tete-a-tete with Maxwell, Les had been summing up the situation. Eddie was standing in front of Maurie with a heavy on his left. Les had one close to him on his left and another a little further away to the right. Les also surmised Eddie was going to take Maxwell's briefcase no matter what. So why not start the ball rolling?

The heavies were all big men. But the one on Norton's left had a bit of a gut poking out from behind a blue shirt tucked into his corduroy jeans. Les twisted just a little to the left, crouched slightly and speared a straight left directly into Blue Shirt's solar plexus. It wasn't quite full strength. But it was enough to knock Blue Shirt cockeyed and stop him dead in his tracks. The other heavy went to grab Les. Norton simply knocked his arms up, then smashed a right hammer punch down on his collar bone, snapping it like a stick of celery. The heavy grunted from the unexpected burst of pain as almost in one movement Les slammed his right elbow into the heavy's jaw, smashing it across the other side of his face. Blood bubbled out of the heavy's mouth, his eyes rolled and his knees started to buckle as Les finished him off with a left hook that spun what was left of the heavy's jaw round the other side of his face. The heavy's eyes closed then he fell back against the bar and crashed to the floor onto his elbow, unconscious. Blue Shirt was still doing his best to breathe while he tried to find some movement in his limbs. Les stepped across and slammed a right uppercut under Blue Shirt's chin; full strength this time. It split the skin to the bone, shattered all Blue Shirt's front teeth and sent him somersaulting backwards over the bar out cold, where he landed with a horrible thump next to the bartender.

As soon as Eddie saw Les go into action, he snatched the briefcase off the bar with his right hand and slammed it into the first heavy's balls. The heavy bent forward to clutch at his groin just in time for Eddie to crunch a perfect headbutt right into the bridge of his nose. A shard of white bone stuck out and claret started pouring down the heavy's face. As the heavy's eyes screwed up with pain, Eddie stepped back, and slammed three, quick short lefts into his mouth, mulching it to a crimson pulp. The heavy slid down the bar, landing solidly on his rump at Maxwell's feet. Eddie brought his right foot back and kicked the heavy flush in the face. His head wobbled for a moment and that was it. This left a profusely sweating Maurie Maxwell standing alone at the bar with spilt drinks all over the front of his suit. Eddie changed the briefcase into his left hand, then reached under his jacket and whipped out the VP.70 with his right.

Eddie shoved the barrel up Maxwell's bulbous nose. 'Now listen to me, you fat turd,' he hissed. 'If I ever so much as fuckin hear from you again, I'll come back and kill you. You understand?' Maxwell looked cross-eyed down the gun barrel and nodded his head. 'Not in here,' said Eddie. 'Somewhere else. But I will kill you. You got that?'

'Yeah. Sure Eddie,' sweated Maxwell. 'Sorry mate.'

Eddie brought the gun back as if he was about to swat Maxwell across the face with it. 'Don't fuckin mate me. You arse.'

The bartender stood next to the unconscious heavy with his mouth open while the few patrons in the bar looked at the other unconscious heavies with their mouths hanging open also. At that moment the bouncer came running up the stairs. Eddie brought the gun around and aimed it at his face.

'Now unless anybody's got any objections, we'll be on our way.' Eddie jabbed the barrel of the VP.70 at the bouncer. 'What about you Knackers? Have you got any objections about us leaving?'

The bouncer brought his hands up by his side and shook his head. 'Would you like me to get you a taxi?'

Eddie turned to Les. 'Come on. Let's fuck off.'

Les nodded and smiled pleasantly at the few people in the bar. 'Goodnight everyone,' he said. Eddie put the gun away. Les put his hands back in the pockets of his jacket and followed the little hitman down the stairs.

Back in the Commodore, Eddie tossed the briefcase onto the rear seat and started the car. Quickly, but smoothly, he reversed around and drove out of the McDonald's parking area. The lights were with them and in a few moments Les and Eddie were cruising back along the same wide, flat road they were on earlier; seatbelts secured, well within the speed limit.

'Well, that wasn't so bad, Eddie,' said Les.

Eddie gave a little chuckle. 'No. It was a doddle.' He looked at Norton for a second. 'Jesus Les. That wasn't a bad uppercut you landed on that poor mug's chin.'

'Yes,' agreed Les modestly. 'But I still like your short lefts.'

Eddie opened and closed his fist. 'Yeah. I think I've still got it,' he winked.

Before long Eddie drove back up Bolton Street and pulled round behind Norton's Berlina. He switched off the lights and motor then took a hanky from his pocket and wiped a smear of blood from the knuckles on his left hand.

'Well thanks for that, Les,' he said. 'You've come to the rescue again.'

'That's okay, Eddie,' shrugged Les. 'Anytime mate.'

'Bad luck about that other thing. But at least we got back okay.'

Les shrugged again. 'That's showbiz.'

'Anyway,' Eddie said putting his hanky away, 'I'd better give you your five grand.'

Les nodded impassively. 'And don't forget the twenty for the fish.'

Eddie reached behind him and got the brown, leather briefcase. He opened it between them and started counting the contents.

'Hello, hello, hello,' said Eddie. 'What have we got here?' Eddie gave the money another quick check. 'Well I'll be. Sixty-five thousand buckaroonis.'

'My goodness Eddie! You have had a good night,' said Les.

'Yeah.' Eddie seemed to think for a moment. 'Right. Maurie owed me thirty-five grand.' Eddie took that out. 'Less five grand for you.' He handed Les his five thousand dollars. 'That leaves thirty over.' Eddie looked at Les for a moment more. 'Fifteen each.' He dropped another fifteen thousand dollars in Norton's lap. 'There you go. Twenty grand. Not bad for a quick trip into Newcastle.'

'Not bad at all.' Les was chuffed. 'Thanks Eddie.'

'No worries,' winked the little hitman.

Les took two thousand dollars and put the other money back in the briefcase. 'I'll keep this. And I'll pick the rest up when I get back to Sydney.'

'Okay Les. Good idea.'

Les shoved the money inside his jacket, got out of the Commodore and walked round to the driver's side window.

'Okay Eddie. I'll see you when I get back home. We'll go and grab a bite to eat or something.'

'You got me,' smiled Eddie. He started the car and slipped it into drive. 'I'll see you back in the old steak and kidney.'

'Enjoy those fish. And say hello to Lyndy for me.'

'Will do.' Eddie tooted the horn and drove off towards the highway.

It was a much happier Les Norton who drove back up Hunter Street. Twenty grand, he chuckled to himself. Like Eddie said, not bad for a couple of hours sightseeing in Newcastle. He looked around him for a familiar landmark. Now, how the fuck do I get out of here?

Somehow Les managed to find the two bridges he crossed on the way in and it wasn't long before he was back on Nelson Bay Road heading for Shoal Bay. The tape played itself out and in what seemed like no time, Les was back at the flats. He locked the car and walked upstairs.

The first thing Les did was stash the two thousand dollars under the mattress. Satisfied it was safe, he changed down to his jox and T-shirt, then walked out to the loungeroom to switch the TV on and maybe watch something for half an hour or so while he had an Ovaltine. Instead, he yawned, switched off all the lights and went into the bathroom to clean his teeth. I don't know, he yawned again, looking at himself in the mirror. All this killing and bashing people and driving at night makes you tired. Especially driving at night. Les clicked off the bedroom light and climbed into bed. Despite the fact that he'd just put two men in hospital, helped send another two to a watery grave, and almost been eaten by sharks, it wasn't long before the big Queenslander was snoring peacefully.

Les rolled out of bed around eight the next morning feeling pretty good. A night off the booze, plus a lazy twenty grand falling in, made quite a difference. And he was still alive. Well and truly. Les had a scratch then walked out onto the sundeck to see what the weather was doing. It was pretty much like the day before, with maybe a few more clouds around. The radio was playing, but there was no sign of the girl next door; or Australia's answer to Elmore Leonard. Below him, the early morning traffic went past and a few people were walking around while across the road there seemed to be a bit more activity on the water than the day before. Les went to the bathroom then made a cup of coffee and decided to go for a run. Nothing too strenuous. Just a lazy jog down to the Memorial Club, back to Zenith Beach and home. Get the old blood circulating and clear away any cobwebs before breakfast. Les changed into his Nikes and his old training gear, did a few stretches on the sundeck, then armed with his sunglasses and an old sweatband walked out the front.

It was quite pleasant jogging along under the trees with the ocean on his right. A few people went past; Les gave them a smile along with a hello and got the same back for his trouble. He soon made it to the smoked glass windows of the Memorial Club and turned back. Les wasn't thinking about all that much as he trotted along. Just that the club had looked pretty good and he might check it out that evening for a bit of action. While that was drifting across his mind, the sun sparkled on the blue waters of Port Stephens, birds sang in the trees above and a flock of pelicans hovered in the air for a few moments before landing smoothly on the ocean where they bobbed around looking down their beaks at each other with big, soft pelican eyes. Bugger it, thought Les. It's not that bad up here, and I'm all cashed up. Why not stay till Monday? Drink piss and pig out on fresh prawns and lobsters till they're coming out my ears. Kick back, maybe smoke some of that mull that turned Kastrine Kreen into a serial rapist and get into a bit of music. Bondi'll still be there when I get back. With a new slant on things, Les picked up the pace and headed for Zenith Beach.

Les was barely puffing when he reached the gate next to the swimming pool. But as he did, his ankle rolled slightly on a small rock. Les cursed quietly to himself and leant against the wall to rub his foot. The pain had stopped when a bloodcurdling howl rang out from the buildings built along the water at the end of the drive.

'Aieeeoowoooowwwow.'

'Jesus Christ! What was that?' Les almost jumped a metre in the air. A second or two later the first howl was answered by another one. Louder and longer.

'Ahhhoooowwhooowhooowaieeeoow!' The hairs rose on Norton's neck as the second scream echoed right up to the top of the mountain to be quickly followed by a third. Bloody Hell! What have they got in there? Werewolves? Les forgot about his ankle and with a quick look over his shoulder, ran back to the flat.

Norton's hunger pangs soon managed to put the incident by the gate out of his mind and in next to no time he was showered and changed into his Levi's shorts, and a blue Endeavour Resort T-shirt he got in

Cooktown, and staring into the fridge. He shook his head and closed the fridge door. Stuff cooking anything. That little coffee shop in the plaza looked okay. I shall get the paper and breakfast there, like the true gentleman that I am. Les jammed his *South Park* cap on his head, got his sunglasses and walked back down to the street.

There was no one in the paper shop. Les handed the lady the correct money, tucked a newspaper under his arm and skirted round the landscaping to the coffee shop. It was neatly furnished with flowers, mirrors on the walls and comfortable chairs and tables with crisp, white table cloths. However, a table full of young, out of town trendies had decided to share several boxes of cigarettes with everyone else in the restaurant while they tried to eat. Les walked over to a dark-haired bloke in a white shirt frothing a cappuccino behind an espresso machine and ordered a fresh OJ and a flat white for starters, followed by scrambled eggs with everything else you could fit on a plate, plus grilled tomato and toast, then pointed to a table outside. Les had time to make himself comfortable and spread his paper out when the OJ and coffee arrived. He drank his OJ first and checked out the headlines.

Along with some lame-brained footballer crapping all over the wall of a hotel room, Les and Eddie's little escapade had managed to make the front page as well. There were side by side photos of Fishbyrne and Zaccariah, and whether the shark that did all the damage was a great white or not, whoever

119

covered the story was definitely in favour of it being one; at least six metres long to boot. They'd even managed to drag up a witness who saw the great white. Some bloke called Jack who owned an oyster lease at Tea Gardens. Les finished his OJ, chuckled to himself and looked at the people around him. Isn't it amazing, he thought. All these people reading the news, listening to it on the radio, discussing it or whatever, and sitting slap bang amongst them is one of the villains responsible for the foul deed. Six metre, white pointer though. Les shook his head. Why didn't they say it was a pod of killer whales and be done with it? At least they got the names of the two blokes that were killed right. Les read on, then the smile vanished from his face. 'Believed to be.' was now, 'The victims remains had been positively identified by immediate members of both families.'

Les read it again and scowled. Immediate members of both families meant close relatives. Like mothers, fathers, sons, daughters, sisters, brothers, whatever. That bloody Eddie said Zaccariah had no family. Now Les had murdered some poor bloke in cold blood and there were people out there grieving. And you could imagine what the family would be going through. Christ! Identify the remains. What? An arm? A piece of leg? A couple of heads? Yuk! Les scowled into his coffee. No. Fuck Eddie and fuck Price too, he cursed to himself. Allright, Fishcake was no fuckin good and would have finished up in gaol where the cunt belonged, but what did the other poor stiff do? Nick a lousy hundred grand from a club.

Blokes did it all the time. It wasn't as if he was a heroin dealer or running a child pornography ring or something. The gravity of what Les had done began to sink in and it started to turn him right off his day. There was plenty more to the story in the paper plus photos and a feature article on both men. However, Les didn't bother going through it. As far as Norton was concerned, he'd read enough.

Les may not have been able to read all the newspaper article. But he did manage to eat all his breakfast; and down another flat white. He surmised that unless Forbes Zaccariah came into the world an orphan or arrived in Australia as a refugee, he was bound to have some kind of family somewhere. Les should have known that. It didn't ease his guilt all that much. But it was better than nothing. He paid the bill, dumped his newspaper in the nearest garbage bin and walked back to the flat.

Hakin was sitting on his sundeck drinking a coffee. Les ignored him and stared out at the ocean, drumming his hands on the railing while he figured out what to do with himself. It was just a little cool to go swimming and snorkelling wasn't even worth considering. It was too early in the day to get full of turps and he certainly didn't feel like getting stoned. The light bulb above Norton's Wylie Coyote head lit up. Why not go for a drive? Cruise around in the grouse Berlina with the stereo blasting, check out the area and have a nice lunch somewhere. Les tossed his camera, road map and a few tapes in his backpack, locked the flat and walked down to the car. Ten minutes later, Duke Robilliard had taken his harp to *No Time* and Les had taken Government Road to Salamander Bay.

Driving like Grandma Duck with the stereo bopping away in the background, Les cruised around Bagnalls Beach then Salamander Bay and Wanda Beach. It was absolutely beautiful. Nothing but calm, clear water washing gently against lovely stretches of sandy beaches shrouded with trees. Some expensive looking houses faced the bay with the odd shopping centre, club or resort here and there and as Les drove past he still couldn't believe how big Port Stephens was. It was absolutely enormous. He pulled up at Soldiers Point just round from the Marina and gazed across to North Arm Cove then on to Tahee where the Karuah River fed into Port Stephens. It was all gentle little headlands and peninsulas, backed by rolling mountain ranges thick with trees that like Port Stephens itself, seemed to go on forever. Les found his camera, got out of the car and walked over to a fish cleaning bench to get a drink of water and take a few photos. He wasn't there a minute when he was besieged by seagulls and pelicans hoping he had some fish. Even a few cheeky magpies and a couple of Willie wagtails put their beaks in.

'Sorry fellas,' said Les, as they squawked and swarmed around him. 'All I got is a new camera and a roll of film. I'm just another pain in the arse tourist.'

Les snapped what he thought were several good photos then said goodbye to his feathered friends and got back in the car. A couple of minutes later Dr Bob was swinging into *All I Want* and Les was cruising along Salamander Way looking for the One Mile Beach turnoff.

The turnoff was a pleasant drive past scatterings of homes and old farmhouses. The entire foreshore was part of Tomaree National Park, so there were enough trees, native shrubs and reserve to make an army of environmentalist Nazis think they were in greenie heaven. Les pulled up at One Mile Beach then walked between a caravan park and a restaurant down to the sand. One Mile Beach probably got its name because it looked to be around 1.6 kilometres of clean, white sand. The wind was blowing slightly off shore and there was a hot surf running. The waves broke outside then formed up again making for a long smooth ride with a neat shorebreak. Along the entire beach were four waxheads picking the eyes out of what were already perfect waves. Les snapped another couple of photos then got back in the car and headed for Boat Harbour.

Unlike round Sydney's shoreline, there were no rugged cliffs. It was mainly low headlands and sheltered bays with easy access to the crystal clear water. Les was sorry he had the wind up about diving, because it all looked like a snorkel sucker or scuba diver's delight. The last stop was Birubi Point then nothing but Stockton Beach — fifty kilometres of undeveloped beach, with a seemingly endless desert of rolling sandhills behind, running all the way back to Newcastle. There was a scattering of houses around Birubi Point, but apart from that the only signs of life were a few people fishing and a couple of windsurfers drifting in and out amongst the waves, about half a kilometre down the beach. Les found a tiny cemetery tucked amongst the scrub overlooking Birubi Point and wouldn't have minded seeing how old some of the headstones were. However, snooping around graveyards in his present frame of mind seemed a little fatalistic. He did take a photo and a couple of Stockton Beach, then a rumbling inside told him it was well and truly lunchtime. Les had a last look around the peaceful, almost eerie desolation of Birubi Point, got in the car and headed for Nelson Bay.

He drove down the hill past the marina then came back via the roundabout and took a left at the hotel into the shopping centre. He was about to park and thought he might as well do a victory lap and see what Nelson Bay had to offer. There were lots of neat little shops, some restaurants, banks, a supermarket and a pie shop with forty varieties of pies. The local picture theatre was at the back of a small arcade; and stuck in the middle of town, amongst all the new shops and malls, was an old thirties-style block of flats you still see round the back streets of Bondi. Same mottled, brown bricks and the same bit of yard round the front, only with a few small palm trees and camellias pushing up through the woodchips. How did they ever escape the developers, wondered Les. He finished his victory lap past the local pawn shop and podiatrist then angle-parked outside a chemist, locked the car and mingled in with the other people in the street.

Despite being able to afford the best meal in town and wash it down with French champagne if he wanted, for some reason Les felt like a feed of plain old fish and chips. He found a fish shop in the mall that looked okay and ordered three pieces of sea perch, chips and a bottle of lemonade. Opposite the fish shop was a blue council seat. Les plonked himself down, spread his fish and chips out to cool off then got into them while he had a people perv.

The passers-by were groups of unemployed, young people; one lot following a bloke carrying a slab of VB like he was the pied piper; a sprinkling of tourists; women doing their shopping and retirees filling in time. Pretty much what you would expect to find in a small, laid-back coastal town. Les could pick the local men though. They all seemed to be in their fifties or sixties, wearing shorts and thongs, with huge stomachs, bandy legs, and ruddy faces that said their lives revolved around three things — boats, beer and fishing. Les finished his fish and chips, dropped his rubbish in the nearest bin, then walked back to the car and drove home. All up, it hadn't been a bad afternoon. He'd seen another beautiful part of Australia, got some good photos; and he could recommend the fish and chips.

Les pulled up in the garage and turned off the motor just as Dave Edmunds finished pounding the soul out of *Something About You Baby*. Norton stared through the windscreen and drummed his fingers on the steering wheel. What to do now, he pondered. Go upstairs and make myself a cup of coffee then sit on my big fat arse and have a read for a while. Les patted his stomach. No. The best thing would be to take a walk along the beach. Give my legs a stretch and walk off all those greasy fish and chips. He locked the car, adjusted his cap then walked round to the front of the flats and crossed the road. Les was standing on the grass, cleaning his sunglasses while he looked for a path down to the sand, when over to the right, he thought he saw a familiar figure sitting on a picnic table with her feet resting on the seat. She was wearing an old pair of jeans and a grey sweatshirt and staring out across the bay with this enigmatic look on her face that made it hard to tell if she was laughing or crying. She was obviously very deep in thought and never noticed Les watching her. She shook her head for a moment and a quick swirl of shoulder length, black hair caught the afternoon sun like finely spun satin. Hello, Les smiled to himself. It's Cher Bono from the paper shop. I wonder what she's doing here. Les continued to look at her as she stared out across the bay. S'pose I may as well go over and say hello. See how she's going. Besides, she still owes me two dollars.

'So there you are,' said Les. 'I've been looking everywhere for you. The woman in the paper shop told me you'd skipped town.'

The girl turned to Les as if she was coming out of a dream. 'I beg your pardon?'

'The two dollars I gave you. Where is it? Or do I have to call the police?'

'Two dollars?' When she spoke, the girl had a slightly high pitch in her voice, almost like a child's. 'Oh wait a minute. You're the nice man in the paper shop who gave me the money.' She smiled that perfect white smile again and her lovely green eyes flashed simultaneously.

'I'm glad you referred to me as a nice man,' said Les.

The girl looked at Les for a moment then went for her pocket. 'Hang on, I've got it right here.'

'No. That's allright,' smiled Les, shaking his head. 'I was only joking. I saw you sitting there, so I just thought I'd say hello. That's all.'

'Oh.'

'I'm not disturbing you, am I?'

'No.' The girl shook her head. 'Not really.'

'Allright then,' Les smiled again. 'How are you?'

'I'm . . . I'm fine.'

'That's good,' said Les. 'Fine's fine enough.'

'Yes. I suppose it is.' The emerald eyes took Les in. 'How are you?'

'I'm . . . pretty good thanks,' replied Les. 'Can't complain one little bit.'

The girl looked at Les a little suspiciously. 'Are you from around here?'

Les shook his head. 'No. I'm from Sydney. I'm staying in those flats on the corner.'

'You're on holidays?'

'Yeah. I got here Wednesday. I'm going back . . . Monday.'

'Oh.'

'What about yourself? You from up here?'

The girl shook her head also. 'I live in Newcastle.'

'Can't say I've ever been there,' said Les. 'So what brings you to Shoal Bay?'

The girl looked at Les for a moment. 'I come here quite often. But I've just been to see my father.'

'Oh? And how was he?' Les imagined her father was old and retired and not feeling too good.

'How was he?' The girl's face changed expression as if she was impressed with Les politely inquiring about her father. 'The last time I saw dad. He was ... fine. Just fine.'

'Like I said,' smiled Les. 'Fine's fine enough.'

'Yes. You're absolutely right,' the girl nodded.

'Anyway. My name's Les.' Norton offered his hand.

'I'm Digger.'

'Digger?'

'That's what everybody calls me.'

'Okay Digger. Pleased to meet you.'

'You too Les.' Les shook the girl's hand. It was soft, warm and lovely to hold.

'So ... what do you do, Digger? If you don't mind me asking.'

'I'm a veterinary assistant.'

'That's a good job,' said Les. 'Being involved with animals.'

'A good job?' echoed Digger. 'Yes. If you like sticking thermometers up dogs' behinds, pulling stitches out of their stomachs, and listening to little

128

old ladies who think their cats and canaries can speak perfect English. It's wonderful.'

'Oh?' Les was taken off guard. 'Oh well. Fair enough Digger. I never thought of it that way, I suppose.'

'I'm tossing it in shortly,' continued Digger, 'I'm joining the National Parks and Wildlife Service. Give me marsupials any day.'

Les shook her hand again. 'Well good on you Digger. I'm proud of you. Those people do a damn good job.'

'Thanks.' Digger let go of Norton's hand and looked at him. 'So what do you do, Les?'

'What do I do?' Les gave Digger the sort of look Basil Fawlty gives Cybil when she catches him with his hand in the till. 'I'm ... involved with the church, Digger.'

Digger's green eyes lit up. 'You're a priest? A minister?'

'No,' replied Les slowly. 'Though they often call me Deacon Les. We're more like a mission. We take in the underprivileged around Kings Cross and offer them ... solace. Among other things.'

'Oh isn't that wonderful.' Digger shook Norton's hand. 'I'm proud of you too Les.'

'Thanks Digger,' smiled Norton.

'And what's your church called Les?'

'Called? We're called the Mob, Digger. MOB.'

'MOB. That's an unusual name for a church,' said Digger.

'Yes. It stands for Music Of Brotherhood. We're

involved a lot with music. Our patron saint is Saint Price of the Grasping Hand.'

Digger looked interested. 'And how do you run the church Les? With government help?'

'No Digger,' replied Les. 'We have a lot of wealthy benefactors who like to remain anonymous. They're always giving us large donations. Through Saint Price.' Les smiled serenely. 'In fact one of our benefactors owns the block of flats across the road where I'm staying.'

'Isn't that nice.'

'Yes. It certainly is, Digger.'

'I go to church regularly,' said Digger.

'You do?'

'Yes. We're The Church Of The Peaceful Sea. There's one not far from here. You can come and pray with us this Sunday morning if you like, Les.'

Les suddenly felt like a bit of a fool. He'd tried to be a smartarse and got tripped up by a decent girl for his trouble. 'Why thankyou Digger,' he said. 'I'll keep it in mind.'

'Good. You'd like our little church up here.'

Les felt stuck for something to say. He gave Digger an oily smile. 'Are you going back to Newcastle tonight, Digger?'

Digger shook her head. 'No. I'm staying at my cousin's house. He lives just behind the hotel.'

'Right.'

Digger turned away and stared out to sea again. She wasn't ignoring Les. It was more like whatever had been on her mind before Les came along had suddenly surfaced again. Les looked at her side on for a moment. He couldn't tell what it was about Digger. But there was something.

'Are you doing anything tonight, Digger?' Les seemed to ask her the question before he even knew he'd said it.

Digger turned around slowly. 'No,' she replied.

'Neither am I. Look, I hope you don't think I'm being rude. But would you like to go out somewhere tonight?'

Digger stared at Les for a moment. 'Allright then.'

'T'rrific. Where would you like to go? Dinner? A movie? Anywhere you want, Digger.'

Digger stared at Les again and a little smile seemed to flash for an instant across her lovely, emerald eyes. 'I'd like to go to the Port Stephens Memorial Club.'

'Sounds good to me. What time would you like me to call around for you?' asked Les.

'Are we going in your car?'

Les nodded. 'It's only just down the road. If I have too much to drink, I'll leave it there and we can get a taxi home. Is that okay by you?'

'Sure.'

'Do you drink, Digger?'

'A little.'

'Okay. What time?'

'About eight o'clock. Is that allright?'

'Perfect.'

Digger told Les her address and he said he'd be there by eight. She was quite happy with that.

'Righto Digger,' said Les. 'I was just going for a walk. So I'll leave you to whatever it is you're doing. And I'll see you tonight.'

Digger gave him a lovely smile. 'Allright Les. I'll see you then.'

'See you then Digger.' Norton turned and left her on her own.

There was a short path to the sand behind two small trees; Les took it and walked down to the water's edge. The tide was out leaving the sand firm underfoot and Les was half tempted to take his gym boots off and get his feet wet. But having to wipe sand and shell grit from between his toes made him change his mind. The bay curved gently around ending at a small, tree-covered headland beneath Nelson Bay Lighthouse. At a leisurely pace, Norton set off towards the headland.

Well don't that beat all, thought Les, as he strolled along to the rhythmic sound of tiny waves lapping against the sand and shell grit crunching beneath his Nauticas. I've got a nice little friend for company tonight. Digger. Les chuckled to himself. What sort of name is that? Les pictured her sitting on the picnic table, gazing out at the ocean. She didn't appear to be any raving beauty. But she had something going for her besides her shiny hair and emerald eyes. She definitely looks like a little Miss Goody Two Shoes, bible-basher though, thought Les. But what's wrong with that? Les started chuckling to himself again. What did she say when I asked her if she drank? A little. Christ! Wait till she's in the rissole tonight and Deacon Les meets the demon Jack. Hang on. Did I just take the Lord's name in vain then? Shit! I'd better watch that. In fact I'd better watch my p's and q's all around tonight. Digger's obviously a decent person and I've already managed to put my foot in it as it is. Before Les reached the headland he decided to turn around and head home. When he climbed back up the trail, Digger had gone. Les crossed the road and walked up to the flat.

The walk along the sand left Norton feeling very relaxed. He made a cup of tea, then took it out on the sundeck. A few more autumn clouds had drifted across the sky and from next door he heard the sound of someone pounding furiously on a portable typewriter. Les finished his tea, then got Charles Bukowski and made himself comfortable on the double bed. Les nodded off about the same time Chinaski started giving the white wine an awful nudge at Harry Friedman's birthday party. When Norton woke up, the room was in semi-darkness; the only light, a row of fuzzy, orange strips, cast through the vertical blinds by the corner street lamp. Les blinked at his watch. Getting on for seven. 'Just nice,' he yawned, stretching his arms above his head. He got up from the bed and ambled into the shower. Shortly after Les was standing in the kitchen in his jox and T-shirt eating toasted sandwiches while he half watched the ABC news.

They were the number three item on the news now; after the war in India and some disgruntled ex-postal employee in Hog Slop, North Carolina, who'd just shot twenty people then blown himself up in a synagogue. Divers in steel cages had recovered more remains of the shark victims and there were now two white pointers on the loose. Les watched disinterestedly for a few moments then changed channels. He took his time cleaning what little mess there was and had another cup of tea. When he'd finished Les found himself in front of the mirror wearing a green polo shirt with a denim collar, a pair of green suede Reefs and his best jeans with a thousand dollars stuffed in the front pocket and reeking of Fahrenheit. He gave himself a once up and down then blew a kiss at the mirror. I should be whipped and beaten for looking that good. Hallelujah brothers and sisters. He cleaned his teeth, gave himself one last detail, then locked up and walked down to the car.

Digger's cousin's house wasn't hard to find. It was an old, white, fibro weekender with a galvanised iron roof a block behind the hotel and two houses down from the next corner. A short set of steps ran side on up to a verandah at the front where two chipped windows faced the street either side of a faint light coming from the front door; and it looked as if no one lived there. The grass out the front was waist high, a skinny, leafless tree pushed up through the weeds and a rickety garage at the end of a side passage was just a dark opening to a jumble of old rubbish. There were two cars parked in the passageway — a white Holden utility and a rusty, blue Ford Laser. Les left his car out the front, and with one eye open for snakes, walked across the front yard and up the steps. The front door was partially open behind an old flyscreen. Les could hear music and voices coming from the rear of the house and make out a dim light coming from somewhere in the front loungeroom. He rapped on the flyscreen and waited. He rapped three times and still no one came. Les didn't want to knock too hard in case the flyscreen and everything else might have collapsed all around him. Oh well, he thought. Why not? He creaked the old flyscreen open and stepped inside.

Sitting on a skinny layer of dusty, orange carpet, an old, grey Chesterfield lounge faced a cheap stereo and a small TV set with a lampshade on top. Several abstract paintings hung on the walls then a hallway led past what appeared to be bedrooms on the right towards a square of light coming from another room at the back. Les walked softly towards the sound of a radio and voices then stopped at a white wooden door to the kitchen.

Inside, the stand-out furnishings were faded, blue lino on the floor and worn out, red laminex around the shelves. An old, round-top fridge stood against the wall on the left, across from a single tub sink, sitting next to an electric stove under a window with a single pot plant on the sill. The only bright spots were a couple more paintings on the walls. Digger was standing near the fridge, wearing blue eye shadow, red shoes and a loose-fitting, red and blue mini dress. The mini dress buttoned up over a nice little pair of boobs, almost to her chin.

But the hemline almost came up to her navel. And if Digger's mini dress wasn't filthy enough, she had a great pair of legs and a backside that almost broke Norton's heart on the spot. Les felt his mouth gape open as he gave her a double, triple blink. Some taller bloke, about the same age, wearing a pair of old, blue shorts and a plain white T-shirt, was standing behind her. He had his left arm across Digger's boobs while he pinned one of her arms behind her back with his other. The bloke had fair hair and a grainy face, with a short straight nose under a pair of soft hazel eyes. They both seemed engrossed in whatever it was they were doing and didn't appear to notice Les standing at the door. Les waited a moment or two then knocked.

'Hello. I'm not disturbing anyone, am I?' They both looked up at the sound of Norton's voice. The bloke immediately let go of Digger, who wiggled around and began to straighten her dress. As she did, Les managed to glimpse a pair of glossy red knickers.

'Sorry to barge in,' said Les again. 'But I knocked a couple of times and no one answered.'

'Oh hello, Les,' she said, a little self-consciously. 'How are you?'

'I'm good,' replied Les. 'How's yourself?'

'Fine.' Digger's eyes turned to the bloke who was now standing beside her. 'Brendon was just showing me how to get out of an arm bar.'

Les nodded. 'Yeah. They can be tricky things to get out of. Arm bars.'

'Yes,' replied Digger. 'Les, this is my cousin Brendon. Brendon. This is Les. The man from the paper shop.'

'Hello Brendon. Nice to meet you.'

'Yeah. Same here.' Brendon shook Norton's hand and shuffled on one foot. 'I used to learn judo,' he said.

Les nodded again. 'That's a handy thing to know, Brendon.'

Brendon smiled at Les a little odd. Like his eyes didn't quite seem to square-up. 'You do any martial arts, Les?'

Les shook his head. 'I did a bit of boxing at school, that's all. And I used to play football.'

'Right,' replied Brendon slowly, giving Les a once up and down.

'Les is a deacon, with a church in Sydney,' said Digger.

Brendon looked directly at Norton. 'Really?'

Les shuffled on one foot too. 'It's more like a mission than a church, Brendon.'

'I'm in the church with Digger,' said Brendon.

'Yes. Digger told me,' said Les. 'The Church Of The Peaceful Sea. Sounds ... enlightening.'

'It is,' replied Brendon, not offering Les the same invitation to come happy clapping on Sunday morning as Digger had done. 'What's yours called?'

'The MOB,' answered Les. 'Music Of Brotherhood. We work up the Cross. I mean. We're located in Darlinghurst.'

'Can't say I've heard of it,' said Brendon.

'We tend to keep things a little low key,' smiled Les, thinking it was time to change the subject. He had a quick look around the kitchen. 'So what do you do for a living Brendon? If you don't mind me asking?'

Brendon glanced at his cousin. 'I'm an artist,' he replied.

Les nodded and tried not to smile. 'I thought that's what you might have been.'

'You noticed my paintings?' said Brendon.

Les nodded to an abstract mass of colours hanging above the fridge. 'That. And it looks as if you've sold your lawnmower so you can eat,' Brendon and his cousin exchanged glances. 'Can't you get a grant or something?'

Brendon shook his head. 'I work at the painting shop down the road.'

'That's why he's like he is,' cut in Digger. 'It's ruining his health.' She turned to her cousin. 'I've told you time and again. You have to get out of there Brendon.'

'I know, Digger,' replied Brendon. 'But I need the money.'

Les sensed Digger wasn't bagging her cousin because it looked like his tent had a few pegs missing. She was genuinely concerned for his health. Les had got a whiff of the fumes coming from the painting shop when he passed by. So he could imagine what it would be like spending a whole day in there.

'Yes. Well you know what they say about money, Brendon,' said Norton, benevolently. 'It's the root of all evil.'

138

'Too right,' agreed Brendon. 'And I could do with a couple of good roots right now.'

'Brendon. Please.' Digger's cheeks reddened.

'Sorry Digger,' said Brendon, dropping his head slightly.

Shit! We do have Miss Prissy here don't we, thought Les. 'Anyway,' he said to Digger, 'if you're ready Digger, we might get going. There's no mad hurry though,' he added.

'No. Good idea,' replied Digger, picking up a black, leather sling bag from the kitchen table. 'I'll see you when I get home Brendon. I won't be late.'

'Righto,' replied Brendon.

'Nice to have met you, Brendon,' said Les.

'Yeah. Have a good night, Les.' Brendon turned to his cousin and smiled. Beneath the smile Norton noticed something else. A look of gentle understanding mixed with deep affection. 'You too Digger.'

Digger gave her cousin the same look in return. 'I'm sure I will,' she said.

Les followed Digger to the front door and opened the flyscreen. He ushered her down to the car, opened the passenger side door then went round and got behind the wheel. As Digger put her seatbelt on and straightened her dress, Les couldn't help himself. He just managed to catch another glimpse of her knickers. They weren't red. They were blushing pink.

'So we're off to the rissole, Digger,' said Les, as he took the back street up from the flats.

'Yes,' she replied. 'It will be a first for me. I've never been there.'

'Me neither,' said Les. 'It looks pretty good from the outside.'

'Yes. It does.'

It was only a short drive to the Memorial Club. Les didn't bother about a tape. He just let the radio play and some old Moody Blues song came through the speakers.

'So how was your day, Digger?' he asked.

'My day?' Digger turned to Les. 'Good thankyou. Very good.'

'Fair enough,' said Les.

'What about you, Les? How was your day?'

'Mine? I had a very pleasant day Digger.' Les told her what he'd done including having a feed of fish and chips in Nelson Bay.

'Well, it sounds like you had a really good day.'

'A good day?' said Les. 'Digger, it was that good at times I was wishing I was schizophrenic. So I could have had someone to share it with.'

Digger looked at Les for a moment. 'You and Brendon would get on very well together, I think.'

'I hope so. He seems like a nice bloke.' Norton turned into the club parking area and started looking for a vacant space. 'Be nice if he could crack it with his paintings though. It's a pretty tough game art.'

'He will,' said Digger. 'He's a very good artist actually. The main reason he's never got any money is because he spends it all on his boat.'

'Boat?' Les nosed the Berlina in behind a Holden panel van and cut the engine.

'Yes. He bought an old fishing boat. We often go diving. Do you dive, Les?'

'I haven't got my PADI, if that's what you mean. But I'm a keen snorkel sucker.'

Digger smiled at Les and started undoing her seatbelt. 'There's nothing wrong with snorkel sucking.'

Les felt his eyes drawn to the hem of Digger's mini again. 'No. It's good.'

'I suppose you heard about the shark attack?' said Digger tentatively.

'Yeah. That was awful, I don't even want to talk about it,' replied Les, dropping the subject.

'No. Me neither.'

By the time Digger got out of her seatbelt, Les was round her side of the car with the door open. He followed her the short distance to the club foyer, where they were welcomed inside by smiling men and women wearing black and white to sign the little dockets for their temporary membership. The bottom part of the club was to left of the front desk and a set of stairs on the right led up past a brown, woollen tapestry on the wall of a war scene — complete with flashing red lights for the explosions — to the main auditorium. Les followed Digger up the stairs, his eyes burning holes in her shapely little behind as it swished slightly from side to side under her filthy mini dress. Right. That's it, Les told himself. I've got to stop looking at Digger as nothing more than a sex object. Enough is enough. She's obviously a decent, God-fearing young woman. And any wickedness manifesting in my evil mind has to cease. Immediately. I'll only end up making a complete prick of myself. But Lord have mercy. What a dress. What an arse. Doesn't the rotten little bible-basher know how good she looks? Hasn't somebody told her? She must own a mirror or a camera surely? However Digger appeared completely oblivious to Les perving on her or anything else. She just walked up the stairs taking everything in around her, a precocious little smile on her face as if her night had begun already.

At the top of the stairs, a bistro and dining room stood on the left and a wide doorway on the right led into the auditorium. Les gestured, then stepped inside behind Digger. The auditorium was quite large with rows and rows of brown chairs and tables offering extensive views over Port Stephens, while several banks of brightly-lit poker machines whirled and tinkled away in the background. On the left, a bar with a giant TV screen at one end was showing Friday night football, and out from the bar a few steps led down to a sunken dance floor. In the corner another set of stairs ran up to a circular cocktail lounge above. A console and mixer were on a table next to the steps and on a small stage at the back of the dance floor, a band had set up beneath a black, velvet banner with Whizz-Key Variety Band blazoned across the front in white and gold letters. Alongside the chrome railing running round the dance floor several rows of chairs and tables were set aside for non-smokers. There was a reasonable crowd of very casually dressed, Friday-night-at-the-rissole punters; with a number of couples, some single girls and plenty of blokes already getting into the cheap booze. Les had a quick, professional look around and it took him about two seconds to realise that as far as looks and clothes went, Digger was ten lengths in front of any girl in the place. It took all the blokes drinking in the club the same time to realise it too as their eyes started riveting into Digger's backside like Black and Decker drills.

Les nodded to the bar upstairs. 'You feel like a cocktail for starters, Digger?'

'Okay,' she replied. 'That would be nice. Thankyou.'

Les ushered Digger through the chairs and tables and the envious looks from the blokes, to the stairs at the side of the dance floor.

The cocktail bar was called Emotions and there were more brown chairs and tables with a semicircle of windows giving an even better view of Port Stephens at night than what you got downstairs. Framed glass posters for Drambuie, Tia Maria and Johnny Walker ringed the walls and one near the bar said Jack Daniels. Our Benefactor. Couples and foursomes occupied most of the tables, but at one table sat six of the ugliest girls Norton had ever seen in his life. They dressed ugly, looked ugly and smoked ugly cigarettes with their ugly fugly drinks. One lump-headed brunette was wearing an imitation black leather jacket over a blue slip with green and white football socks slopped into chewed-up gym boots. Les found a table and turned his back on them before they put him off his night.

'What do you fancy, Digger?' he asked once they got comfortable.

Digger looked at the cocktail list then turned to a small blackboard on the bar. 'I'd like a Tropical Sunrise please.'

'Good thinking Ninety-Nine,' said Les. 'I might have one of those myself.'

Les went to the bar and came back shortly with two red and yellow drinks in long stemmed glasses decorated with little umbrellas and lumps of fruit.

'Well Digger,' he said, removing an umbrella and a piece of pineapple on a tiny, plastic sword. 'Here's looking up your old address.'

'Yes.' Digger clinked Norton's glass and took a look around her. 'To ... absent friends.'

'That'll do.' Les took a mouthful of his cocktail and almost gagged. It was dead flat and tasted like watered down Bacardi overdosed with sugary fruit cordial. Digger however, got stuck into hers like it was 1927 Bollinger.

'These are nice,' she said.

'Yeah,' replied Les, looking for an indoor plant he could tip his into. 'They're not bad, are they.'

Les forced his down while Digger sipped away steadily on her elbow-shaped straw. She didn't say much. She seemed quite happy just taking in the surroundings, though Les kept getting the impression she was looking around for someone or hoping someone might walk in and see her there with Les, like an ex-boyfriend. Or maybe one was working there. Something along those lines. Les finished his cocktail a little behind Digger. All the while, the Jack Daniels poster near the bar kept beckoning to him like a long lost friend. A tape of old fifties music drifted up from below, playing through the band's speakers.

'Well what do you reckon, Digger,' said Les. 'That cocktail was nice. But how about we go downstairs? The band should be starting soon.'

'Allright. Do you mind if we sit in the non-smoking section?'

Les gave her a wink. 'I would have insisted on it Digger.'

They left the cocktail bar and walked down to the auditorium. A few more punters had arrived, but they had no trouble finding a table just to the right of where the console was set up above the dance floor. They sat down and Digger placed her sling bag on the table.

'What would you like this time, Digger?' asked Les.

Digger went to open her bag. 'I'll get them,' she replied. 'It's my shout.'

Les placed his hand gently on Digger's and looked at her very sagely. 'Digger,' he said. 'I don't wish to be pushy. But we have a thing in the MOB. Our church. We're not allowed to accept money from women on the first night out.'

'Oh?'

'Oh yeah. It's strictly against our religion, Digger. The second night or whatever, maybe it's okay. But the first night is strictly taboo. Now you wouldn't want to go against my religious beliefs would you?'

'No Les. Absolutely not. Never.'

'Thankyou, Digger. I appreciate it. However,' Les pulled out a fifty and dropped it on the table, 'if at some time during the evening you wish to go to the bar yourself and get some drinks with the MOB's money, we can accept that.'

Digger stared at Norton's wad of money as he stuffed it back in his jeans. 'Les. How much money did you bring with you?' she asked.

'How much?' replied Les innocently. 'Enough I hope. I'm not sure what the drinks are in here.'

'Heavens. You could buy every drink in the club with that.'

'Sounds good to me.' Les thought it might be better if he took a different tack. 'What I really mean is, Digger, this money has to last me till at least Monday. And I didn't want to leave it at the flat.'

Digger looked slightly bewildered. 'I think your church is a little different to ours,' she said.

'Yes. Well we are a pretty solid bunch Digger. Build on the rock and all that.' Les smiled at her. 'Now. What can I get you?'

'I'd like a scotch and dry please.'

'Coming right up. Ice and slice.'

Les walked across to the bar and ordered a JD and ice, another two with diet coke and a Johnny

Walker Black Label for Digger. I think I'd better start watching myself with Digger, Les told himself while he was waiting. It's fun having her on about the church thing and all that, but throwing money around in front of her isn't all that smart. Even if that's the way we are in the MOB. I'd like to stay friends with Digger. She's a one off and she's gorgeous. And I don't think she'd be very impressed if she found out I'm not much more than a murdering gangster. Les gave the barman a fifty and hoofed his JD and ice. When he got his change, Les looked at it and frowned. After paying top odds at all the drinking holes around Bondi and the city, the drinks in the club were about a third. Bloody hell! Talk about give you the shits. I got a little sex pot with me I can't pork and a pocket full of money I can't spend. The warm glow from the Jack Daniels spread through his body. I knew I should have stayed home. Les picked up the drinks and eased his way back to their table.

'There you go Digger,' he said when he sat down. 'Cheers mate.'

'Yes, cheers Les. Thankyou.' Digger took a sip. 'Ooh this is nice.' She peered at Norton's glass. 'What are you dinking?'

'Jack Daniels and unleaded,' replied Les. 'He's my personal benefactor.'

'How come you got two?'

'The other one's in case the schizophrenic comes out in me again.'

'Like I said Les, I think you and Brendon would get on well together.'

'Does your cousin drink?'

'Yes. But only beer. It's not good for him.'

He's full of spirits as it is, thought Les. 'Fair enough.'

Digger got into her Scotch and had another good look around her as if she was either looking for someone or having simply a wonderful time. Or both. She looked so contented Les left her to it. She turned back to Les and smiled.

'Well who would have thought I'd finish up in Nelson Bay Memorial Club with a deacon,' she said, partly to Les and partly to herself.

'Fair enough,' said Les. 'And who'd have thought I'd finish up in a rissole on Friday night with a digger.'

Digger gave a little chuckle and raised her glass. 'I like you Les. You're funny. You're also genuine. I can tell.'

'That's me, Digger. Fair dinkum in a funny sort of way. You've hit the nail right on the head.'

They got into a bit of chit-chat. Digger was a *South Park* fan same as Les. Her favourite was the Charles Manson episode. Les said his was Chef Aid and he bought the CD. He didn't sing her any bars of *Chocolate Salty Balls* and he didn't dwell on Mr Hankey.

Digger knocked over her Scotch pretty smartly, picked the fifty up from the table and insisted on going and getting the next drinks.

'Please yourself,' said Les. 'Can you get me two while you're there? Plenty of ice.'

'I may as well get four.'

'Whatever you think's a fair thing.'

Les sipped the last of his JD and watched Digger walk across to the bar. From where he was sitting it looked as if her dress had somehow managed to inch up even further. Les also noticed that as soon as Digger got to the bar, a scrum of boozey blokes seemed to hit it at the same time. A few even started putting the hard word on her. Digger simply smiled and replied politely, seemingly a little blasé as to what was on their minds. Les couldn't help feeling pleased with himself in one respect. But drunken blokes. Digger in that mini. And him on his own. If he didn't act promptly, Les could sense trouble. Leaving a lot of lewd remarks and gestures in her wake, Digger returned with the drinks on a tray and sat down.

'Thanks Digger,' said Les.

'You're welcome.' Digger took a healthy sip from one Scotch then wrinkled her nose slightly. 'That's funny,' she said. 'This one doesn't seem as nice as the other.'

'It might be the ice,' said Les. 'Mine's okay though.' He leant across the table and placed his hand on Digger's again. 'Digger. There's something else I have to tell you about our religious beliefs in the MOB.'

'Heavens! What is it this time?' she said. 'I haven't done something wrong have I?'

'No. Nothing like that,' assured Les. 'It's just that I can only let you go and get the drinks once on the first night too.'

'Oh? That's odd.'

'Yes. I should have told you before. But I forgot.' Les gave Digger a contrite smile. 'I hope my religious beliefs don't offend you Digger?'

'No. Not at all,' replied Digger. She looked up at Les and her eyes started to swim. 'I just don't know how I'm going to handle all this pampering.'

'Don't worry about it, mate,' said Les. 'But I admit, we do have a habit of pampering in the MOB.' Les smiled back at her. 'And like I said, we are a pretty solid congregation.'

'And you stick to your beliefs too. I think that's wonderful.'

Les was about to say something when there was a shuffle of drums, a couple of chords sounded on a guitar and Whizz-Key got ready to go into action. Les glanced across the dance floor. On stage were four musicians wearing black trousers and black polo shirts, with the band's name on the pockets in gold lettering. They were no spring chickens. The bass player was as bald as a billiard ball and the rest all looked a bit on the square side even for Friday night in a country rissole. Les expected the worst. Someone whispered: One-two. One-two-three-four. Then this: Boom. Boom boom. Boom. Boom boom, started and their lead singer appeared at the top of the stairs holding a remote microphone. He had black hair, combed up in a pompadour; an oily, showbiz smile plastered across a jowly face and was a dead ringer for Tommy Lee Jones. Like the band, he was wearing black trousers and shoes, only he had a white shirt on opened a few buttons down the front and a pair of Elvis Presley sunglasses. Gold chains dangled round his neck, chunky rings sparkled on his fingers and next to a gold chain on one wrist was a watch the same size as the conning tower on a nuclear submarine. Round his waist shone a silver belt buckle as big as a wok. Les couldn't believe it. He looked like a cross between Neil Diamond and a Las Vegas used car salesman.

The singer gave his shoulders a flourish, poked out one arm and started into the old Tom Jones classic *It's Not Unusual*. He moved into the song with great hand gestures, wiggled his pelvis, shuffled his feet and tossed the mike from one hand to the other like Mr Showbiz himself. He was a shocking lair and an awful bodgie. Yet for all the hype and strained facial expressions, he had a sensational voice and the band were great. He finished the first song and maybe it was the Jack Daniels, but Les found himself clapping and cheering like there was no tomorrow. Moving confidently around the room, as if he was Wayne Newton working The Sands at Las Vegas, the singer cut into *Cold Kentucky Rain* complete with all Elvis's mannerisms better than The King himself. He finished that song and Les whistled and clapped again as the singer slipped smoothly into:

'Another little song I'd like to do for you. *Love Grows Where My Rosemary Goes*.'

'Hey Digger, what do you reckon?' laughed Les. 'They're not bad.'

151

Digger nodded enthusiastically over her Scotch and dry. 'Yes. They're good.'

That song finished then the band slid into a hot version of *Unchain My Heart*. Norton could feel the Jack Daniels pumping and his feet tapping.

'Would you like a dance Digger?' he asked.

'Mmmhh. My word.' They took a last slug of booze each and hit the dance floor with the other punters.

There was plenty of room and the rules appeared to be anything goes. Les got into a bit of a boogie with a style that was all his own. Digger just seemed to do her best; wiggling her incredible behind, shaking her shiny black hair and waving her arms around. All completely out of time with the music. However, with her tight little figure tucked into that incredible mini dress. No matter what Digger did, she could do no wrong. Whizz-Key slipped into *Crunchie Granola Suite* and Les and Digger did a bit of rock'n'roll, while the singer worked the room better than Neil Diamond at The Greek Theatre. Then the band kicked back with *Come Monday* and Les and Digger eased into a bit of cheek to cheek combined with a clumsy two forward and one back. They had a couple more dances then sat down.

'That was fun, Les,' said Digger. 'You're not bad on your feet, for a big man.'

'Yes,' conceded Norton. 'And you're not bad yourself — for a runt.'

'Runt? You cheeky thing.'

Digger went to the ladies and Les got some fresh drinks. He got back to the table before Digger and noticed she even got monstered by drunks walking back from the toilet. Just keep looking boys, nodded Les. But don't touch. Norton was sipping on a delicious as she sat down.

'You know what, Digger?' said Les. 'I'm sorry I didn't bring my camera. I'd love to have taken some photos. The night's turning into a hoot.'

'I brought mine,' said Digger.

'You did?'

'Yes. I thought I'd put it in my bag just for fun.'

'Unreal,' said Les. 'Do you mind if I have a look at it?'

'No. Here it is.' Digger got her camera from her bag. It was a Canon Z.135. Same as Norton's.

'Hey, these are good cameras, Digger,' said Les. 'Mine's exactly the same. Where did you get yours?'

'In Newcastle. I got a student discount.'

'Good on you.' Les handed Digger back her camera. 'Well, we should get some good photos, if you want to.'

'I'm hoping we will.'

They got into some more drinking and laughing and for some reason, Digger seemed to be trying to keep the same pace as Norton. She had that many Black Label Scotches, her emerald eyes were starting to turn ebony. But she claimed she was allright. The band started up again and this time the singer returned in all black with silver trim, wearing another belt buckle bigger than a satellite dish. He slipped into *Concrete And Clay* and started working the room again, easing nonchalantly through the chairs and tables picking out people to join him in a few songs. The punters loved it. He got one young girl up from her table and started walking her round the room while he crooned *Let It Be Me* in her ear. The girl must have thought it was Elvis himself serenading her. She buried her head in the singer's chest and cried buckets of tears, much to the chagrin of her pimply-faced boyfriend left sitting at their table sucking moodily on a cigarette and a schooner. The singer's act was that corny, you could have boxed it and sold it for breakfast cereal. But it worked and he had a terrific set of pipes.

Les borrowed Digger's camera and took some photos, then when the singer drifted over to their table, Les made Digger get up and join him in a couple of bars of *I Am I Said*, while Les took a couple more photos. Digger might not have been any great shakes on the dance floor, but her singing was even worse. Les handed the camera to some punters at another table and got them to take a photo of Digger and him, then the band slipped into *Let's Twist Again*, so they hit the dance floor. They twisted to that, boogied to *Old Time Rock 'n' Roll*, did their best to *Calendar Girl* and *River Deep Mountain High*. They even stomped to *Surfing USA*. Again Digger had about as much rhythm as a cattle stampede. But it made absolutely no difference. All she had to do was stand there in her mini, tap one foot and wiggle her bum a few centimetres from side to side. That was more than enough. They had one more dance then sat down. Digger headed for the ladies. Les went to the gents and came back via the bar with fresh delicious.

The band finished on *New York New York* with Les, Digger and the singer high-kicking round their table. The singer managed to drop the mike a couple of times and Les had a sneaking suspicion he was trying hard to see what Digger had on under the mini. Les couldn't blame him. He would have done exactly the same thing. Les clapped and cheered and gave the singer a standing ovation. So did Digger. Then they sat down and a jolly, splendid night was had by all. Next thing the lights went out around the poker machines, and a nasally voice came over the PA system saying all gambling had finished and the bar was now closed. Goodnight. This left Les and Digger with a bit of a sweat up and a table full of empty glasses sitting in front of them. Les felt he'd had enough and Digger looked totalled, though she was doing her very best not to show it.

'Well Digger. I had a pretty good night, mate,' said Les. 'What about you?'

'It was fantastic,' she answered. 'One of the best nights I've ever had.'

'I can't see me driving home though.'

'No,' she agreed. 'I don't think that would be a very good idea.'

'So it looks like a taxi.'

Digger rocked forward in her seat, almost knocking over a couple of glasses. 'Why don't we walk home? It's not very far.'

'Righto,' shrugged Les. 'I wouldn't mind a bit of fresh air to tell you the truth. I've got Jack Daniels coming out of my ears.'

'I feel allright,' said Digger.

Les shook his head. 'I don't know how you do it. You're a marvel.'

'It's ... it's easy,' said Digger. She picked up her bag, managed to knock over a couple of glasses this time, and they headed for the door.

Les could see Digger definitely had her wobble boot on, so he gently took her by one arm and deftly guided her through the chairs and tables. This walk home should be fun, he told himself. I'm almost shot myself and I got a feeling I'll end up having to carry Digger most of the way. But it's been a hoot of a night. And you never know. Little Miss Goody Two Shoes might even give me a quick kiss goodnight, if I'm lucky.

There was a bit of a crowd round the door filing out so Les slowed down for the other punters. He noticed Digger was still getting plenty of looks and remarks from the drunks. But everything seemed cool. They were getting near the door when two blokes about thirty-something stubbed out their cigarettes and eased themselves away from the bar. They'd had their eye on Digger and were giving each other plenty of nudge nudge, wink wink. Les half noticed them, but he was too busy keeping an eye on Digger. The tallest one was wearing a bright red shirt and black trousers with a gold chain round his wrist. He had dark hair, combed back from a sallow, grainy face and looked like he fancied himself. His shorter mate had on a cheap black leather jacket, jeans that were a size too long and a blue T-shirt with Goodyear Tyres on the front. He had scrubby brown hair, googly eyes and moved around like he was trying to act tough. Les sensed them giving him a once up and down from behind, but didn't bother turning around. They just looked like a couple of would be's and they weren't going to do anything while he was there. The two mugs shuffled around Les. The taller one blended in with the other punters for a smother, then winked at his mate, reached across and jammed his fingers right up Digger's backside.

Digger gave a high pitched squeal then spun around red-faced and glared at Les. 'Ow! What was that?' she shrieked. Then she noticed Les glaring daggers at Red Shirt.

Norton couldn't believe his eyes. What he'd just seen wasn't only plain, moronic ignorance. He was with Digger and it put him completely on show. Les was completely ropable and ready to smash the pair of them right on the spot.

'You having a good time? You goose,' he seethed at Red Shirt.

'What's up with fuckin you?' said Red Shirt, winking at his mate.

'You arse. I just saw what you did then.' Les turned to Digger. She was as red-faced as Norton was. 'Are you allright, Digger?'

Digger looked quite shocked. 'I think so,' she said. 'What's . . .?'

157

Les turned back to Red Shirt. 'How would you like it, if I grabbed you by your greasy stinkin' throat. You piece of shit.'

'How would you like to try? Dickhead.'

Leather Jacket suddenly appeared on the scene. 'You lookin' for a blue are you? You want a fuckin blue?'

'Fuck him. He's just a big suck,' said Red Shirt.

Les had a quick look around, then eyeballed Red Shirt. 'I'll see you and your short-arsed little mate out in the car park. Come on, Digger.'

Les started moving Digger down the stairs with the two mugs following not far behind. They were laughing between themselves and looked fairly confident. But Norton couldn't have cared if they were Mike Tyson and George Foreman. Norton was boiling. And there was no way they were getting away with what they just did. Not to an innocent little sweetheart like Digger. And not right under his nose.

'What was that all about?' asked Digger.

'You know what happened upstairs,' replied Les.

'Yes. That horrible man did something awful to me.'

'My oath he did. The . . .' fumed Norton.

'He had no right to do that, Les. And it hurt too.'

'Exactly. Now he has to be taught the error of his ways.'

'You don't mean there's going to be a fight?'

'I'm afraid so, Digger.'

'Goodness!'

'You see, this is another of the MOB's religious beliefs. If the woman in question is insulted, then the deacon must defend her honour.'

'Oh. Isn't that lovely.' Digger suddenly looked concerned. 'But there's two of them, Les.'

'I know. But fear not, woman. We have a method of fighting at our Shao Lin temple that's not too bad.'

'Allright. But if I can help you, I will.'

Les couldn't believe what he'd just heard. There wasn't all that much of Digger. But she was willing to get in and have a go for him. What a gal. 'Okay Digger,' he said. 'But it might be best if you just keep out of the road. You can cheer me on if you like. In the name of the Lord.'

'I will Les. I'll pray for you.'

'Thanks Digger,' smiled Les. 'Now I know I can't lose.'

Les stormed through the club foyer and out the front door then headed left for the parking area. The two mugs were only metres behind. Les remembered where he'd left his car, so he thought he may as well fight them there as anywhere else and walked towards it. A few cars had driven away when he found it so there was plenty of room to move around. All the time, Les had been watching the two mugs out the corner of his eye and he had an idea what their move would be. The smaller bloke would probably get behind him and tackle him round the legs. The bigger bloke would be the hitter. Les also knew that although he was wild as all hell and he had plenty of ability, he also had a massive belly full

159

of delicious on board and his reflexes would probably be a bit off. So be extra careful.

Les found a spot to his liking and turned around. He was right. Leather Jacket started circling round to his right while Red Shirt came in on his left. Les had a quick look to see where Digger was and took another look at how far away Leather Jacket was. Les was right about something else too. His reflexes were off a little. Red Shirt and his mate had obviously done this before and they weren't wasting any time. Red Shirt fired off a fairly solid right straight at Norton's face. Les just caught it out the corner of his eye and was able to ride it. But the punch still collected him above the right eye, splitting the skin and making Les see a few quick stars. Les rolled under it and went into a crouch, spinning round to his left. He saw Leather Jacket come in to tackle him and slammed his right knee up into his face. Leather Jacket gave a groan like he'd been hit by a car and slumped straight down on his backside.

Les kept turning round to his left then came up just as Red Shirt got ready to throw another one. Unfortunately, he'd left himself wide open and Les was able to sink a short right rip deep into his solar plexus, paralysing him on the spot. Red Shirt just had time to open his mouth for air that wasn't coming, when Les slammed his left elbow into it smashing all Red Shirt's front teeth. Les grabbed him by the collar and was going to follow up with a power-laden, short right, but claret started bubbling out of Red

Shirt's mouth. So Les thought that might be enough blood for the time being as he didn't want to freak poor little Digger out. It might be better if he went for a bit of fancy stuff. Red Shirt was completely out to it. The only thing keeping him up was Les holding him by the collar. Les took Red Shirt by the front of his shirt, pulled him forward, turned him to the left then kicked his legs away. Red Shirt flipped up in the air, Les let him go, and he slammed down onto the concrete on the base of his spine. Les heard the thump and laughed to himself as he thought how Red Shirt would feel when he woke up in the morning. Like a cattle stampede had gone over him. And he'd be like it for a month. Leather Jacket was still sitting on his behind watching the blood pouring from his nose. Les walked behind him, lifted up his leather jacket and gave him six hammer punches in the kidneys. Leather Jacket howled like a banshee and screwed his face up with pain. Les let go of his leather jacket and left him lying on his side, moaning into the concrete.

Les turned around to look for Digger. She was leaning up against his car with her bag in one hand and her camera in the other. 'Well Digger,' he said. 'What did you think of that?'

Digger looked at Red Shirt and his mate lying on the ground. 'Very good.'

'Your honour has been defended. And the sinners have been vanquished.'

'I can certainly see that.'

'But, it could have gone the other way.'

161

'Don't worry, Les,' said Digger. 'I was praying for you.'

'I knew that, Digger. I could feel the power in me.'

Digger held up her camera. 'And I got some great photos too.'

'You did?' beamed Les. 'Unreal.'

Digger's expression changed and she put her hand up to Norton's face. 'Oh Les. You're bleeding.'

'I am?' Les dabbed at his eye and got a tiny smear of blood.

'And you got that defending my honour. You're so brave.'

'Any God-fearing Christian man would have done the same thing, Digger. Don't worry about that.'

Digger had another look at the tiny cut above Norton's eye. 'That needs a bandage. Are you sure you're allright?'

Les had been hurt worse playing Monopoly. But he thought he might as well go along with it.

'Well, to tell you the truth, I don't feel like walking home.'

'No. We'll catch a taxi,' insisted Digger. 'And I'll patch you up at your place. Have you got any bandages?'

'There's a first aid kit in the bathroom.'

'Good.'

They started back towards the taxi rank at the front of the club. 'Thanks Digger. You're a real sweetheart.'

Digger put her arm in Les's. 'You're the sweetheart.'

There were two taxis out the front of the club and they climbed in the first one and drove off. Les didn't say much. He just dabbed a hanky at his eye while Digger looked at him with boozy concern. A few minutes later Les had opened the front door of the flat and turned the lights on in the kitchen and lounge.

'Get your first aid kit and I'll put the kettle on,' said Digger. 'And bring a towel with you.'

'Yes mother.'

Les went to the bathroom and came back with his Big W first aid kit. He turned the cassette on and slipped in a laid-back tape. By the time Digger had the water boiled and poured some in a bowl, Graeme Conners was happily crooning *The Pacific Hotel*. Les sat down at the kitchen table and Digger gently wiped away the small amount of blood caught in his eyebrow.

'I don't think it needs stitching,' she said.

'That's good,' said Les.

'It's still nasty though. Goodness. What dreadful men those two were.'

'Utter rotters,' agreed Norton.

Digger poked a cotton bud in the bottle of iodine. 'This might sting a little.'

'I'll be brave.' It did sting. Barely. Les thought he'd better add some sound effects. So he grunted an expressionless 'Ouch.'

'Sorry.' Digger gave his eyebrow another dab then applied a bandaid. 'There you are, Les. All finished.'

Les felt the bandaid with his finger. 'Thanks very much Digger. You're a sweetheart.'

'It's the least I could do.' Digger hung the towel over a chair and started tidying up.

Les got to his feet. 'Can I get you something Digger?' he asked. 'A cup of tea? Some coffee?'

'What have you got to drink?'

'Drink?' Les looked at her for a moment. 'All I got's white rum and pineapple juice.'

'Can I have one of those, please.'

'Okay. In fact I might have one myself.'

Les made two drinks, not too strong and with plenty of ice. For a little Miss Goody Two Shoes, Digger didn't mind the demon drink. But Les felt she'd had more than enough. Digger had made herself comfortable on the lounge. Les handed her a drink, pulled the coffee table over and sat down next to her on the right so they both faced the ghetto blaster. 'Well. Cheers again, Digger,' he said.

'Yes. Cheers Les.' Digger took a sip. 'Ooh. These are nice.'

'Yeah, they're not bad are they.' Les took another sip. 'Just take your time Digger. And I'll walk you home when you're ready.'

'Thankyou.'

Les had another mouthful of rum, rested the back of his head on the lounge and smiled. 'Well. Apart from those two dills spoiling things a bit, I thought it was a pretty good night. What about you?'

'Yes. It was fun,' replied Digger.

'And I really enjoyed your company, Digger. Thanks for coming out with me.'

'I'm glad I did,' smiled Digger. 'In fact I'm glad I met you Les. I had a couple of things on my mind. And ... you're something else, Les.'

Les returned her smile. 'You're something else too Digger. I can guarantee you that.'

'Me? How do you mean?'

'Your eyes,' shrugged Les. 'Your beautiful hair. The way you smile. Your clothes.'

'Clothes? I don't know what you're talking about,' said Digger. 'I just wore something comfortable. That's all.'

Les glanced down at the mini dress barely covering her thighs and wished he had X-ray vision again. 'Yeah, you're right. Forget the clothes. My mistake.'

Digger looked at Les for a moment. 'I'll bet you take lots of girls out.'

Les shook his head. 'Not really,' he replied. 'I work most nights.'

'At the mission?'

Les nodded. 'At the mission.' Digger had put her drink down on the coffee table. Les put his drink down next to hers. I know I shouldn't do this, he told himself, but what can you do? She looks like an angel. And I can't see the good Lord striking me down for one lousy little kiss. 'Digger,' said Les, 'did I tell you about another religious belief we have at the mission?'

'No Les,' replied Digger. 'What's this one?'

Norton slowly rubbed his hands together. 'On the first night out, if the lady in question has had her honour defended, then the defender — namely the Deacon — is entitled to ask the lady in question for a tiny kiss.' Les held up an index finger. 'However, if the lady in question says no, then it's still allright. And her honour still remains defended. To the max.'

Digger smiled up at Les. 'Let me get this straight, Les. You're entitled to ask me for a kiss. Because you defended my honour?'

Les nodded enthusiastically. 'That's right. Article seventy-one. Paragraph ... splimty two.'

'Allright then,' smiled Digger. 'You can kiss me.'

'I can?'

Digger gave a little nod. 'Mmmhh.'

Les looked at her for a second. 'Love that article seventy-one.'

Les put his arm around Digger's waist and drew her gently towards him. Digger put her hand on Les's other arm and tilted her face up. Les closed his eyes and very, very softly placed his lips on hers.

Digger had the sweetest, loveliest little mouth imaginable. Soft, warm, moist and possibly just that bit yielding. She opened her mouth a fraction and kissed Les back. Les softly stroked her face and ran his fingers though her gorgeous dark hair. Maybe there was a bit of forbidden fruit syndrome running through Norton's mind regarding Digger. But Les thought he'd found heaven. Digger slipped an arm around Norton's neck and Les gently massaged her scalp while Digger's lips moistened some more. Les was kissing Digger for nothing more than the sheer enjoyment of kissing her; she was that nice. But evil Mr Wobbly had other ideas. Mr Wobbly had been getting evil ideas ever since Les knocked on the door of Brendon's kitchen and Mr Wobbly spotted Digger in her mini and got a glimpse of her pink knickers. Now he was rattling his cage and wanting to do all sorts of awful things.

Les kept kissing Digger then, like a crack of sunlight coming from behind a sky filled with clouds, Digger opened her mouth just the teensiest, weensiest bit more and Les felt the barest tip of her spicy, warm tongue. A shiver went down his spine and Mr Wobbly started to go spare. Les ran his fingers down Digger's spine then rested his hand on her behind and felt the line of her knickers under her dress. That was the end of Mr Wobbly. He ripped the door off his cage, snarled around him and started frothing at the mouth. Les kept kissing Digger and Digger kept kissing Les back. He put his hand on her thigh and worked it around in front of her knee. Digger spread her legs slightly and moved into Les. Their kissing intensified and Les worked his hand up her leg. He was miles away, not even knowing what he was doing. Only whatever it was, it was bliss. Digger gave a little moan, then suddenly moved her head back and pushed herself away from him. Les opened his eyes and let go off her.

'Are you allright?' he asked her.

'I . . . I'm fine.' Digger shook her head. 'I think I've had a little too much to drink, that's all.'

Les nodded in agreement. 'Yes. You managed to put a few away tonight sport.'

'Oh dear.' Digger blinked her eyes around her.

'Are you sure you're allright?' asked Les.

Digger put her hand on Norton's arm. 'Do you mind if I lie down for a while?'

'No. Not if you're crook. Would you like me to get you a glass of water? You're not going to be sick are you?'

Digger shook her head. 'No. I'd just like to lie down.'

'Okay. Give me your arm.'

Les led her into his bedroom and pulled back the doona. 'There you go, mate,' he said, and ruffled the pillows. 'You'll be okay in there.'

'Thankyou.'

Digger kicked off her shoes and climbed into bed. Les pushed a pillow behind her head and brought the doona up under her nose. Just to be on the safe side, he got a glass of water from the bathroom and lay a towel down at the side of the bed.

'You allright now?' he asked.

'Yes thankyou,' she answered from beneath the doona.

'Okay. There's a glass of water there if you want it. If you need anything else, just give me a yell. I'll be out in the loungeroom. And if you want to crash out, that's okay. I'll doss in the other room.'

'Thanks Les. You're so sweet.'

Les turned the light off, left the door slightly ajar and went back out to the loungeroom. He picked up his drink, took a sip, stared at the ghetto blaster still playing softly and smiled. Poor little bastard. It's half my fault too, pumping all that bloody Black Label into her. But, it takes two to tango and I didn't ask her to keep up with me. I just get the taste. Christ! I'd hate to have her head in the morning. Les laughed out loud. I'd rather have her head than Red Shirt's back. Or his mate's kidneys. Serves the pricks right anyway. Les shook his head. Bloody hell! There's some in this world, isn't there. Les picked up his drink, took a sip and stared blankly at the ghetto blaster as John Paul Young hung back into *Groovin'*. That finished and Norton's head slipped forward a little as he found the Sandman kicking sand in his eyes. 'Shit! I think Digger's got the right idea,' he yawned. I might hit the sack myself. I can't see Digger surfacing before dawn and that bottom bunk will do me nicely. Les chuckled. I hope she doesn't snore too loud. Les drained the last of his rum and looked at the glass. Bloody Digger. What a little fox. You don't find many girls like that these days. Les smiled at his empty glass. It wouldn't surprise me if she still had her cherry. Innocent as the day is long. But that much sex appeal, she makes Elle Macpherson look like the bride of Frankenstein. Oh well.

Les put the glasses in the sink, turned off the ghetto blaster and started switching off the lights. A few minutes later he'd cleaned his teeth and was down to his T-shirt and jox spreading blankets on the bottom bunk in the spare room.

The bunk was a little longer than Les thought and was quite comfortable. He scrunched up a couple of pillows, turned off the lights and crawled in. Ohh yes, he thought, as he stared into the darkness. How good's this? Les yawned and was about to drift off, when he found he still had half a boner. Mr Wobbly was refusing to lay down. Christ! I'm half a mind to have a three bagger, he thought. Charles Bukowski's always at it. And Madonna's given tampering with yourself the green light. So it's all kosher. Les gave his old boy a rub. Shit! It's a thought. No. Imagine if Digger got up and found me in here with a full hand going alone. I'd definitely be brushed from the prayer meeting on Sunday.

Les lay back, closed his eyes and began to drift off. He recollected on the night for a few minutes thinking what a good time he'd had and smiled as he pictured the singer leading the crying girl around the auditorium. A few minutes later, Les was entering the twilight zone, somewhere between awake and sleeping. Next thing he was on a boat with Eddie at the controls. They were towing a rubber ducky. On the rubber ducky was a used car. Les could see the price written on the window. $20,000. Four Elvis impersonators got out of the car and started singing *Love Me Tender*. Red Shirt and Leather Jacket drifted among the Elvis impersonators wearing waiters uniforms. Les turned to Eddie to find Eddie dressed as an Elvis impersonator; white cape, sunglasses, the lot. Les was wearing his wetsuit and it was all covered in fish scales. Les was about to ask

Eddie what was going when from miles away someone started calling Les's name.

'Les. Les. Are you awake, Les?'

Like he was dragging himself out of quicksand Les opened his eyes. It was a woman's voice. 'Uhh?'

'Les. Are you awake?'

Les blinked into the darkness. 'Digger. Are you allright?'

'I'm fine. Are you awake?'

'Yeah. Yeah, I am now,' muttered Norton. 'What's wrong?'

'Les. Would you do something for me?'

'Sure Digger,' Les called out. 'What is it?'

'Would you come and lay down next to me for a little while?'

Les blinked into the darkness again, wondering what was going on. 'Yeah, okay,' he said.

Les swung his legs over the bunk and stared at the floor for a moment. Digger must be a bit scared or something, I won't bother putting my pants on. Bugger it. Les walked across to the main bedroom and opened the door. Digger was lying under the doona with the pillows beneath her head. Les sensed her watching him in the darkness. He pulled back the doona then got into bed with her and put one arm around her. Apart from a little blue eyeshadow, Digger was stark naked. Les nearly fell back out of the bed.

'Digger. What's going on?' he asked her.

'Nothing's going on,' she purred. Digger put her arms around Norton's neck and kissed him. Les kissed her back as Digger discreetly slipped the tongue in. A chill ran up Norton's spine and Mr Wobbly immediately snapped to attention.

'Digger. This is a little unexpected,' said Les.

'What is?'

Les ran his hands across Digger's behind. 'This is.'

'Don't you know what to do, Les?' said Digger.

'Well, sure I do. But . . .?'

'Well, what are you waiting for?'

Still feeling a bit drunk, Les looked at her for a second. 'Not much at all, I suppose.'

Les had his T-shirt and jox off in an instant. He kissed Digger on the mouth again then kissed the smoothness of her neck, working his way down to her small, firm breasts and kissed the two, tiny pink circles that formed her nipples. They felt softer than marshmallow. Les ran his tongue around them and kissed them some more then slowly worked his way down to her navel. Digger's legs were barely apart but the small, neat bush of her ted looked very inviting. Norton couldn't help himself. He pushed his face between her knees and eased his way up towards it, kissing and sucking, pushing his tongue in as far as he could. Digger hardly moved or made a sound. Les glanced up in the darkness and noticed her holding onto the pillow; eyes closed, her face to one side, her top lip slightly curled. For all the work Les was putting in, she didn't look aroused or horny. It was as if suddenly she'd changed her mind and wished she hadn't called Les in. But she wasn't pushing Les away or telling him to stop and Les was certainly horny.

In fact by now Les and Mr Wobbly were both basket cases. Les ran his tongue back up over Digger's navel and around her nipples again. Still, she was very restrained and quiet. Les even sensed she seemed a little scared or something. Les couldn't quite figure it out. But he'd got this far without forcing her and Digger still wasn't saying no. Les got between her legs and pushed.

After Kastrine Kreen's double garage, Digger's was like a little mouse hole. She was no virgin. But she was beautifully firm and moist. Les started working away while Digger lay back on the bed, barely breathing let alone moving. She didn't spread her legs or bring her knees up. She just kept her eyes closed curling her top lip, looking as if she'd be glad when the ordeal was over. Les pushed and shoved as carefully as he could and got a bit of a rhythm going. But even though Digger had invited Les in and pretty much told him to go for it, to Les it felt like he was having sex with Digger against her will. Almost as if he was raping her. It might have felt good, but somehow it didn't feel right. Les got about halfway inside Digger, gave a few more shoves and that was it. Les was too worked up. He shuddered, gave one great moan of ecstasy and poured himself into Digger. After a few seconds Les rolled off and got started getting himself back together. Digger still hardly moved or made a sound. It was very strange sex. Satisfying. But not stimulating. And there definitely didn't appear to be much sharing. The only person that seemed to have enjoyed himself was

Mr Wobbly. And now that he was happy, he crawled back in his cage and went to sleep. Les picked up the towel he left earlier at the side of the bed, gave himself a wipe then put it between Digger's legs.

'Are you allright?' Les asked her.

'I'm fine,' answered Digger.

'You're not feeling sick or anything?'

'No. I'm fine.'

'Okey doke.'

Les settled next to Digger with one arm around her. It was quiet and peaceful in the room and the bed was warm. Les closed his eyes for a moment and found himself drifting off again. He blinked his eyes open and looked at Digger. 'Do you think it might be an idea if I got you home?' he asked her.

Digger looked back at Les. 'You just want to get rid of me now, don't you?' she said.

Les nodded. 'I knew you were going to say that. Allright. I'm not going anywhere. I'm just going to lay here and snore until you get down on your knees and beg me to take you home. And I'll have an extra pillow, too.' Les took a pillow away from Digger and put it under his head.

Digger leant over and kissed him. 'No. I have to get going soon. Brendon will only worry if I don't come home.'

'That's what I said in the first place,' smiled Les. 'But oh no. Yadda, yadda, yadda. You can't win, no matter what you do.'

They got off the bed and started putting their clothes on. Tired and all as he was, Les managed to make a slow pretext of finding his clothes while he perved on Digger getting into hers — knickers first, then her bra followed by her little mini dress and red shoes. Digger went to the bathroom while Les climbed into his blue tracksuit and tied up his gym boots. Soon they were both standing in the loungeroom. Les put his arms around Digger and gave her a cuddle. Digger slipped her arms around his neck.

'Well. That was the night, that was,' smiled Les.

'Yes. It certainly was,' replied Digger.

'I can't wait to see how those photos turn out.'

'No. I've got a few more on the roll before I get them developed. But I expect they'll be good.'

Les gave her a little kiss. 'Come on.' He picked up his keys and opened the door.

Everything was closed and it was only a few minutes walk to Brendon's house. One or two cars went past and a few people were walking along the grass opposite the hotel, or sitting on the picnic tables talking, just having a hang. The night wind gently ruffled the trees and above the ocean the moon peeped through the clouds turning any whitecaps on the bay into silver. Les was tired and so was Digger. He had his arm around her as they walked along, while Digger rested her head on his shoulder as if she was sleepwalking. Norton left her to her thoughts until they turned the corner for Brendon's house.

'Are you doing anything tomorrow, Digger?' he asked her.

'I'm not sure,' answered Digger. 'I have got one or two things to do.'

'Would you like to go for a drive or something?'

'I'll think about it.'

'Maybe we could have lunch somewhere?' suggested Les.

'I suppose so.'

Les gave her a squeeze. 'That sounds like a definite maybe to me. How about I call round at twelve or so? See how you're feeling.'

'If you want.'

They got to Brendon's front gate. Les let go of Digger and held her tiny hand in his huge mitt for a moment then smiled down at her.

'There's no need to walk me to the door,' said Digger.

'Okay,' said Les. He bent over and gave her a little kiss on the lips. 'Well. Until tomorrow, Digger. Goodnight. And ... God bless.'

'Yes,' replied Digger, avoiding Norton's eyes. 'And God bless you too, Les.' Digger stepped inside Brendon's excuse for a front gate and closed it behind her. As she started up the path Digger suddenly turned around. Les didn't need X-ray vision to see the tears in her eyes. 'You're the only real man I've ever had, Les,' she said. Without waiting for an answer Digger turned around and walked up the steps. Les waited till she was in her front door then started walking back to the flat.

By the time he got home, had a shower then dried off and changed into a clean T-shirt and jox, Les had started to figure out just what sort of a bloke he was. A good look at himself in the bathroom mirror and

Les knew exactly what sort of a bloke he was. A bit of a rat. He'd lied his shifty head off to an innocent, young Christian girl. Got her drunk and porked her. A harmless, little veterinary assistant, who was going to join the National Parks and Wildlife Service, because she loved animals the same as she loved God. And Deacon Les got her pants off. Well done Deacon Les. Okay, he didn't tear her clothes off or anything like that, but she was that drunk and gullible she would have believed anything he told her. Article seventy-one. Plus she liked him. He was funny. And what else was he? Genuine. Yeah. That'd be right. She wanted to show Les she could drink like him at the club. Then back at the flat she wanted to show him she wasn't just a little Miss Goody Two Shoes either. She knew what it was all about. That's why she lay back against the pillows, like a piece of wood with her face all twisted up while some drunk slobbered all over her. And the only reason she came back was to patch up an almost non-existent cut over his eye because she was concerned about him.

The rat looking back at Les in the bathroom mirror's eyes got meaner and its tail got longer. And what were Digger's last words at the gate when she was crying, besides, 'God bless you too Les. You're the only real man I've ever had.'? That's because normally she'd keep her legs together and the only sex she's probably ever had has been an innocent little romp with a boyfriend from the church. Now she might even finish up pregnant for her trouble as well. Wouldn't that be great. Yeah. You're a real man allright. But the main thing is, Les. You had a terrific night. You got pissed. Got yourself a root. And you made a decent little girl cry. Don't forget to run down the pub as soon you get home and tell all your mates. Norton looked at himself in the mirror for the last time, then turned off the lights and crawled into bed, dragging his rat tail behind him.

As Les pulled the doona up over him he found some of Digger's fragrance still clinging to the pillow. This put a bit of a smile back on his face. Oh well. Maybe I can make it up to her tomorrow? I'd sure like to. Even if she didn't sound all that keen on seeing me. I'll try and slip her poor, loopy cousin a few bucks from that money I got off Eddie before I go back too. So he can get his lawnmower out of hock, or wherever it is. Brendon didn't seem like a bad, poor bloke either. Les yawned and let out a great sigh. Digger. What a number. How did I ever find her? Blowed if I know. Les chuckled to himself. Look at that. She's even got me cutting down on my swearing. Les touched the bandaid above his eye. One thing for sure. She was definitely worth fighting for. Les stared up into the darkness. Before he knew it, the Jack Daniels had started to take over and soon he was snoring peacefully.

Les rolled out of bed around eight-thirty the next morning with a dry throat, a fuzzy brain and a slight headache. However, compared to hangovers he'd had in the past it was almost nothing. He shuffled to the bathroom then, still wearing what he'd slept in stepped out on the sundeck to check out the weather. Kastrine Kreen was sitting on her balcony in a loose yellow dress next to Hakin in his jeans and T-shirt and some bloke wearing a shirt and tie, holding a biro and notebook, who looked like a journalist. They all managed to totally ignore Les. Les was going to totally ignore them in return, but decided he wouldn't even bother doing that. He placed a hand over his eyes and looked around. It was like a summer's day. The sky was an electric blue, the air quite warm and a light breeze coming from the north west gently swirled across the smooth waters of the bay. A haze hung over the hills and despite the breeze, there seemed to be a strange stillness in the air, as if a storm was approaching. Les blinked at the sunlight for another moment or two then walked back to the kitchen and nuked some instant coffee in the microwave, tarting it up as best he could with Carnation and raw sugar.

The first few mouthfuls didn't taste too bad and Les found he wasn't feeling as remorseful as he had been when he went to bed. He still didn't feel like tap-dancing around the flat over what happened with Digger. But things could have been a lot worse and there was still a chance he could put a smile back on her sweet little face. Then Les glanced at his watch and a couple of things dawned on him. As well as calling round to see Digger at twelve, he had to retrieve his car first. And allowing for his karma, the local car thieves had probably taken the stereo and stripped it down to the axles by now. He sipped his coffee and another thought struck him. It was a beautiful day outside. Why not jog down and sweat out a few litres of last night's stale delicious while he was at it? Les finished his coffee and changed into yesterday's damp training gear. He pulled the bandaid off his eye, did a few stretches on the balcony then got his keys, walked down the front and trotted off.

The Berlina was still sitting where he'd left it in the car park the night before and nothing was missing. There wasn't even any bird shit on the roof. Pleased that his karma was in after all, Les decided to keep going. He jogged past the club and the cannon on the corner, took a right past some houses and units, then followed the trees through a caravan park and round the edges of Little Nelson Bay. A fairly steep hill ran up to Nelson Head Lighthouse. Les looked at it for a moment and shook his head. Stuff it. He was on holidays. Maybe some other time. He jogged back to the car, hooked his feet under the front bumper bar and finished off with a series of punishing push-ups and sit-ups. When Les finally got to his feet, his chest was heaving, but compared to when he first got up, he felt one hundred per cent. He watched nonchalantly as the sweat dripped down his chin and onto the asphalt. I reckon you could put that in a glass with coke and ice, he mused. And start all over again. Something else caught his eye and Les couldn't help an evil smile forming on his face. Three patches of deep red near the back of the car, still sticky and glistening in the sunshine. Hello. It looks as if some poor bastards have cut themselves.

I wonder who? Tch, tch. Les peeled his sweat band off, opened the driver's side door and wound down the window. He was about to climb behind the wheel when he realised what a dill he was. If I'd have had any brains, he frowned, I would have walked down and got the car then gone for a run after. Now if I take Digger for a drive or something it's going to smell like a Mongolian wrestling team's change room. Good one mate. Les took his wet T-shirt off, wiped as much sweat as he could from his back and drove home to the flat with the windows down. He didn't bother locking the car. Just left it in the garage as it was, then went upstairs and had a shower.

When he got out, Les felt even better again. He wrapped a towel around himself, made a pot of tea and some toasted sandwiches and took them out on the sundeck. The neighbours had gone and what started out as a beautiful day only seemed to be improving. Yet there was still something odd about it. The traffic was light and for a Saturday there didn't seem to be many people around. Possibly Shoal Bay was a bit quiet this time of the year? But it just seemed too quiet. And there was something missing. Or conspicuous by its absence. Les looked around and shook his head. Buggered if I can figure it out. Maybe I'm just getting paranoid. He glanced across the bay to Jimmy's Beach and a quick memory of the shark attack flicked across his mind. That's what it must be. I've gone from schizophrenia to paranoia. He finished his sandwiches and went back inside. After cleaning up what little mess there was, Les changed into his jeans, Nauticas and a blue T-shirt he'd bought in Jamaica, then walked down to the car and headed for Digger's cousin's house via the beachfront. As he drove past the hotel, there was a sign out the front saying Reggae Party Tonight. Shit! What a coincidence. I reckon I could finish up in there this evening. Might even catch up with a few old rastas from Mo' Bay. I wonder if Digger might like to come with me? You never know. He turned the corner and pulled up outside Brendon's sumptuous villa.

The Holden utility and the old Laser were still parked in the driveway and the grass round the house looked even longer and more tangled in the daylight. Les walked up the front steps, knocked lightly on the flyscreen and hoped for the best. A moment or two later Digger answered the door wearing a pair of faded jeans and a white T-shirt with Save Our Wildlife on the front.

'Hello Les.' Digger's greeting seemed fairly cordial. But she didn't make a great deal of eye contact.

'Hello Digger,' replied Les. 'How are you?'

'I'm fine.'

'That's good.'

'Do you want to come inside?' said Digger.

'If it's okay with you?' answered Les.

Still avoiding Norton's eyes, Digger creaked open the flyscreen. Les wiped his feet and like he was walking on egg shells followed her into the kitchen.

'How's your eye?'

'It's allright thanks,' replied Les.

Digger was sipping a mug of tea. 'Would you like a cup of tea?' she offered.

Les shook his head. 'No, I just had one thanks.'

He had a quick look around. 'Where's Brendon?'

'He's at work.'

'That's right. At the paint shop,' nodded Les. 'What time did he have to start?'

'Eight-thirty.'

Les subconsciously glanced at his watch. 'He'd be right into it by now.'

Digger frowned into her tea. 'I wish he wasn't,' she said.

Shit! That didn't go over too good, thought Les. Maybe I'd better watch what I'm saying. I got a feeling I'm only in here on sufferance as it is. He tried for a smile. 'So, how were you when you woke up this morning, Digger?'

'Quite woozey,' she answered. 'But I went for a swim.'

'A swim?'

'Yes. One of the managers at the hotel is in the church. He lets me use the pool when I'm up here and I do laps.'

'Oh. Good on you,' said Les. 'I ended up going for a run myself. I jogged down to get the car. And it was such a nice day I decided to keep going.'

'Yes. It's almost like summer outside,' said Digger.

'Yeah. It's a top day allright.' Les looked at Digger. 'So what's doing?' he said tentatively. 'Would you like to go and have a bite to eat? Or go for a drive, or something?'

'It's nice of you to ask me. But I have to drive over to Salamander Bay and pick up a whipper snipper.'

Les held his hands up. 'Hey look. I was only joking, what I said about your cousin's front yard last night.'

'That's allright,' replied Digger. 'He was supposed to pick it up last week. But his car was off the road.'

Les nodded to the two cars in the driveway. 'Which one's Brendon's?'

'The Laser.'

'You drive a Holden ute, Digger?'

'Yes. What's wrong with that?'

'Nothing,' replied Les. 'I used to have a Ford ute. But it got stolen.'

'They're very handy,' said Digger. 'Working at the mission. I imagine you'd know all about that, Les.'

'Too right. I miss the old ute. We'll have to get another one.'

Digger looked up at Les from under her eyebrows. 'Would you like to come for a drive out with me in mine?'

'Yeah. Allright. When were you thinking of going?'

'Now. I want to catch Glenda before she goes to work.'

'Okay. Let's get going then.'

'I'll get my keys.'

Digger locked the front door, Les followed her out to the driveway and got in the ute. Inside was as neat as a pin. There was a Wilderness Not Woodchips sticker on one side of the rear window and a fish symbol on the other. A small cross on a chain hung from the rear-vision mirror. Digger started the engine and reversed down the driveway then took the back street to Shoal Bay Road. As they went past Norton's flat, she turned the radio on and an old Skyhooks track started playing through some speakers behind the dash. The ute was a T-bar automatic and Digger was a careful, confident driver. She zipped effortlessly along with the traffic and soon they were past Nelson Bay Marina approaching Corlette.

Les didn't say anything about last night for the time being, or try cracking any corny jokes. He thought he might leave it till if they had lunch somewhere. Digger wasn't saying much either. But Les soon got a feeling something was on her mind and she was holding back pent-up anger. She kept breathing heavily through her nose and every now and again her mouth would tighten and she'd snort out noisy little bursts of air. Something was literally up her nose allright and any tick of the clock Les was expecting her to let rip and give him a blast about something. The houses and water went by and Les thought he recognised a couple of places from the day before. Then Digger took an off road and they drove along a street full of trees and a number of houses with For Sale signs out the front. The radio played, they went over a couple of speed humps, then Digger pulled into the driveway of a house on their side of the road with a concrete mixer and a pile of timber in the front yard. A blue station wagon was parked in the drive next to some kids' bikes. Digger cut the engine just as a woman came out the side door wearing a white shirt and a black dress.

Les turned to Digger. 'Can I give you a hand?' he offered.

Digger shook her head. 'No. I'll only be a minute.'

Les sat in the car and listened to the radio as Digger walked up to the woman in black and white. They were all smiles for a few moments then the woman went to the garage at the end of the driveway and came back with a whipper snipper. They were all smiles again, then the woman got into the station wagon, Digger put the whipper snipper in the back of the ute, started the engine and after giving the woman a little toot on the horn, reversed round and drove off.

'What about two-stroke?' asked Les.

'Brendon's got some in the garage,' replied Digger.

'Right.' Les would have loved to have asked Digger if Brendon sniffed that too?

They drove off again. Still nothing was said and still Les could feel Digger's suppressed anger. They went back the way they came, then Digger took another road that turned into a four lane with a few roundabouts and not so many houses. The traffic was fairly light, the weather was beautiful and Les was enjoying the drive amongst the trees and fields. Driving in the outside lane, Digger came to a roundabout. She went through it, and further on hit her blinker and changed back into the inside lane.

Next thing there was the sound of screeching brakes and a horn blasting as an old, brown Fairlane swung up behind them. The driver was speeding and trying to overtake Digger on the inside and as she changed lanes she'd accidentally cut him off. The driver kept blasting on his horn and started flashing his lights. The Fairlane was right up Digger's rear and Les turned around for a look. The driver was a solid, brown-haired bloke with a moustache, wearing a dirty white T-shirt. He was red-faced and shaking his fist at Digger, pointing for her to pull over.

Digger looked in her rear-vision mirror. 'What's wrong with him?'

'I think he's got some idea in his head that you cut him off,' said Les.

'Oh piffle. I had my blinker on. I never cut him off at all.'

'I know,' said Les. 'He's just a mug. Ignore him and he'll go away.'

Digger gave another little snort. 'Too bad if he doesn't.'

Les gave Digger a double blink. My goodness. Is this the same little Miss Goody Two Shoes I know and love from last night? The bloke in the Fairlane was still going off his brain, bipping his horn and flashing his lights. He roared around Digger, pointed for her to pull over then swerved in front of her, hit the brakes and stopped. Digger was forced to hit the brakes also, and pulled in behind him. She turned off the motor, looked up at the Fairlane through her eyebrows and snorted through her nose again.

Les started undoing his seatbelt. 'Digger. I think you'd better let me handle this.'

'It's quite allright, thanks,' said Digger. 'I can handle it. Stay in the car.'

'Digger. He's a nutter. He's one of those road rage idiots you read about.'

'I don't care what he is. Just stay in the car please Les.' Digger sounded adamant.

Les shook his head reluctantly. 'Allright. If you say so.'

Digger started to open her door. As she did, Les saw her take something from the door tray. It was a bottle of hair conditioner. Terrific. She's going to wash his hair then rinse and condition it for him. Digger got out of the ute as the road raging nutter stormed out of the Fairlane brandishing a steering lock in his right hand. He was about six foot three, florid faced with a bit of a gut and looked somewhere in his early twenties. Under his dirty white T-shirt he was wearing a pair of old blue shorts and equally old thongs. What a hero, scowled Norton. A girl half his size and he needs a steering lock in his hands. Les opened his door a little ready to jump out and wrap the steering lock around Blue Shorts's head.

'You dopey fuckin moll,' he bellowed. 'You just cut me off. Now I've fucked up me radiator.'

'I did no such thing,' replied Digger. 'And watch your language.'

'Fuckin bullshit,' roared Blue Shorts. 'You were all over the fuckin place.'

'Well I'm sorry. But I wasn't. And I didn't. So there.'

'Pig's fuckin arse.' Blue Shorts pointed a big, beefy finger at Digger. 'You just fucked up my radiator. So I'm going to fuck up your headlights.'

Digger stood her ground. 'You think so?'

'I fuckin know so.' Blue Shorts glared at Norton. 'And I'll give your fuckin wimp boyfriend some of the same. If he wants to put his fuckin head in.'

Norton saw red. He gripped the door handle as Blue Shorts raised the steering lock. Digger brought the bottle of hair conditioner up at the same time with the top off.

'You see this?' she said. 'This is unleaded petrol.' Digger squirted some into the crutch of Blue Shorts's stubbies.

Blue Shorts looked down and his jaw gaped. 'Huh?'

'And this.' Digger held up her other hand. 'This is a Bic lighter.' Digger clicked it and a blue flame shot out the top.

Blue Shorts rubbed his crutch, smelled his hand then looked at the lighter burning in Digger's hand. 'Oh Christ! You're fuckin kiddin'.'

'No I'm not kidding. And don't you take the Lord's name in vain either. You horrible man.' Digger gave Blue Shorts another squirt of petrol in the crutch.

Blue Shorts panicked. He dropped the steering lock and grabbed at his crotch just as Digger pushed the lighter into it and set his stubbies on fire. Blue Shorts screamed in horror and started slapping at the flames. But instead of putting the fire out, all he did was whack himself in the balls. Les watched completely rapt as Blue Shorts fell back against the front of his car banging away at the flames only to get more pain for his trouble. Screaming and blubbering, Blue Shorts fell to the ground and started tearing off his burning stubbies. Underneath he was wearing a pair of filthy old BVDs and they were on fire too. Luckily Digger never used enough petrol to give Blue Shorts third degree burns. But the family jewels weren't going to be much use to him for a long, long time. Digger watched Blue Shorts rolling around on the ground for a moment or two, then put the cap back on the bottle and returned to the ute. She put the container and lighter back in the door tray, started the engine and drove off. Les stared at her, wide-eyed with admiration.

Digger looked up through her eyebrows as Blue Shorts disappeared in the rear-vision mirror still grovelling about in the dirt. 'Well, Deacon Les. What did you think of that?' she said.

'What did I think of that?' replied Les. 'I think I'm in love with you, Digger. You're sensational!'

Digger now had a definite gleam in her eye. 'Not bad for a little girl hey? And he deserved it too. The foul-mouthed, horrible big thing.'

'My very word he did.' Les smiled at Digger. 'And that's not a bad fighting technique you've got in your Shao-Lin temple either, sister.'

Digger looked evenly at Les. 'We're not the MOB. But we do have our moments.'

'Do you what.' Les wanted to burst out laughing. 'So where to now?' he asked. 'Home?'

'No,' said Digger. 'I want to go to Nelson Bay first.' She turned to Les and smiled. 'I've decided to buy you something. When's your birthday?'

'My birthday? What do you want? My star sign?'

'No. Not your star sign. Your birthday. The month and the day.' Les told her. 'Thankyou Les. That's all I need to know.'

None the wiser, Les sat back and enjoyed the drive. Watching the way Digger shortened that big goose up was one of the best things Les had ever seen. And Digger was definitely a changed girl. Any anger, or whatever it was she had bottled up inside her, was now gone. She stopped snorting and started quietly whistling along with an old Beatles song playing on the radio. Les started whistling it too. Before long Digger had driven the back way into Nelson Bay and pulled up outside a bottle shop round the corner from Bi-Lo.

Digger wound up her window and looked impassively at Les. 'I still owe you two dollars, don't I?'

Les returned Digger's impassive look. 'You don't think for a minute I'd forgotten, do you?'

Digger looked back at Les as if she'd just taken the perfect squelch right on the chin. 'Come on,' she said.

They locked the car and Les followed Digger across the main street to the small arcade that led to the local picture theatre. On one corner was a surf shop and inside was a butcher, a restaurant, and several other shops. Past a clothes shop on the left, before the entrance to the theatre, was a new age gift shop. The window was full of crystals and little statues and carvings from overseas and books about health and yoga. Inside were clothes, rings, sunglasses and other trinkets and more books. Near the door was a rack full of strange postcards. Digger started going through the cards till she found what she was looking for.

'There you are,' she said, and handed Les a postcard.

'What's this?' Les started reading the card as Digger flicked through the others on the rack.

On the top, it said Aztec Astrology. Beneath that was a colourful Aztec drawing of a figure covered in plumes, headdresses, amulets and coloured leggings. Next to the little figure it said *The Monkey. Ozomatli. Number 11. Beneficial colour. Golden yellow.* Les read on. *As man's counterpart, not his opposite. The Monkey is halfway between the wildness of nature and the order of human culture.* It then went on about how the Monkey gave man the gift of fire. The next paragraph was interesting. *First and foremost, you cunning and hard working Monkeys have the good taste not to take yourselves too seriously.* Yes. That could be me, thought Les. *Even if it means scattering your talents and turning inventions into charming deviltry and sleight of hand.* Les looked at Digger for a moment. Does this girl know something about me? *You are an individualist, unselfish, yet expert in manipulation.* Yes. I have been known to bend people round to my way of thinking, agreed Les. *With your natural elegance you are a tranquil aesthete.* I'm buggered if I know what that means, though. *Your freedom is always very precious to you.* Les reflected back on getting arrested on Wednesday night. Yeah. My bloody oath it is. *Above all, the Monkey likes surprises and unexpected occurrences.* What? Like shark attacks? *Impulsiveness and spending money. You also have a pleasant, friendly, physical appearance.* Well, I'm fit. I suppose. The card went on and finished with, *The Monkey's mood is usually happy, with good-natured humour.* Yeah, nodded Les. I'll drink to that. Maybe those Aztecs were on to something?

Les handed Digger the card. 'Yeah. That's good. I especially like the part that says I have a pleasant, friendly physical appearance. With general good-natured humour.'

'There's a few other things that are fairly accurate about you too,' said Digger.

Les looked at some of the other cards. 'So what are you?'

Digger shook her head. 'You wouldn't want to know.'

'Yes I do,' said Les. 'Come on. You know everything about me. What's your story?'

'Oh allright then.' She took a card and handed it to Les.

There was a similar little drawing on the front, only with more plumage. 'The Wind,' said Les. 'Eecatl. Number 5. Beneficial colour, brown.' Les looked at the price. 'How much are they? Two dollars.' He handed Digger the cards and two dollars. 'How about buying both of them. Then we're square. And I'll read all about you in the car.'

'Very well.'

Digger went inside and paid the lady who put the two cards in an envelope. Digger handed the envelope to Les and they walked out to the car. As Digger drove back to the house Les read Digger's card.

The Wind was extolled by the Aztecs in the form of an enigmatic divinity. The card went on. *The bird boasts the virtues of a well travelled guide and is just as much at ease in water as in the sky. Those of you born under the Wind are also masterful investors, showing incredible ingenuity and forthrightness, as well as being unrivalled in your physical flexibility.* Yes, thought Les. That was pretty ingenious what she did with that bottle of hair conditioner today. *The nature of the Wind also lies in its ability to circumvent obstacles. Therefore the Wind's natives sometimes prefer to evade the issue, choosing to drift in the cloudy air of ambiguity which can feed the indecisive, inconsistent side of this sign.* Digger's hiding something. She's not really in the church. She works at a massage parlour. It went on about overcoming whimsical dalliances and being of unusually high intellect. The last sentence got Les. *The Wind rises up in the victory cry of a benevolent squall as your passions are united with a like-minded partner.*

Les nodded at Digger. 'Yes. I can see a bit of this in you. An enigmatic divinity. You like the water. You're ingenious. I don't know about evading the issue though. You're one of the most ball ... gutsy women I've ever met.'

'They're good the way they do them but. Aren't they?' said Digger.

'Yeah. They're not like a horoscope. You can be born on any month of the year. Just so long as it's those two or three dates. And that's your profile.'

'That's right,' said Digger. 'The Aztecs used to judge time and events by solar flares and the planet Venus. I like some of their theories.'

'What? Like human sacrifices and tearing people's hearts out while they're still alive. You're not like that in The Church Of The Peaceful Sea, are you Digger?'

Digger shook her head. 'We just believe in love and God Les. And peace to all.'

'Unless some one comes at you with a steering lock.'

Digger seemed to think for a second. 'Let's just say I wanted that man to have a burning desire for something. Besides me.'

Les gave her a wink. 'He certainly found himself cast into the flames Digger. That's for sure.'

They pulled up in Brendon's driveway, Digger switched off the engine and they got out of the ute. Les held up the two cards in the envelope.

'Do you mind if I have both of these?' he asked Digger.

Digger shook her head. 'No. I'd like you to have them.'

'Thanks.' Les watched as Digger took the whipper snipper from the back of the ute. 'So what's doing now?' he asked her. 'You feel like something to eat?'

'To be honest Les, I'm not very hungry,' she replied. 'And I promised Brendon I'd clean the house for him. Especially the garage.'

'Would you like me to give you a hand?' offered Les.

'How do you mean?'

'I'll help you. You do the garage and that and I'll whipper snip the yard.'

Digger looked puzzled. 'You don't have to do that Les.'

'I know I don't,' replied Les. 'But I'm not doing anything this arvo, and I'd only be sitting around on my big fat date. So I may as well give you a hand.'

'Well, allright. If you want to. But ...'

Les moved towards his car. 'I'll go home and change into some old gear. I'll be back in about fifteen minutes.'

'Okay.' Digger flashed Les a smile that lit up the big Queenslander's heart. 'Thankyou Les,' she said.

'No worries. I'll see you when I get back.' Les got in the Berlina and drove round to the flat.

Back in his room, Les placed the envelope on the dressing table, stared at himself in the mirror for a moment then walked out onto the sundeck and looked up at the sky. It was a beautiful day outside, he had a pocket full of money and there was a top hotel two minutes down the road. Plus he had a bag of pot and a stack of good music. And what was he doing? Going round to clean up some bloke's yard. Some bloke he hardly knew and would probably never see again, once he went back to Sydney. I know what you're thinking boss — I've either got a pumpkin for a head, or there's an ulterior motive. But it's not quite like that. His training gear was almost dry where he'd hung it out on the sundeck. Les got changed back into it then had a quick glass of milk and a sandwich. He threw a carton of pineapple juice and his camera into his backpack, then locked the flat up and walked round to Digger's.

Brendon's garage was an unbelievable mess. Apart from all the junk in there, it looked like there'd be a day's work just getting rid of the cobwebs. Digger was inside wearing an old pair of shorts and one of her cousin's paint spattered T-shirts. She'd tied a band round her hair and put on a pair of gardening gloves. The whipper snipper was lying on the driveway, filled with two-stroke and ready to go.

'Looks like you've got your work cut out for you,' said Les.

Digger turned around. 'Have you ever seen such a mess in all your life?'

'Can't say I have. But you want to keep your eyes open. You might find anything in there.'

'I already have.' Digger held up a bundle of old *Phantom* comics. 'These could be worth something.'

'Ghost who walks. And his faithful dog Devil.' Les took his backpack off. 'Could you do me a favour, Digger? I brought some pineapple juice. Would you put it in the fridge for me?'

'Sure.'

Les handed Digger the carton of pineapple juice and she took it inside. When she came back Les had his camera out.

'What are you doing?' asked Digger.

'Taking some before and after shots. Come on. You can get in them.'

'Like this?'

'Yeah. I'm not doing a photo shoot for *Vogue*.'

Les took a few photos of the waist high weeds. He got one of Digger near the front steps and got her to take one of him holding the whipper snipper near the dried-up tree. Les put the camera away and looked at the whipper snipper. It was much the same as the one he had at his house in Bondi. Les set the choke on Close, wiggled the rubber nipple so some two-stroke came through and locked the accelerator. Two good pulls and it roared into life.

'You obviously know what you're doing,' said Digger. 'It takes me all day just to get those things started.'

'That's because you're only a woman,' said Les.

'Oh, of course. It's a wonder I can clean my teeth and run a tap at the same time.'

'Have you got any more work gloves?' Digger went into the garage and came back with another pair of gardening gloves. 'They'll do. Thanks.' Les put the gloves on, adjusted his sunglasses and gave the whipper snipper a rev. 'Allright woman. Out of the road. This man's got work to do.' Digger waved Les off and walked back into the garage as Les started zapping the driveway.

Digger probably thought Les was either mad or just trying to curry favours, giving up his afternoon to clean a yard that had been neglected for ages. But secretly, Les was having fun. He liked whipper snipping. He'd bought one for the yards at home but they were that small. By the time he started, he was finished. Les used to end up doing the front of the houses next door and he'd often go over and do Mrs Curtin's yards for her which were even smaller than Norton's. Now Les had hit the big time. Something he could get his teeth, or weed eater, into. Les zapped and revved away blasting the tall weeds and shrubs aside in his path. Sometimes he'd start at the top and work down shredding them slowly. Other times he'd just make great sweeps around him. Les felt like the Terminator. Soon shredded grass and weeds were blasted into his legs, arms and face, turning him green. Les kept going; stopping only for a drink of water or to change the cord and refill the tank.

Brendon had a good-sized yard and cleaned up it could look allright. Les uncovered some rockeries, an old hose connected to a tap, ceramic pots, a rake, and a few other odds and ends. He gathered up some bottles and tins people had thrown over the fence and zapped about twenty dog turds out the front into clouds of white dust. Les lost all track of time and it didn't seem long before he'd finished. He switched the whipper snipper off, splashed some water over his face and surveyed his effort. Yes. The place actually looked like somebody lived there now. He pushed his sunglasses on top of his head and walked round to the garage.

Digger hadn't been idle either. She'd cleaned all the windows, stacked or removed every piece of junk in the garage and swept up. When Les walked in, she was covered in dirt and grime and standing next to three, bulging garbage bags looking as if she'd finished for the day too.

'Hey. Not a bad job,' said Les, looking around. 'You wouldn't recognise the place.'

Digger pursed her lips. 'I don't think I've ever seen so much junk in my life. Brendon must collect it.'

'Did you find any lost Rembrandts or Picassos?'

'No. But I did find those.' Digger pointed to a bundle of old *Playboy* magazines sitting on the work bench. The one on top was dated November 1971 and the over made-up girl on the cover was wearing leather boots and hot pants.

'You're cousin's got great taste in literature and women's fashions,' said Les.

'I've got to get him out of that painting shop,' said Digger.

Les hooked a finger. 'Come and have a look at this,' he said. Les led Digger round the front. 'Well. What do you reckon?'

'Good heavens. I don't believe it.'

'He's actually got a garden hose and there's a couple of rockeries over there. Bit of work here and there and this could look allright.'

Digger shook her head. 'I don't know what to say. Brendon will think he's come home to the wrong house.' She took Norton's hand and smiled. 'Thankyou Les.'

Les gave her a John Wayne salute. 'Any time I'm in town little lady. Now. I'm going to get my camera. Would you mind getting me that carton of pineapple juice?'

'Sure. Do you mind if I have some?'

'Help yourself.'

Les got his camera out as Digger returned with the pineapple juice and two glasses. Les took some photos of the yard, got Digger to get in one then got Digger to take one of him. They were near the front steps finishing the pineapple juice when Digger smiled at Les.

'How do you feel now, Les?' she asked.

'Feel?' replied Les. 'Allright. Why?'

'You're not tired?'

'No.'

'That's good. Because I want to take you for a walk. A climb. While we're still all messy and dirty.'

'A climb?' asked Les. 'Where?'

Digger pointed to the mountain above Zenith Beach. 'Up Tomaree Head. I want to show you the view. And something else. Virgin Island.'

'Virgin Island? They still got one up here have they?'

Digger looked at Les impassively. 'Brendon and I are going diving out there tomorrow. In Brendon's boat.'

'Yeah? Sounds like fun,' said Les.

'Why don't you come with us? The island is absolutely beautiful.'

'Well, I'd love to Digger,' said Les. 'But I haven't got my PADI.'

'That doesn't matter. Just come for a snorkel. You'll love it.'

'Okay. Sounds good,' said Les, trying to sound enthusiastic. 'What time are you leaving?'

'Around ten. When we get back from church. Would you still like to come to church with us in the morning, Les?'

'Yeah, sure. That sounds good too,' answered Les.

'Wonderful. We can both read from my bible.'

Bloody hell, thought Les. That's all I need. I'm not game to put my face in a sink full of water at the moment, let alone go snorkel sucking round some island out in the middle of nowhere. And I can't remember being in a church since my christening. If the sharks don't get me a big hand coming out of the sky will.

Digger clapped her hands together. 'Allright. I'll get my cap. And bring your camera with you. You'll get some great photos.'

'Righto.'

Digger got rid of the empty drink carton. Les tidied himself up a little and checked to see how much film he had left, then Digger came out of the house wearing a peak cap with Newcastle University on the front.

'Allright Les. Are you ready?' she asked.

'Yep. Let's go.'

They left the house and started walking down the hill. Shit! It's a good thing there's not many people around, thought Les, as they turned right into Shoal Bay Road. Digger's covered in old spider webs and all the crap under the sun and I look like the Incredible Hulk's red-headed understudy. They got to Zenith Beach and the start of the brick pavers that formed the trail leading up to Tomaree Point. They were about to start climbing when Les stopped.

'Hey Digger,' he said. 'Have you noticed anything about today?'

Digger thought for a moment. 'Only that it's quite warm for this time of the year.'

'Yeah. But have you noticed how quiet it is?'

Digger looked around. 'Yes. It is. When you come to think of it.'

'You know what it is?'

'No,' shrugged Digger. 'What?'

'There's no birds. Have a listen.'

Digger had another look around. 'You're right. There isn't.'

'I noticed it early this morning.'

'I wonder why that is?' said Digger.

Les shook his head. 'I don't know.'

'Anyway. Let's start walking while there's still plenty of light.'

203

'I'll follow you.'

Even in an old pair of shorts covered in dirt, Digger's backside was still a heartbreaker as she bounced along the trail like a little rabbit with her hair streaming out from under her cap. Les followed behind keeping one eye on the surroundings and another on Digger and telling himself after what happened last night, he shouldn't even be thinking lecherous thoughts about her. But Les couldn't help it. He was also having other thoughts about Digger. Les had never met a girl like her. She was an enigma. A simple little churchgoer who didn't swear. Yet oozed sex appeal and liked *South Park*. She liked animals and you could bet she wouldn't hurt a fly if she could help it. But the way she sorted out that big goose in the Fairlane. Even Eddie wouldn't have thought of that. Then just when he thought she hated him, she stopped at Nelson Bay especially to get him that lovely card. Now she wanted him to come skindiving tomorrow. Digger was an enigma allright.

The trail kept going up, and so did Digger. Les knew he was in good shape. But so was she; and there was no taking it easy if he wanted to keep up. They came to a council plaque on the side of the trail telling them where they were and how much further to the top. It also showed another part of the trail leading to some old gun turrets. Digger suggested they have a look at them on the way back. Around them was nothing but trees, logs, native shrubs and boulders pushing up to the top of the mountain. The meandering trail wasn't all that steep, but it was certainly steady and Les was starting to get a sweat up. Then the pavers stopped at a set of metal steps going straight up. They climbed the steps till they came to a sign saying the scaffolding was still under construction and to take the trail on the right. Les kept following Digger as the mountain fell away behind them and the view began to open up. Now Les could see Zenith Beach below them, another two beaches and all of Shoal Bay, including the little jetty where Eddie picked him up in the runabout. The trail was all rocks now and a lot steeper. It levelled off then stopped at more vertical, metal steps. They climbed them before finally stepping off at the top.

Les found himself in a clearing ringed with small trees and shrubs and the concrete remains of an old gun turret sitting in the middle. A clump of boulders led up to a higher level at one side. Les climbed the boulders behind Digger then they stopped and looked around while they got their breath.

'Well ... what do you think, Les?' said Digger.

'What do I think?' replied Les. 'In a word, Digger, absolutely, positively fantastic.' Les took his camera out of its case and started looking around, wondering what to take a photo of first.

To the south was Zenith Beach and the two adjacent beaches then a spit ran out to an island dotted with tiny, rocky islands at the front. Beyond the spit were more tiny islands and beaches, backed by a coastal mountain range leading to Stockton Bight and the sandhills running to Newcastle. To the west was Shoal Bay and Nelson Bay then the vastness of Port Stephens opened up before fading into more distant mountain ranges. On the ocean side, the steep grey cliffs of Tomaree and Yacaba Heads tumbled down to the ocean, facing a trio of rocky, green islands jutting out of the sea. Looking north across Port Stephens, Jimmy's Beach clung to a long spit of white beach connecting it to the ocean by a few metres of scrubby sand dunes and inland from the spit was Hawks Nest and the start of Myall Lakes National Park. Looking further north, seemingly endless kilometres of beach ran off to the North Coast and out from the beach near the start of Myall Lakes was a bigger island with two hills sticking up at the ocean end. Digger pointed to it as Les switched on his camera.

'That's Virgin Island,' she said. 'Isn't it lovely?'

'Yeah. It sure is,' agreed Les. 'So that's where you're going tomorrow?'

'We're going,' corrected Digger. 'We'll take some lunch with us and everything. There's even an old wreck out there.'

'Is that what you and Brendon are doing? Going diving on the wreck?'

Digger shook her head. 'We've seen it a million times before. But it's really good for snorkelling.'

Yeah. And I'll bet it's full of bloody sharks too, thought Les. 'Sounds good to me, Digger,' he smiled.

Digger held her arms out. 'When you see something like this Les, you have to believe in God. Don't you?'

'You sure do Digger.'

'Are you glad I brought you up here?'

'Of course I am. In fact I'm going to get a photo of you with Virgin Island in the background.'

'Like this?' protested Digger. 'I look awful.'

'No you don't. You look good. Healthy good.'

'Oh piffle.'

Les had a quick look around and raised his camera. 'Okay Digger. Stand next to that tree on your left and say ...'

Les was about to say cheese when this horrendous CRRAACKKK thundered through the air. Les had never heard a noise like it. It was as if an artillery shell had exploded somewhere beneath the mountain, except it sounded a hundred times louder. An eerie silence followed for a second as Les and Digger stared at each other in astonishment. Before either of them had a chance to say a word, there was a strange rumble and Tomaree Point began moving. The boulders they were standing on started to vibrate spilling small rocks over the edges while the surrounding trees shook from side to side. Dead branches crashed to the ground as the air filled with dust and swirling leaves. Les grabbed Digger and put his arms around her. He was too shocked to be scared and wasn't sure if she was holding onto him or he was holding onto her. But as the ground rocked violently beneath their feet, he felt certain the whole mountain was going to tumble into the sea and take both of them with it. Les stared across at Yacaba Head. It looked like gigantic bowl of green jelly wobbling in the sun. Several huge boulders came loose and crashed down into the ocean followed by an avalanche of smaller ones flattening any trees in their path. Holding onto Digger amidst all the noise and confusion, Les found himself facing across the heads towards Virgin Island in the distance. The sand along the entire coastline was moving and all the water from the heads to the island had turned a shimmering silver. How long everything lasted Les wasn't sure. Probably only a few seconds. But it seemed like an eternity. Then as suddenly as it all started, it stopped. The sea turned blue once more, another boulder toppled into the water off Yacaba Head, the trees stopped shaking and everything settled down. Les loosened his grip on Digger and they stared at each other. Les knew the answer to his question before he asked her.

'What in the . . . was that?' he said.

Digger's eyes were like two green plates. 'I think it was an earth tremor.'

Norton's were like two brown ones. 'Earth tremor? How about earthquake? Bloody hell!'

Digger was still holding onto Les. 'I don't think I've ever been so scared in my life.'

'Me either. Did you see those boulders hitting the water?'

Digger nodded. 'Yes. It looked like the end of the world.'

Les was going to add something to that when he was cut short. It was the birds. They'd been silent all day and now it was time to open up. So they did. Every kookaburra, magpie, currawong, seagull, Willie

208

wagtail, anything with feathers and a beak started whistling, squawking or chirping as loud as it could.

Les stared up at the trees. 'Remember what I said about the birds before? Listen to that.'

'They knew all the time,' said Digger.

'Yeah. That's mother nature for you.' Les noticed his camera was still hanging round his neck, switched on and ready to go. 'I never got any photos,' he said.

'I think you'd best take them and we'll get going,' said Digger. 'I don't wish to be up here if there's an aftershock.'

'Yeah, you're right,' said Les. 'Neither do I.' Les snapped a couple of quick shots and put his camera back in its case. 'Come on. Let's make tracks.'

The metal stairs had moved in places and there were some dead trees lying by the side of the trail. In other places they could see where rocks had been shaken loose and had rolled down the side of the mountain. But apart from that the trail was much the same as when they walked up. The birds had settled down as they made it to the start of the pavers when Les heard the first howl echoing up the slopes from the building below. It was followed by another and another till it was a chorus of anguished wails.

'Hey Digger,' said Les. 'What's that building down there? It sounds like Dracula's castle.'

'It's a government psychiatric centre for young people with mental problems,' said Digger. 'The patients helped build it.'

'That earthquake sure stirred them up,' said Les, as another chorus of howls echoed up the mountain.

'Yes. The poor things,' said Digger. 'It must have been terrible for them.'

A piercing shriek split the air rising above all the others. 'Be nice if there's a full moon tonight,' said Les.

They got back to Zenith Beach and started along Shoal Bay Road. There didn't appear to be any damage to the buildings, but people were out of their homes, standing around talking and gesturing. Outside the hotel another mob had formed on the street. They were all holding onto their beers, so the earthquake hadn't affected their drinking. Les and Digger rounded the corner and went straight up the hill. When they got to her cousin's house and walked up the driveway the door was still locked.

'I wonder where Brendon is?' said Les.

'Still at work I imagine,' replied Digger. 'When I have a shower I might walk down and see if he's allright.'

'He's probably wondering the same about you.'

'Probably,' agreed Digger.

Les picked up his backpack from where he'd placed it just inside the garage and put his camera away. 'Well, that was certainly a day with a difference,' he said.

'Yes. It certainly was,' agreed Digger. 'I won't forget what we just saw in a hurry.'

'There's a couple of things I saw today I won't forget in a hurry,' said Les.

Digger smiled at him. 'And thanks so much for doing Brendon's yard Les. That was really decent of you.'

'That's okay,' said Les. 'That was just my way of thanking you for those two little cards you gave me.'

'I'm glad you liked those,' smiled Digger.

'They're not all I like about you Digger.' Les looked at Digger standing by the side steps in her old clothes. 'Digger. Remember last night, I was almost asleep and you called out, "Les, would you do something for me?"'

Digger turned her eyes to the ground. 'Yes. I remember.'

'And I did.'

'Yes.'

'Well Digger. Now it's my turn. Would you do something for me?'

Digger looked up at Les. 'It all depends.'

'There's an Italian restaurant just down the road. How about having dinner there with me tonight? And afterwards they've got a reggae band on at the hotel. We could have a look for a little while. We won't drink too much. And when you're ready I'll bring you straight home. We can still be up bright and early in the morning for church and to go diving. What do you say?' Digger seemed to be thinking. 'Come on, you can't leave me on my own tonight. I was there when you needed me.'

Digger gave Les a kind of wistful once up and down. 'Allright then.'

'Hey! Unreal,' said Les.

'But only because you're a monkey.'

'Yeah. But I'm a nice monkey.'

'Mmmhh. I don't know so much.'

'I do,' said Les. 'It's written on the wind.'

Digger shook her head and looked away. 'What time do you want to call round?'

'No later than seven-thirty. I'll be starving by then. And I'll walk round.'

'I'll see you at seven-thirty, Les.'

'See you then, Digger.' Les threw his backpack over his shoulder and walked home.

After he peeled off his dirty clothes and got in the shower, it seemed to take Les hours to scrub away the green gunk blasted into him by the whipper snipper. Besides being all over his arms and legs, it was in his ears, his hair, up his nose; it had even worked its way round his date. And there was no shortage of nicks and scratches that needed swabbing with iodine. But Les didn't mind. It had been fun. And he'd got a chance to square things with Digger. Plus, how often do you get a bird's eye view of an earthquake? After a shave and a liberal dousing with deodorant, Les wrapped a towel around himself, got a glass of OJ from the kitchen and put the TV on.

The earthquake made the lead story on the news. It was described as an earth tremor measuring 5.5 on the Richter scale. The epicentre was twenty kilometres north of Port Stephens and there was some minor damage around the Myall Lakes area. Newcastle never got hit.

'Five point five,' Les snorted at the ABC newsreader. 'You should have been standing where I was, old mate.'

212

Les sipped his OJ and watched the TV as they interviewed some punters in a caravan park then switched it off. Bad luck Digger was holding onto me for dear life. I would have liked to have got some action photos. Though in retrospect, I think it was the other way around. I was holding onto her for dear life. And the way the sea was shimmering. That was amazing. And I've got to go diving in that tomorrow. Well, the diving I can handle, I suppose. If it's not over my knees. But I don't know about church in the morning. If they give me a bible I'm likely to start reading it backwards.

By the time Les ironed his jeans, patched up his scratches and whatever it was time to get going. He tucked the same Jamaican T-shirt into jeans under his bomber jacket then gave himself a last detail in the bedroom mirror. When he'd finished, Les had another look at the two cards Digger had given him. So I'm a tranquil aesthete, eh. I still don't know what that means. But I'll consider it a rap. And Digger's an enigmatic divinity. I don't think you have to be an Aztec to work that out. Any sheila that can stop me swearing all day has got be an enigma. Les shoved some money down the front of his jeans, got his keys and walked round to Digger's via the beach front. As he went past the hotel he had to laugh. The sign out the front was now changed to Reggae Earthquake Party Tonight. Heh, heh! They sure don't muck around up here, do they. The Laser was gone, but the utility was in the driveway when Les got to Digger's. The front door was open as usual and Les rapped on the flyscreen. He heard Digger call out from inside.

'I'm in the kitchen. Come in.'

'Righto.'

Les opened the flyscreen and walked through the lounge. Digger was standing near the refrigerator with a hair brush in one hand and a blow dryer in the other. By some miracle of science, she'd squeezed herself into a pair of black leather jeans that hugged her gorgeous behind like a Ferrari. Les had a quick peek at the way the leather jeans slotted between her legs and felt like picking up the refrigerator and throwing it straight through the kitchen window. Tucked into her leather jeans was a crisp, white collarless shirt and on her dainty little feet were a pair of denim boots.

'How are you?' rasped Les.

'I'm fine,' replied Digger. 'Are you getting a cold?'

Les shook his head. 'No. A bit of dust went down my throat, that's all.'

'I won't be long,' said Digger, running the brush through her hair. 'There's still a few nits and knots in here. And they give me the willies.'

'Take your time,' said Les. 'Where's Brendon?'

'You missed him by ten minutes. He's gone round to a friend's house.'

'How is he? Was there much damage at the paint shop?'

'A little bit. He said to thank you for doing the yard. He couldn't believe it when he came home. He wants to give you a painting.'

'Fair dinkum?' Les nodded to a painting on the

214

wall of the kitchen. 'Do you mind if I check out some of his paintings?'

'Not at all,' said Digger. 'There's more in the lounge.'

Les walked into the loungeroom and had a look around. There was only the light from the lamp on the TV. But Les could see Brendon wasn't too bad an artist. It was all very abstract and out there somewhere, however Brendon had a good eye for colour. Les checked them out then had a look through Brendon's modest CD collection. He was mostly a Motown freak. Diana Ross and the Supremes, Otis Redding, Wilson Pickett, James Brown. Both Commitments CDs. Then something else caught Norton's eye.

Stacked in a case near the TV was a collection of war videos. *The Battle For Dien Bien Phu*, *VJ Day*, *Steel Tigers*, *Focke Wulf Fw 19*. *Desert Storm*. *Long Tan The True Story*. *The World At War*, and others. On a book shelf were books on the military and military uniforms. *Fighting Skills Of The SAS*, *The Western Front*, *Toku Tai*, *The Final Journey*. Les picked one out. *The Scars Of War* by Hugh McManners. He had a quick look, replaced it and walked back out to the kitchen.

'You never told me your cousin was a neo-Nazi.'

'He's not,' laughed Digger. 'Brendon used to be in the army.'

'The army? He never went to Vietnam, did he?'

Digger shook her head. 'He did two years in the infantry. That's all. But Brendon's always been a bit of a war buff. Ever since he was little.'

'Right.'

Digger switched off the hair dryer. 'Well, I'm ready.'

Les gave her a quick once up and down. You sure are, he thought. 'Are you hungry?' he asked.

'I am now.'

'Good. So am I.' Les looked at Digger for a second. 'You know, I just thought of something. I wouldn't mind taking some photos of this reggae night. Do you mind if we walk back to my place while I get my camera? Or you can wait for me in the restaurant if you like.'

'No, I'll walk back with you,' said Digger.

'It'll only take us a couple of minutes.'

Digger put the brush and hair dryer away and got her keys. She locked the house and they took the back street to Norton's flat. On the way they chit-chatted about the earthquake and how scary it was up on the mountain. Digger had also watched the news, and like Les, she too agreed that if the earthquake measured only 5.5, Richter needed a new scale.

They strolled past the bakery on the corner and were crossing the street when Les noticed a police car sitting out from one of the bays in the car park at the back of the flats. It was unmarked. But after working at the Kelly Club, Les could smell a police car unmarked or any other way. And if there was a police car outside his block of flats, it was odds on who they were there to see. He had a quick look in the front just to be sure and noticed a two-way radio and a spotlight. I think I'll forget about my camera for the time being, thought Les. What'll I tell Digger? Les was wracking his mind for an excuse as they got to the front door, when this dreadful commotion came howling down the stairs. Next thing, the two detectives who had driven him home on Wednesday night walked out the front with Emmett Hakin and Kastrine Kreen in handcuffs. Hakin looked like he was about to burst into tears. Kreen was screaming her feminist head off.

'This is totally fucking outrageous,' she howled. 'How fucking dare you. Do you know who I am?'

Digger's jaw dropped. Les put his arm round her for protection as Stewart caught Norton's eye.

'Stand back sir,' said Stewart. 'We've just arrested a major drug dealer.'

'A what?' Les turned to Digger then back to Stewart. 'A drug dealer. Here? In my block of flats? Good Lord!'

Hakin's face was a twisted mask of anguish and fear. He'd finally met the people he wrote about and didn't like it. He saw Les standing next to Digger.

'Les,' he cried out. 'That's my neighbour. Les. Tell them who I am. You know me.'

'Do you know this man, sir?' asked Stewart.

Les gave an indifferent shrug. 'I've spoken to him on the balcony a couple of times. That's about all. My goodness! I didn't know he was a drug baron.'

'You dopey, fucking moron, Emmett,' howled Kreen. 'You and your fucking big mouth. How could you be so stupid. You fucking imbecile.'

'What about the woman, sir?' asked Grant.

Kreen glared at Les. Les looked back at her and shook his head. 'Sorry. Never seen her before in my life.'

'Thankyou very much, sir,' said Stewart. 'You've been most helpful.'

Les stood back to let them past. 'Anytime officer. I'm only too willing to help the police. I know what a difficult job you have.'

Grant set his jaw. 'It's a constant vigil.'

Grant and Stewart led Kreen and Hakin out to the parking bay and pushed them into the back seat of the Holden. Kreen was still bellowing as the door shut on her.

'My goodness!' exclaimed Digger. 'What was that all about?'

'I'm not sure,' said Les. 'Looks like the police have arrested some dope dealer.'

'Do you know who that woman was?' said Digger.

'No. I saw her on the balcony a couple of times. But she never spoke to me.'

'That was Kastrine Kreen. The author. I'm sure it was.'

Les shrugged. 'I wouldn't know her from a bar of soap. I'll get my camera.'

Les jogged up the stairs laughing fit to bust. Not just because he saw the police cart Hakin and Kreen away, but with relief knowing it wasn't Deacon Les they were after. The way Stewart and Grant tipped him into the gag was a hoot too. Les had his camera and a more thoughtful look on his face when he came back down. He was just in time to see the police car's tail lights turning the corner into Shoal Bay Road. Whoever was driving gave the siren a quick blast for effect. Digger was standing outside the bike shop.

'Looks like we took out the quinella today, Digger,' said Les. 'First we walked into an earthquake. Then we walk in on a major drug bust.'

'Kastrine Kreen though,' said Digger. 'I can scarcely believe it.'

'Well. If she wants to get into drugs and hang around with drug dealers, that's what happens.'

Digger looked up at Les as they rounded the estate agency corner. 'Have you ever done drugs, Les?' she asked.

'Me? I've smoked marijuana, Digger. Nothing else though. What about you?'

Digger shook her head. 'No. Nothing.' She smiled at Norton. 'At least you're honest, Les.'

'Always Digger.'

'I don't like liars, Les.'

'Me neither,' said Les. 'They're the worst.'

'You wouldn't lie to me? Would you Les?'

Les stopped walking. 'Digger. Look at me. Is this the face of a liar?'

Digger smiled up at him. 'No. Of course it isn't.' She slipped her arm in Norton's and they continued on the short distance to the restaurant.

Luigi's had windows on the street and tables out front, either side of a rickety screen door, with plenty of room inside. Les opened the door and they found a wooden table with directors chairs in the middle. The restaurant had soft lighting, speakers playing light music, and two blackboard menus on the walls between posters and photos of old Italy. It was fully licensed and at one end of the counter next to a fat red candle was a huge array of spirits and liqueurs. Everything from Wild Turkey to Blue Sambuca to Ferro China Bisleri. They settled in and a smiling, dark-haired girl in a white shirt, black slacks and blue apron came over with the menus and wine list.

'Do you want a bottle of wine?' asked Les.

Digger shook her head. 'I wouldn't mind a bottle of Lemon Ruski.'

'Okay. Make that two Lemon Ruskis thanks,' Les told the waitress.

By the time the drinks arrived they were ready to order. Les went for Zuppa Del Pescatore and Pollo Cacciatore. Digger ordered Scallopini Ai Funghi. And garlic bread for two. Neither Les or Digger worried about glasses. Les held up his bottle of Lemon Ruski.

'Well. What will we drink to, Digger?' he asked her.

Digger thought for a moment then gave her head a little toss. 'I'll leave it to you.'

'Okay.' Les looked evenly at Digger for a moment. 'To honesty, hearthquakes, and hallelujah. We're still here, Digger.'

Digger clinked Norton's bottle. 'My sentiments exactly Les. Cheers.'

'Yep. Cheers.'

They had a mouthful of drink, looked around the restaurant for a moment then their eyes found each other.

'Digger.'

'Yes Les.'

'When I took you home the other night. And I dropped you off at the gate. Were you crying?'

Digger looked at the table for a moment. 'A little bit.'

'Well Digger. If I did anything to hurt you that night. I'm truly sorry. I certainly didn't mean it. And I certainly didn't mean to make you cry. In fact to be honest. I've been feeling pretty bad about it.'

'You didn't do anything to hurt me, Les. It was ... something else.'

'It wasn't me?'

'No. It definitely wasn't you.'

'Okay. Just as long as I know.' Les clinked her bottle again. 'I feel better now.'

Digger smiled up at Les and placed her hand on his. 'I think you're a decent man, Les. You know that.'

Les returned her smile. 'I'm not perfect Digger. But I do the best with what I've got.'

The garlic bread arrived along with Norton's fish soup. It was grey and brown and looked horrible, but quite rich and tasted good. They nibbled on the garlic bread then the mains arrived. Norton's chicken was allright, and Digger enjoyed her veal. Plus they got plenty of pan fried vegetables, wedges and a neat salad. They ordered another Ruski each and nattered about different things while they ate. Digger was paying off an old house in Merewether and had a student boarding with her. She didn't say anything about her family, whether she had any sisters or brothers. Apart from the church she didn't appear to have a lot of friends. She liked reading and coming up to Shoal Bay to be with Brendon. She was on two week's holiday at the moment. Les got an idea Digger was a bit of a loner and cousin Brendon was her best friend. Digger seemed more interested in Les. So he told her about his house in Bondi and the scene there. About going to Jamaica and finding the old Manse. He skirted around the mission thing at the Cross, knowing that if you wanted to be a good liar, you had to have a good memory. And he'd already forgotten half of what he'd told Digger when he was drunk. Digger said she and Brendon were going for another dive at Virgin Island on Tuesday. Les said he would have loved to have joined them but he had to leave for Sydney first thing Monday morning. Digger didn't feel like sweets and neither did Les. But he suggested a liqueur to finish things off and ordered two nips of Ferro China Bisleri because he liked the bottle. It turned out to be very strong, with a taste like coffee and vanilla essence. Digger wasn't too chuffed about it and neither was Les. He got the waitress to take a photo of them, then fixed the bill. Digger offered to weigh in. Les told her, 'next time'.

'Well that wasn't too bad a feed, Digger,' said Les.

'No. It was nice,' said Digger. 'Thankyou Les.'

'That's okay. Now what say we have a look at the band?'

'Allright.' Digger picked up her bag and they left.

It was only a short walk to the hotel and Les found himself discreetly yawning on the way. The two Ruskis, the liqueur and the meal had weighed him down. Plus he'd had a big one the night before and the day hadn't actually been spent sitting around. Les wasn't sorry he was having an early night.

The hotel had partitioned off the dining room and entry was out the back through the beer garden. Les led Digger through the chairs and tables then took a left at the door near the kitchen. It was five bucks entry and they were having a Cubano promotion. Les paid and they joined the throng.

Inside was packed and everybody was primed on Bacardi with lime and coke and well into party mode. Most of the men were wearing Hawaiian shirts, T-shirts and jeans with a smattering of Jamaican beanies. The girls wore mainly coloured jeans, dresses and flowery tank tops or T-shirts. There were big ones, little ones, fat ones and thin ones. Digger wasn't the only good sort in the place. But she was in the top three. The blokes all looked like blokes. Besides the locals, there was a visiting football team, a bunch of golfers and some people in town for a triathlon. Against the wall was a three-piece band; two men and a woman, wearing batik shirts and featuring congas and steel drums. At the moment they were zipping into Bob Marley's *Lion In*

Zion and the dance floor was jumping. There were black and red posters for Cubano all over the walls and several girls in Cubano T-shirts were behind the bar or walking amongst the punters. It was buy one, get one free. Which between that and everything else, was probably why everyone was roaring.

'This doesn't look too bad,' said Les.

'No. It's good,' replied Digger.

'Would you like a drink?'

'Okay. Why don't we try a Cubano?'

'Righto. Why not.'

Les went to the bar and came back with two bottles and a docket for the next two. They found a spot near the kitchen that was away from the crowd and sipped their drinks next to some tall bloke with red hair and crooked teeth, wearing a yellow Hawaiian shirt. He was with a dark-haired woman who was as fat as he was tall. She was wearing a black dress and had a backside like an old water tank that had popped a few rivets.

Digger looked at her bottle. 'These are allright. But I think I'd rather those Ruskis,' she said.

'Yeah, me too,' agreed Les. 'The lemon tastes better.'

The band was good and the dance floor had thinned out, so Les asked Digger if she wanted a dance. She said yes. The band was playing reggae, yet somehow they twisted. Digger was flat out twisting, but in her black leather jeans, she could have stood there plucking chickens and still looked great. However, that was the last song for the time being.

The band took a break and Les and Digger went back to where they were standing. Les took another mouthful of Cubano then got his camera out and clicked off a couple of photos of the crowd. The fat woman in the black dress had a little camera with her too, and asked Les if he'd mind taking a photo of her and her boyfriend in the yellow shirt. Les was only too happy to oblige then got the woman to take a photo of them.

Everything was going along cosy. Some music was playing through the band's speakers and despite everybody being drunk, they were a happy crowd and it didn't look like there were any mugs wanting to grab Digger on the backside. Les was relaxing and checking out the punters when a sour-faced little bloke with greasy black hair came weaving through the crowd from the men's toilets. He was wearing a drink splattered, blue polo shirt over a pair of jeans and looked belligerently good and drunk. He had his eye on the woman wearing the black dress talking to her boyfriend in the yellow Hawaiian shirt. Polo Shirt pushed his way through the crowd till he was right behind her, then stepped back and kicked her in the arse. She clutched at her ample behind and spun around screaming blue murder. Her boyfriend glared at the bloke in the polo shirt, before grabbing him by the throat, picking him up bodily and carrying him above the crowd to the side door, where he flung him out into the street. Yellow Shirt straightened himself up then came back to his girlfriend who was still rubbing her backside and started fussing over her. Les and Digger exchanged surprised glances.

'What was that all about?' asked Digger.

'I'm not sure,' said Les, shaking his head. 'But I don't think it's all over yet.'

Polo Shirt had picked himself up, dusted himself off and was now standing at the side door with murder in his eye. He couldn't miss Yellow Shirt. He came charging through the crowd, knocking drinks everywhere, then jumped up on Yellow Shirt's back and started punching him round the ears. Yellow Shirt punched back and tried to get hold of him. Yellow Shirt's girlfriend saw what was going on and started putting a few good ones into Polo Shirt herself. She landed a couple more lefts, when another fat woman in a black dress that could have passed for the first one's sister, came waddling through the crowd from somewhere near the bar.

'Hey bitch!' she yelled. 'That's my fuckin husband you're hitting.' Then the second woman started laying into the first woman and her boyfriend in the yellow Hawaiian shirt as well.

Les surmised Polo Shirt must have come out of the toilet drunk and thought the first woman was his wife pitching up to some bloke. So he's given her a boot up the date and got thrown out for his trouble. Now he wanted to carry on with it. Les watched as they all punched and kicked into each other, till the tall bloke tottered over taking Polo Shirt and the rest of them with him into the Cubano-soaked crowd. That was all it took. The footballers were the first to jump in. Then the golfers, followed closely by the triathletes. The locals had to protect their turf, so they jumped in as well. And what should have been a good rockin', easy skankin' reggae dance party quickly turned into a punching, kicking, drink spilling, shirt ripping, chairs over the head, all in brawl, like something out of a Clint Eastwood movie.

Les took Digger by the arm and got in front of her as the brawl intensified. The management and the bouncers all ran in. But by the time they figured out where to start they were fighting just to stay on their feet. A full can of beer came sailing across the room towards Les. It was only moving slowly, so Les was able to palm heel it away. Unfortunately, he palm heeled it that hard, it went sailing back across the room, hit some woman in a coloured T-shirt behind the ear and knocked her flat.

Les gave Digger an urgent look. 'I don't think this is for us, mate,' he said.

'No. Me either,' she replied. 'Let's get out of here.'

Digger picked up her bag and with Les's arm around her they headed for the door. Les stopped to take a quick photo of the fight, but they were swept through the beer garden and out into the street where the brawling continued around the front of the hotel. Les took Digger's hand and they started walking down the street.

'Well. So much for Saturday night, Digger,' said Les, as the fighting raged behind them.

'Yes. What a shame,' replied Digger.

'I'd better get my car and drive you home too. Just to be on the safe side.'

'It's a bit early to go straight home,' said Digger. 'Why don't we go back to your place for a while. Listen to some music and have a talk.'

'Okay. If that's what you feel like.' Hand in hand they strolled past the restaurant and round the real estate agency corner.

Les opened the front door, turned on the lights and they stepped into the lounge. The same laid-back tape was still in the ghetto blaster, so Les switched it on. Digger was leaning up against the bar, and Les was round the other side in the kitchen as Boxing Gandhis cruised into *Sun Don't Shine On Everyone*.

'What can I say, Digger?' said Les. 'As well as taking out the quinella we ended up with the trifecta — earthquake, drug bust, then an all-in brawl. And if you want to throw in that bloke with the Fairlane, we got the quadrella.'

'Yes. It's certainly been a funny old day allright,' agreed Digger.

'Anyway. What can I get you? Tea, coffee. Would you like an Ovaltine?'

'What have you got to drink?'

'Drink? Rum and OJ. That's about it.'

'Allright. I'd like one of those please.'

'Okay. But only one,' said Les, pointing a finger. 'Don't forget we're going diving tomorrow. Not to mention church in the morning.'

'One will be fine thankyou,' said Digger. 'Heavens. You'd think I was an alcoholic.'

'Well, you did give it a good nudge last night, Digger.'

'Oh? And what about you Deacon Les. And your friend Jack Daniels?'

'Yeah. But I'm a big ugly bloke. I'm allowed to drink like that. You're just a sweet little girl. You have to go easy.'

'Oh piffle.'

'Digger. Watch your language, please. There could be ladies around.'

'Phooey!'

Les made two white rums and OJ with plenty of ice and not too strong. He handed one to Digger then came round into the lounge, smiled at her and clinked their glasses.

'Well, thanks for coming out with me tonight, Digger. I just felt like a bit of company. Especially yours.'

'Thankyou for taking me out, Les,' replied Digger. 'And I enjoyed your company too.'

'Bad luck the reggae night turned into a bun fight. We were just starting to show those squares how to twist.'

'Yes we were too,' smiled Digger. 'But what about that horrible man coming up and kicking that poor woman in the behind. Goodness that must have hurt.'

'Reckon. One thing for sure. He couldn't miss it.'

'No. That's true.'

'Don't you ever finish up with a backside like that, Digger,' said Les. 'I'd probably still talk to you. But you wouldn't get me on the dance floor.'

Digger half-turned around, looked at her tight behind under the leather jeans and gave it a pat. 'I think I'm safe for a little while yet.'

Les raised his glass to Digger's heartbreaking behind. 'I'd say so.'

Digger moved over to the ghetto blaster. 'This plays CDs doesn't it, Les?'

'It sure does. But I only brought tapes with me.'

Digger turned to Les. 'Would you do me a favour?'

Les smiled at her. 'I'll think about it. I could even make that an I suppose so. I suppose.'

'I've got a CD in my bag. Would you play a track off it for me.'

'Sure.'

'And then would you dance with me to it out on the balcony?'

'Dance with you? Okay. What's the CD?' Digger got a CD from her bag and handed it to Les. 'Rodriguez? *Cold Fact*,' said Les. 'I don't think I've heard this.'

'It was big in the seventies,' said Digger. 'Play track eight.'

'Righto. In fact I'll rearrange the acoustics a little better.'

Les opened the door to the sundeck then moved the coffee table over in front of it so the ghetto blaster was facing away from the loungeroom. They took their drinks outside then Les popped the stereo open and put the CD in.

'Track eight,' said Les. '*I Wonder.*'

'That's the one,' nodded Digger.

Les tapped the forward button to number eight and pressed pause. He took a sip of rum and OJ, then put his glass down and turned to Digger. 'You ready?'

'Yes.' Digger had a sip and put her glass down too.

Les released the pause button then put his arms round Digger's waist and held her gently to him. Digger put both arms around Les and rested her head against his chest as the music started. It was a nice laid-back song with a good beat and a funky little bass riff that made it very easy to dance to.

The lyrics were a little hard to pick up yet one line seemed to stand out from the others. Something about how often have you had sex and if you knew who'd be the next? That's curious, smiled Les, as they danced into the shadows.

They drifted effortlessly around the sundeck, amongst the chairs and tables and along the balcony. Above them, the moon looked like a big, pearly face, smiling out of a cloudless sky spattered with diamonds, as it turned the inky smoothness of the ocean into a platinum mirror. High up in a tree by the sand, a night bird called to its mate. Les looked down at Digger as her beautiful, dark hair moved in the moonglow while they danced. The song didn't go for very long and soon started to fade out.

'Hey. What a good track,' said Les.

Digger smiled up at him. 'Would you play it for me again, Les?'

'Sure. I'd love to.' Les pushed the repeat button and they danced around the balcony again.

The song finished for the second time, but they both kept drifting around comfortable in each other's arms. Les gently worked his fingers into Digger's scalp and felt her face burrow into his chest.

'Digger. This is lovely out here with you. I'm almost lost for words.'

Digger looked up at Norton and smiled softly. 'Les, I've been promising myself. One day. At a special time. In a special place, I'd dance to that song with someone. Someone special.'

'Take it easy, Digger,' said Les. 'You'll give me a swelled head.'

Digger ignored him. 'I can't explain this to you, Les. But the last few days have been awful for me. And before that too. Now I feel my whole life's taken a new direction. And a lot of it's because I met you.'

'Digger. You don't know how good that makes me feel,' said Les. 'But honestly, I'm nothing special. And I'll be gone on Monday.'

Digger gave her head a toss. 'I don't care Les. You've done something for me you'll never know.'

'Digger. Come on. You're making me feel ...'

Digger put her hand behind Les's neck, then reached up and kissed him. Then kissed him again. Les felt a strange electricity surge through every nerve in his body. He was still tingling when Digger eased herself away and looked into his eyes.

'Now take me inside, Les. I want to finish what we started on Friday night.'

Les wasn't quite sure if he heard right. 'Digger, what are you saying? Do you know what you're doing?'

Digger unzipped the front of her leather jeans and placed Norton's hand between her legs. 'Does this tell you if I know what I'm doing?'

Digger was wearing a pair of shiny, tight, maroon knickers with a pale-blue trim. What Les felt underneath made his hair stand on end and peppered his brow in the cool night air with beads of sweat.

'Digger, I don't quite know what to say.'

Digger reached up and kissed Les again, discreetly slipping in the tip of her tongue. 'Don't say anything. Just take me inside.'

Les looked at Digger snuggled in his arms for one fleeting moment. 'Is it allright, if I say okay?'

They left the CD to play itself out and went straight into the bedroom. Digger kicked off her boots and undid her shirt while Les got out of his jacket and jeans. By the time Digger was down to her knickers, Les was standing in his T-shirt with a rock hard boner poking out underneath. Digger pushed her hair to one side then casually bent over and put it in her mouth. Les felt like he'd just been pole-axed as she started sucking and licking like there was no tomorrow. Not only did Digger give Les the most fantastic head job he'd ever had. She relished in it. Moaning and groaning with sheer enjoyment. Les couldn't believe anything could feel or sound so good. Finally she stopped, slid her knickers off and flung herself back on the bed. Les took his T-shirt off, climbed up on the bed then put his face between Digger's legs, gripped the cheeks of her backside and went for it. Digger spread her legs and brought her knees up. She grabbed Norton's head and held his face into her as she squealed and thrashed around on the pillow. Les nuzzled Digger's ted, pushed his tongue in as far as he could, licked it and sucked it till he thought her head was going to cave in. When he finally came up, Digger was heaving and panting like she was about to go into cardiac arrest. Les pushed his mouth onto Digger's and felt her hot, wet tongue slip straight into his. Norton's heart skipped several beats. Well, he told himself. I don't care if she cries. Hates me in the morning. Or I hate myself, and have to live a life of remorse wearing sack cloth and ashes because of what I'm about to do. And I don't give a stuff if the heavens open and the angels take me away in a chorus of trumpets and cast me into the burning pits of hell for all eternity for this. But tonight. Deacon Les is going for it. Les eased Digger's knees up a little more and started to slip Mr Wobbly in.

It took a bit of pushing. But when Les finally did, Digger let out a howl you could have heard up on Tomaree Head. This time however, she didn't lie there like she was being violated. Digger got right into it. She grabbed Les, kissed him, scratched at his back, bucked up and down and kicked her legs in the air. And when she didn't either have her tongue in his mouth or his ear, screamed her head off. Norton went into hyperspace and rode Digger like there was no tomorrow; with a few extra thrusts now and again for good measure. Les often thought some of his sex was the best he'd ever had. But this was. Digger, the little Miss Goody Two Shoes, churchgoer, was the ultimate pleasure machine. Les pumped away as she screamed with delight. Mr Wobbly ate on Digger's screams like they were chocolate truffles. Eventually Les could take no more. He drove deeper and faster then emptied out with one great, gasping shudder, jamming his face into the pillow so he wouldn't bite a piece out of his tongue. Digger gave a last lingering howl and Norton's scrambled brain reflected back to something it said on Digger's Aztec card. The Wind rises up in the victory cry of a benevolent squall as your passions are united with a like-minded partner.

A few minutes later, Les was lying on the bed still getting his breath back. His heartbeat had almost returned to normal and Digger was snuggled up next to him with her head on his chest. Les opened his eyes and saw her looking up at him.

'Digger, I have to ask you this,' he said. 'What got into you?'

Digger gave Les a sly smile. 'I think you did. Didn't you?'

'That's not quite what I meant Digger. It wasn't that liqueur was it? If it was I'll go out and get a forty-four gallon drum.'

'No, it wasn't the liqueur.'

'Well it had to be something.'

Digger gave a little chuckle, then reached up and kissed Les. 'I told you, Les. It was you. Now. More please.'

'What?'

'More please. I want some more.'

'Digger. Who do you think you are? Oliver Twist.'

'No.'

'You're going to have to give me a few minutes.'

Digger chuckled again. 'Okay. Let's have a sixty-niner while we're waiting.'

Les brought his head off the bed. 'A sixty-niner?'

'Yes.'

'Why not make it a seventy-one, while we're at it.'

'What's a seventy-one?'

'A sixty-niner with two fingers jammed in your date.'

'Okay.'

'Forget about it Digger. You want the top or the bottom?'

Digger took the bottom. They both started sucking away and it wasn't long before Mr Wobbly was right back in the swing of things. Digger got into it again moaning and squealing with delight. Les buried his face in her ted and it wasn't long before the big Queenslander was doing plenty of moaning and groaning himself. Digger grabbed his dick and shoved all she could in her mouth as she felt Les starting to let go and swallowed every drop. Les copped all Digger's in the face and came up for air with his eyes spinning.

Les was lying on the bed with a towel over him. Digger went to the bathroom then came back with two glasses of water. Les gulped half his down, Digger drank some of hers then lay up on his chest.

'Have you had a good night?' she asked.

'Let's just say ... it's been intense Digger. No. It's certainly been good allright Digger,' admitted Les. 'I can't ever remember anything like it.'

'That's good.' Digger had another drink of water and looked at her watch. 'I'd better get going soon.'

'Yeah. Fair enough,' said Les.

'But we've still got time for another.'

'Oh I'm sure we have,' said Les. 'But I think I'm a bit like the old saying at the moment Digger — the mind is willing. But the flesh is weak.'

Digger smiled and took hold of Les's dick. 'I'll give you another suck. And we'll see what happens.'

Digger's tongue wove its magic once more and soon Les had a horn that hard, you could bounce hand spears off it. Les rolled Digger over and gave it to her again. It took a while to finish. When it did, it sounded as if Digger had just had her leg amputated without any anaesthetic, while Les was flopped on the bed wheezing and panting like he'd just won a watermelon eating contest. They lay on the bed together till eventually Digger tapped Les on the chest.

'I think I'd better get going,' she said.

Les blinked his eyes open. 'Okay. We'll get the car. Because I don't think I could walk to your place and back.'

Digger snuggled up to Les. 'Don't worry,' she smiled. 'You were fantastic.'

Les looked at her. 'You weren't bad yourself, you know.'

Digger's cheeks coloured for a second or two. 'Come on. Let's get dressed.'

They put their clothes on and went into the loungeroom. Les gave Digger her CD before he forgot then poured two glasses of orange juice and they sat down on the lounge. For all that had happened, Digger hardly had a hair out of place and you'd think she'd come from a walk in the park, while Les looked as if he'd just carried a piano up the stairs. Digger put her hand on Les's leg and looked directly at him.

'Les. You know how earlier. You proposed a toast to among other things. Honesty?'

'Yes. I remember that,' said Les.

'Well. There is something I haven't told you about me. And I think I should.'

'If you want to, Digger. Okay.' Actually Les was rather curious about Digger's sudden turn around from the tearful, little Miss Goody Two Shoes into Madam Lash overnight. This had to be it.

Digger put her orange juice down. 'You've never asked me what my real name is, have you Les? Or why they call me Digger?'

Les shrugged. 'I didn't think it was any of my business. Besides, Digger's fine by me.'

'Well my real name is Anne.'

'Anne?' said Les. 'That's a nice enough name.'

'I used to get Anzac for short at school. Then everybody started calling me Digger.'

'What was Anzac short for?'

'Anne Zaccariah.'

Les gave Digger a double blink. 'Did you say Zaccariah?'

'Yes,' replied Digger. 'That's my full name. Anne Zaccariah.'

'Zaccariah?' Norton's jaw dropped. 'Not the same Zaccariah ...?'

'That's right,' said Digger. 'The man who got taken by the sharks at Jimmy's Beach. That was my father. Forbes Zaccariah.'

Les stared at Digger in horror. 'You're not fair dinkum are you?'

Digger nodded. 'You would have read about it in the papers? Or seen it on TV?'

'Yeah. I did.' Norton felt like he'd just been hit in the face with a shovel.

'Well that was my dad. And the policeman.' Digger looked intently at Norton. 'Are you allright, Les? You've gone quite pale.'

'I just can't believe it,' mumbled Les. 'This is ... I mean. That's awful.'

Digger nodded. 'It's true. I had to go to the morgue and identify the body. There wasn't much left. But I knew it was dad by the tattoo on his arm.'

'Oh no.' Norton's stomach started to heave.

'Remember when I first met you?' said Digger. 'You asked me what I was doing here. And I said I came to see my father. That's what I meant.'

Les opened his mouth, but nothing came out.

'I suppose I sounded flippant. When you asked me how he was,' continued Digger. 'And I said he was fine. But I wasn't myself at the time.' Digger stared at Les again. 'Are you sure you're allright, Les?'

Les put his orange juice down. 'I think something might have been off in that fish soup, Digger.'

Les got up and hurried to the bathroom. He just managed to shut the door behind him, before he started throwing up. After a few minutes he splashed some water on his face then returned to the loungeroom and sat back down next to Digger. Digger stared at him with a worried look on her face.

'Oh Les. You poor thing,' she said. 'I didn't mean to upset you.'

'No. That's allright,' said Les. He picked up his orange juice and took a mouthful. 'It's just finding out on top of all that rich food. It kind of got to me.'

'Oh Les.' Digger stroked Norton's face. 'You're so sensitive. You lovely man.'

'Yeah,' muttered Les.

'But it's all over now. And I know daddy went quickly.'

'Oh shit!' Les dropped his orange juice and ran back into the bathroom. After a while he came out wiping his face again. 'Sorry Digger. I don't mean to be such a wooz.'

'That's allright,' said Digger. She smiled at Les. 'Oh you poor sweet thing. You're so caring.'

Les gave Digger the bleakest look. 'Yeah.'

Digger stroked Les's face again. 'I'm sorry if I upset you,' she said. 'But I felt I had to tell you.'

'That's okay,' swallowed Les.

'We won't talk about it anymore.'

240

'Suit yourself Digger . . . Anne.'

Les went quiet on the lounge and for a moment Digger seemed distracted.

'There was something a bit odd about the way dad died though,' she said.

'Odd?' Les found himself staring at her in horror again.

'Yes. Fishy.' Digger put her hand to her face. 'Ooh! I didn't mean to say that.'

'Come on Digger. I think I'd better get you home.'

'Allright.'

Les found his keys and walked Digger down to the car park. During the short drive to her cousin's, Digger had a sweet smile of contentment on her face while she rested her hand on Norton's thigh. Les was in a state of absolute shock. He couldn't look Digger in the eye and he was almost sick again. He pulled up out the front and switched off the motor.

'My, my. Look at that front yard,' said Digger. 'I wonder who lives here?'

'Yeah,' croaked Les. 'I wonder?'

Digger smiled at Les. 'That reminds of a song.'

Les felt like he was trying to swallow a ping-pong ball. 'Yeah. Don't it.'

Digger placed her hand on Norton's cheek. 'Les. Are you sure you're allright? You look awful.'

'I'll be okay. I just got a bit of a pain in the stomach. That's all.'

'That's no good,' said Digger.

'Digger. Do you mind if I don't come to church with you in the morning?' said Les. 'I might have a sleep in.'

'No. That's fine. I understand,' said Digger. 'But still come to Virgin Island with us. I want you to.'

'Oh yeah. I'll be allright by then. What time do you want me to call round?'

'I'll come and get you at ten. I'll pull up alongside the park on the corner.'

'Righto. I'll be ready.'

Digger peered into Norton's eyes. 'Oh Les ... You look so sad. I hope you're not going to cry over what I told you about my father.'

'No. I'll be okay,' said Les. 'Something like that though. You wouldn't be human if it didn't bowl you a bit.'

'You're sweet, Les. You really are.'

Les gave Digger a sickly smile. 'Thanks.'

She reached over and kissed him softly on the lips. 'You don't have to walk me to the door. Go straight home and have a glass of warm water.'

'Okay,' nodded Les. 'I'll do that.'

Digger smiled into Norton's eyes. 'Les.'

'Yes Digger.'

'I love you.'

Les stared into Digger's beautiful, shining green eyes. The look emanating from them was purely angelic and suddenly Les found himself coming apart at the seams. It was all he could do to stop himself bursting into tears. 'Digger. There's a couple of things I think I have to tell you,' he said.

'Tell me tomorrow.' She kissed Les again. 'I'll see you in the morning.'

Digger got out of the car and closed the door behind her. The last Norton saw was her giving him a dainty wave as she let herself into the house. He started the car and drove back to the garage.

The lights were still on when Les stepped inside the flat. He tossed his keys on the table then walked out onto the sundeck and stared across the water trying to think. An hour ago he was dancing on air. Now he was totally deflated. If he felt like a rat the night before, tonight he didn't know what he felt like. I don't believe this, Les told himself. I don't fuckin believe it. I meet a girl. A decent, honest girl, who tells me she loves me. And I find out I just murdered her father. The poor little bastard. Christ! What she must have gone through. I don't know about tonight. But no wonder she got so drunk and everything on Friday night. She was still in a state of shock. I identified daddy by the tattoo on his arm. Oh shit! Les kept staring across the bay in disbelief. God! How can I face her again? And what did she say? There was something odd about daddy's death. Shit! And what did I say to her? Digger. There's a couple of things I have to tell you. Christ! Why did I have to say that? If she ever found out it'd kill her. She'd probably kill me. Les shook his head in dismay. No. I got to get out of here first thing Monday. Goodbye Digger. Sorry. Sorry for both of us. Les stared at the ocean for a bit longer then went inside.

He got out of his clothes, then climbed into bed and stared up at the darkness. Les couldn't ever remember feeling so rotten in his life. Poor bloody Digger. What have I done? Les lay on the bed staring at the ceiling in sad disbelief as a tear trickled down his cheek. Eventually sheer exhaustion overcame the big, red-headed Queenslander and his worries temporarily disappeared into the night.

Around nine the next morning, Les was sitting on the sun deck in a pair of shorts and a green Sturt University T-shirt staring out across Port Stephens through his sunglasses. It was a bit cloudier than the day before, but still pleasant with a light nor'wester blowing. He'd been up earlier and cooked a feed of scrambled eggs and sausages, now he was sipping on a second cup of coffee having a think while he took in the surroundings. Boats were cutting across the water and people and cars were moving around below. There were even signs of life next door. Kreen had stormed out onto the balcony to retrieve a couple of books sitting on a table and Hakin picked up a T-shirt he'd left out to dry. Kreen gave Les a filthy look and got a ribald smile for her trouble. Hakin sheepishly put his head down and looked the other way. Les ignored him, and figured from the way they were both bustling around they were getting ready to make a hasty departure before AUTHOR ON DRUG CHARGES appeared in the papers. As for the Sunday papers, Les didn't bother; he'd have a look when he got back. At the moment there were other things on his mind.

Finding out he'd murdered Digger's father had knocked Les for a loop. It was bad enough reading about Forbes Zaccariah leaving a family in the first place. Now having it all land fair and square in his lap made things worse again. Especially Digger being such a sweetheart and his feelings towards her. Having to say goodbye to her wasn't going to be easy either. Also unnerving was Digger's stoic attitude and the way she kept feeling sorry for him. Les was used to a bit of harmless chicanery here and there. But absolute deception like this was horrible. Above all though, how was he going to look her in the eye today and what was he going to say to her if she started asking him questions? Another one of those angelic looks and anything could happen. Les sipped some more coffee and stared into his cup. There was only one thing he could do. Put on a brave face and try to be his usual, easygoing self. It wouldn't be easy. But what was it Warren always said about advertising? Sincerity is the most important thing. And if you can fake that, you got it made. Tomorrow he'd be back in Sydney and it would all be behind him; along with the memory of Digger and those beautiful green eyes.

On another note, Les was still curious how Digger could turn from little Miss Goody Two Shoes, church on Sunday, into such a mad raving case overnight. Shortening up that big goose in the Fairlane Les could come to terms with. Digger was a ballsy little girl for her size. She went diving, she did a job that a lot of people couldn't do and she didn't get round in a four cylinder car with Dalmatian seat covers. But the sex thing. That had Les shaking his head. Les also had a funny feeling Digger was on to him somehow. The times there she referred to him as Deacon Les. And. He'd know all about utilities working at the mission. It could be his imagination, but there just seemed to be something in the tone of her voice. Les looked at his watch and finished his coffee. Whatever the outcome, it was time to make a move.

Les washed up then changed into his blue tracksuit and folded his bomber jacket into his backpack just in case it got a bit cool out on the high seas. He put the bag with all his diving gear in it near the door, still unopened since he got back from Jimmy's Beach with Eddie. With any luck he might still be able to get out of going in the water. Maybe he could feign sinus trouble or something? He'd feigned everything else. Les tossed his camera, the OJ and whatever into his backpack then picked up his keys and had a last look around the flat. He was about to draw the blinds when he heard the friendly toot of a car horn. He walked out on the balcony and saw Digger's utility parked across the road. Les waved back. Well, here goes nothing, he thought. Les picked up his bags, locked the flat and walked down to the street.

'Good morning Les,' said Digger happily, as Les tossed his bags in the back of the utility. 'How are you?'

'I'm good thanks, Digger,' he replied. 'How's yourself?'

'Great. Just great.'

'That's good.'

Les climbed in the front and adjusted his seatbelt. Digger was wearing a grey tracksuit, trainers and a plain white T-shirt. Her hair was shiny, her green eyes were sparkling and she looked absolutely radiant. Les smiled at her and Digger gave him a quick kiss on the cheek for his trouble.

'Did you sleep allright?' she asked as they drove off.

'Yeah, not bad,' replied Les. 'That glass of warm water made the difference.'

'I knew it would.'

Les still had trouble looking Digger in the eye. 'So how was church this morning?' he asked.

'Oh. It was fabulous,' beamed Digger. 'If only you could have been there. I sang. I prayed. It was the best morning ever. It was like Jesus had lifted this terrible load from my shoulders.'

'That's fantastic. I'm happy for you, Digger,' said Les.

'Thankyou Les.' They approached the Memorial Club. 'Are you looking forward to going snorkelling with us today?'

'Yes,' replied Les, a little wooden. 'It should be good.'

'It will be. I guarantee you.'

They drove past the Memorial Club and the cannon on the corner. Les wanted to say something, but couldn't quite find the words. Digger seemed to sense his awkwardness.

'Les,' she said, carefully. 'If I upset you last night. Telling you about my father. I'm sorry. I didn't mean to.'

'No. That's allright,' said Les. 'I'm glad you did.'

'But you looked so sad and shocked. It hurt me to see you like that.'

'Forget about it Digger,' he smiled. 'I can be a bit of a wooz at times.'

'I probably shouldn't have mentioned anything,' said Digger. 'But I just thought you should know, that's all. I like to be honest about things.'

'I know you do,' agreed Les.

'You're the same too. Aren't you, Les?'

'Of course. I told you that Digger.'

'That's good.' Digger looked at Les. 'Everything should always be out in the open. Especially with friends.'

'My sentiments exactly.' Les swallowed and found a little sweat had formed in the palms of his hands.

They went down a hill and alongside a tree-covered cliff facing the water, then Digger turned right into a parking area next to a building with a sign that said Nelson Bay Charter Boat Terminal And Kiosk. There was a park then a rockwall led past some concrete jettys before the breakwater at the entrance to Nelson Bay Marina. Several cruise boats were moored on a jetty out from the rockwall and a number of people were fishing off the breakwater. A small bridge closer to the kiosk led out to another concrete jetty with girders built above it and a sign saying Official Weigh Station. The rest of the boats were tied up further down at the main part of the marina.

'Well. Here we are,' said Digger.

'Here we are,' repeated Les.

They got out and locked the car. Les picked up his bags and followed Digger across the park to the bridge leading out to the jetty with the girders. Moored alongside was a drab, green, twelve-metre fibreglass and wood fishing boat, with a cabin towards the front and an open deck at the back. A chrome rail ran round the bow with more chrome railing round the deck. There were a few touches of white amongst the green and an orange lifebuoy was tied to a railing above the cabin next to an aerial. Lashed across the deck was a white, two-metre dinghy and printed in bold, black lettering along the bow was the name *Gainsborough*.

'What do you think?' smiled Digger.

Les looked at the boat then looked at Digger, Righto, he told himself. What's happened, has happened. Time to get my shit together or I'm going to bring myself undone. 'What do I think?' said Les. 'All I can say is, the wind and the monkey went to sea in a beautiful pea green boat.'

'That's us,' said Digger. 'Just like the owl and the pussycat. I remember that old poem from school.' Digger slipped her arm in Norton's. 'Gee you're a romantic, Les.'

'I know,' replied Les. 'The sea air always brings it out in me.'

They crossed the bridge and stepped onto the boat just as Brendon came out of the cabin wearing a pair of faded Levi's, trainers, a blue sweatshirt and an old green cricket cap. He had a bottle of mineral water in one hand and was all smiles.

'Permission to come aboard, captain,' said Les, snapping off a salute.

'Permission granted,' said Brendon, returning Norton's salute. 'How are you, Les?'

'Good thanks, Brendon. How's yourself?'

'T'riffic. Hey thanks for doing the lawns yesterday. I want to see you about that later.'

'That's okay. I was on my way to the pub, but your cousin nagged me into it.'

Digger ignored them both and got straight to the point. 'Is everything together Brendon? The tanks are filled, the radio's working properly, the food's in the fridge?'

'Yes Digger,' replied Brendon. 'Everything's AOK. But you'll be navigator and first mate. So why worry?'

'You just get us out there and back,' said Digger. 'I'll start double checking everything.'

'Where'll I put my stuff?' asked Les.

'Under the bow,' said Brendon. 'Come on I'll show you.'

Les followed Brendon inside the cabin while Digger started poking around all their scuba gear stacked in plastic crates on the deck. Brendon stopped to tie a shoelace, the engine was running so Les had a quick look around.

The cabin was fairly roomy with windows round the sides and enough headroom for a tall person; the colour scheme was blue floor, brown fibreglass walls and wooden panels. Three square windows faced the bow; the ship's wheel, console, compass and radio were on the right and back from the console was a map table with drawers underneath. There was a step down to a small galley on the left and through a doorway under the bow was a small cabin with a foam rubber bench running round it. There was more foam rubber seating on the left side of the cabin with a storage compartment underneath secured by a solid Yale lock. Built into the ceiling were handrails for rough weather and on one wall was a barometer and what looked like an Alice In Wonderland clock. It kept perfect time twice a day.

'In there?' said Les, nodding to the forward cabin when Brendon brought his head up.

'Yeah.'

'Okay.' Les left his backpack on the seat opposite the map table and stowed his bag up front amongst some other gear. He came back up as Brendon started easing the boat away from the jetty.

'You may as well make yourself comfortable while I sort all this out,' said Brendon.

'Righto.'

Les sat down next to his backpack while Brendon spun the wheel, worked the controls and gave the port control their ETA over the ship's radio. Les thought it might be best to leave

Brendon alone for the time being so he kept quiet, sat back and watched proceedings. Out on deck, Digger was still busy doing whatever it was she was doing with the scuba gear. They left the breakwater, Brendon gave the engine a few more revs and then they started chugging through Port Stephens towards the heads. Weather reports were crackling over the radio, but the old diesel motor made it fairly noisy in the cabin and Les couldn't make out one word that was coming through. However, the *Gainsborough* had a gentle, rocking motion and seemed to slice through the water easily. It wasn't long and they were past the houses and shops along Shoal Bay approaching the heads. The swells picked up a little and Les pushed himself back into the seat. Brendon got off the radio and settled behind the wheel. There was no seat, but by Brendon's casual stance and the way his body angled you would have thought there was one. Eventually he turned to Les as they started through the heads.

'You know much about Port Stephens, Les?' he asked.

'Bugger all Brendon,' replied Les. 'Except the earthquakes are good for this time of the year.'

'Yeah. What about that.' Brendon gave Les an offbeat smile. 'Do you want a quick tourist guide?'

'Sure. Why not?'

'Okay.' Brendon pointed to Tomaree Head. 'You see those old gun turrets sticking out on those rocks up there?'

'Yeah.'

Brendon told Les about all the gun turrets on Tomaree Head and how the government at one stage during the Second World War was convinced the Japanese were going to invade Port Stephens. There was considerable Japanese activity around the area during the war years, light planes had flown over Newcastle; there was even a story going round that they'd found Japanese helmets in the sandhills behind Anna Bay. United States naval and infantrymen used to train at Shoal Bay for their landings in the Pacific Islands and despite the area's natural beauty, there were reefs and bomboras all over the place and wrecks everywhere.

'Digger tells me there's a wreck where we're going,' said Les.

'That's right,' said Brendon. 'The *Milton*. It was an old teak and coal steamer. It went down during a storm one night in 1942. It hit this side of the island facing exactly due north. You can line up your compass with it.'

'What happened to the crew?' asked Les.

'They never found the bodies. All eight men. Those that didn't drown, the sharks got.'

'Shit!'

Brendon looked evenly at Les. 'Does it bother you, knowing Digger's father got taken by sharks, Les?'

Les gave Brendon a subconscious double blink. 'Well, I have to admit, it did come as a shock when she told me. That's awful.'

253

'Yeah.' Brendon started bringing the boat left. 'Terrible. Ain't it.'

Les almost lapsed into silence. But he managed to keep going. 'Hey Brendon. Who's Uncle Tom? I heard some bloke mention him on the news.'

'Uncle Tom.' Brendon gave Les a knowing smile. 'He's a local legend. He's a one-eyed white pointer that hangs around here. Especially when the whales are migrating.'

'Have you ever seen him?'

Brendon shook his head. 'No. But I've seen photos. He's eight metres long if he's an inch.'

'Bloody hell!'

'Everybody reckons they've hooked Uncle Tom,' said Brendon. 'But nobody's landed him.'

'Does he hang around Virgin Island?'

'No. There's too many tiger sharks. They keep chasing him away.'

'Ohh, give me a break will you.'

As Tomaree Head started fading behind them, Brendon pointed to a huge slice in the cliff going from the ocean, up through the trees almost to the top of the cliff. 'You see that?' he said.

'Yeah,' nodded Les.

'They call that Mother Murphy's.'

'Mother Murphy's?' Les looked at the darkened chasm cut into the surrounding cliffs. 'Why's that?'

Brendon flashed Les a lecherous grin. 'You figure it out.'

Les stared at the cliff face for a few moments then it dawned on him. The way the rocks folded back at the sides of the fissure, it looked for all the world like a massive vagina. Up near the top, a shale of lighter coloured rock hanging down inside even formed a huge clitoris. It was uncanny.

'Reminds me of a writer I know,' said Les.

'What was that?' asked Brendon.

Les looked up as Digger came into the cabin. 'Nothing.'

'Well,' she said, 'everything seems okay. I'm still not sure about that regulator though.'

'That's okay,' said Brendon. 'It's yours.'

Digger puffed a little air out her nose. 'Thanks Brendon.'

Les smiled at both of them. 'I might go outside for a while. Get some air.'

Brendon started straightening the boat towards Virgin Island. 'Okay.'

Les picked up his backpack and went out on deck. There was a padded seat across one end of the bow and a wooden bench running under the left gunwale. Les sat down on the padded seat and took out his camera.

Digger and her cousin seemed to be getting into an earnest conversation in the cabin. Les left them to it and got a quick shot of Mother Murphy's before it disappeared in the distance then started looking for other targets. Yacaba Head and the small islands jutting out of the ocean in front of Port Stephens faded away behind them as the *Gainsborough* cruised past Providence Bay and the seemingly endless sands of Bennetts Beach. A huge albatross came out of nowhere, skimmed the surface of the ocean for a while then flew off towards the horizon. Les took another quick snap before it was gone and settled back. The sun was out, the ocean was blue and apart from the nor'wester flicking a little sea spray here and there, the seas were fairly calm. Except for one awful thing on his mind, Norton was at peace with the world. The gentle rocking of the boat almost lulled him to sleep when a movement in the water caught his eye. From out of nowhere, the boat was suddenly surrounded by a pod of twenty or more dolphins, including a baby swimming alongside its mother. The pod swam effortlessly around the boat and dived up and down in the wake while bursts of air sprayed from their blow holes making tiny rainbows in the sunshine. Les got to his feet and snapped off two quick photos as Digger came out of the cabin.

'Aren't they lovely,' she said.

'Reckon,' agreed Les. 'Check out the little one.'

The baby dolphin must have realised they were looking at it. So like any cheeky kid, it started putting on a bit of a turn; darting in and out of the other dolphins, spinning around and jumping out of the water.

'Look at that,' said Les, getting a quick photo. 'Cheeky little bludger. Haven't these dolphins got any parental control?'

'If you ask me. He deserves a good smack,' said Digger.

Putting on a turn for his new found audience, the baby dolphin wasn't quite watching what he was doing and swam into another dolphin's tail. Unexpectedly, he copped a solid flick under the snout and went beneath the boat. The keel passed over him and he tumbled out at the stern with the wash from the propeller. The mother and several other dolphins stopped and regrouped around the baby.

'Shit! I hope he's allright,' said Les, as the rest of the pod fell behind the boat.

'Ohh, the poor baby,' said Digger.

Les put a hand above his eyes. There could have been blood in the water. But if there was, he didn't say anything to Digger. 'I think he's okay,' said Les. 'They all seem to be swimming again.'

Digger was about to say something, when her cousin called out from the cabin. 'I'd better see what Brendon wants.'

'Righto.'

Digger went back inside the cabin. Les watched the dolphins fade away then sat down again. He was staring at the ocean, not thinking about much, mainly hoping the little dolphin wasn't hurt too bad, when Brendon sat down next to him.

'Digger told me you were up on Tomaree Point when the earthquake hit,' said Brendon.

'Yeah,' replied Les. 'I thought the whole bloody mountain was going to come down at one stage.'

'I was in the painting shop. And that was bad enough.'

'I'm not in any hurry to see another one,' said Les.

'You're not Robinson Crusoe. Did Digger tell you I want you to have one of my paintings?'

'Yeah. That's good of you Brendon. But you don't have to.'

Les told Brendon about the small yard round his house in Bondi and how he used to do his neighbours half the time, so it was a bit of a buzz ripping into a big one. Les did admit he was also trying to sweeten things up with Digger, for getting her so drunk on Friday night. Brendon said Les had certainly done something for Digger, because she had a big smile on her face at church this morning. Which was good to see, considering what she'd just been through. Straight faced, Les agreed, then managed to switch the subject to Brendon's boat. After that they chit-chatted about one thing and another while the *Gainsborough* moved easily through the swells and whitecaps. Brendon never pressed Les about his work at the mission. But at times Les got the feeling he was trying to catch him out. Next thing it was Digger's turn to call out from the cabin.

'I suppose I'd better get back behind the tiller,' said Brendon. 'We'll be there soon.'

'Okay,' said Les.

Brendon stood up and winked at Les. 'We'll continue our conversation later on, Deacon Les.'

'Yeah. Righto Brendon,' smiled Les.

Les watched Brendon go inside the cabin and take over the wheel. There it is again, thought Les. Deacon Les. And the exact same tone of voice as Digger. Les stared into the swirling water behind the boat then glanced over at the two of them talking in the cabin for a few moments before turning back to the ocean. Les was still staring at the ocean when Virgin Island seemed to loom up out of nowhere, less than a kilometre in front of the boat.

For an island with such an innocent name, it looked wild and rugged and was a lot bigger than Les had first thought. The western tip was about three kilometres from land and the two hills he saw from Tomaree Point were mountains with sheer, grey cliffs tumbling down to the sea. The rest of the island was low, green slopes, thick with vegetation, but no sign of any trees. Away from the cliffs were numerous bays and anchorages and dotted around these were reefs and smaller islands with a few bigger ones in between. From what Les could see on this side, it looked peaceful enough sitting in the sunshine with the calm blue water lapping round the foreshores. But he imagined with a decent swell running and a stiff breeze, let alone a storm, it would be as dangerous and treacherous as any other part of Australia's coastline. He took a quick photo and went into the cabin.

'So that's it, eh?' said Les. 'The beautiful Virgin Island.'

Digger was staring through the front windows. 'Yes. Isn't it wonderful.'

'In a rugged sort of way.' Les turned to Brendon. 'So what's the story, skipper?'

'Well,' replied Brendon, cutting the engines back a little. 'I was going to take you right around the island and give you a good look. But I've been listening to the weather reports coming in and it looks like this nor'wester is going to swing round to the south.'

'When? Now?' asked Les.

'No. They reckon this afternoon,' said Brendon. 'But you never know for sure. So I'm heading straight into Bennetts Bay and anchor near the wreck. Me and Digger want to get two good dives in. Then if the wind does pick up, we'll go straight back to Port Stephens. These reefs can get a bit hairy in a southerly.'

'Fair enough,' said Les. 'I can always come out here again.'

'You sure can,' said Brendon. 'And Digger and I would love to take you. Wouldn't we, Digger?'

'Of course we would,' smiled Digger. 'Anytime.'

Les looked at them both for a moment. 'I might go back out on deck and take some more photos.'

Les returned to where he was before and watched the shoreline approaching, trying not to read anything into what Digger and Brendon had just said in the cabin or the way they said it. Brendon carefully brought the boat past an island of solid rock jutting out of the sea then through the surrounding reefs and bombys and into a bay that had been split into two pebbly beaches by a ridge of volcanic rock jutting out from the shore. All around the boat, the water changed from light blue to dark, showing the numerous deep holes and caves on the bottom. More volcanic holes and channels scoured back into the shoreline and behind the two pebble strewn beaches, low rocky ledges rose up into the surrounding scrub.

Wedged into a deep channel, on the right hand side of the volcanic ridge that split the bay in two, was the wreck of the *Milton*. The old boat was bent near the middle and the front half was pushed up and twisted to the left like a stubbed cigarette butt half in and half out of the water. Some blackened ribs and plates stuck up at the sides and the ship's bridge was still sitting there along with the boiler, riddled with holes and covered in orange rust. Most of the hull was intact. But instead of cargo, it was full of water and shell grit washing around with the tide and the small swells running into the bay. From where Les stood, the *Milton* looked a good fifty metres long and over five metres wide and by the way it was jammed into the rocks he imagined the fully laden boat would have hit like an express train when the storm sent it crashing into the bay. He took a couple of photos then went back into the cabin.

'I suppose that's the *Milton*,' said Les.

'That's it,' said Brendon. 'Right where it landed in 1942.'

'There's some deep holes on the left side of that ridge,' said Digger. 'But if you stay this side of the wreck, it's fairly shallow. And there're a lot of big stingrays that hang around over there.'

'Okay,' nodded Les.

Brendon cut the motors back again while Digger climbed up on the bow. He switched off the engine as Digger dropped the anchor over and the *Gainsborough* swung round with the breeze then rocked gently with the swells, moored roughly a hundred metres from the *Milton*, its bow facing the old wreck's stern. Les checked the depth sounder and noticed they were in five fathoms of water.

'So what happens now, skipper?' asked Les.

'Now?' said Brendon. 'Digger and I go for a dive. You going for a snorkel?'

'Probably. I might watch you two first.'

'Suit yourself.'

Les went back out on deck and sat down at the stern to watch proceedings. Brendon and Digger were obviously anticipating a change in the weather, so they didn't waste any time and were soon down to their costumes, with Digger looking as sexy as ever in a blue one-piece that hugged her in all the right places. Les got a photo of them getting into their plain black wetsuits and BCD jackets. But they didn't take much notice. They were more interested in doing all their safety checks and Les was reminded briefly of his one attempt at going for his PADI. It was a serious business. If you slipped up or ran out of air down there, you drowned. And that was it. However, Brendon and Digger knew what they were doing and soon they had their scuba tanks on, weight belts adjusted and knives holstered to their legs ready to go. They gave themselves one last safety check each, then Brendon moved down to the back of the boat where one end of the stern swung open to reveal a small wooden platform just above the water. Digger shuffled over to join him then they put their flippers on and started cleaning their face masks.

'We should be back in forty minutes,' said Brendon.

'Okay,' said Les. 'And if you're not back in forty minutes, what'll I do? Get the dinghy and come looking for you?'

'That might be an idea,' said Digger.

'And if I don't find you in sixty minutes, can I start eating the food?'

'Just do us a favour. And be back here in forty minutes,' said Digger.

'I'll be here,' said Les. 'Don't worry.'

Brendon and Digger put their face masks on and checked their air hoses. Brendon gave Digger a nod then stepped off the back of the boat and a second or two later, Digger splashed into the water next to him. They floated near the stern for a few moments while they adjusted the air in their BCDs then dived under. Les watched their flippers gently splash the surface followed by two clouds of silver bubbles and it wasn't long before they disappeared into the depths leaving him on his own.

It was strange being out in the middle of nowhere with nothing for company but the wreck of an old ship and the only noise the cries of some passing seagulls and the sound of water slapping gently against the *Gainsborough's* hull. Everything was beautiful enough, yet in an eerie, isolated way. Les peered into the water around the boat. It was ideal for diving and he could make out the bottom easily, even see some fish swimming about. But parts of the bottom disappeared into an indigo blackness and there could be anything lurking near those deep holes. He also thought Brendon and Digger were crazy diving around there on their own. The place would have to be full of sharks and Digger's father had just been eaten. Les peered into one of the holes under the boat. Either that, or they've got plenty of ticker. More than I've got at the moment. Les tapped idly on the gunwale. Well, I've got to do something, he told himself. They'll be finished their first dive before long and they'll think there's something wrong with me if they get back and find out I've just been sitting around like a stale bottle of piss for nearly three quarters of an hour. But I'm fucked if I'm swimming over to that old wreck. They can stick the stingrays up their arse and anything else that's over there. The little white dinghy caught Norton's eye. That's what I'll do — I'll row over to the island and have a quick look around. You never know. There might even be buried treasure somewhere. Arrhh, arrhh. Pieces of eight. Pieces of eight.

Les put his camera in his backpack, then untied the fibreglass dinghy. It didn't weigh much and Les soon had it manhandled over the side and tied to the back of the boat. He put the oars in then dropped his backpack near the seat in the middle and very carefully climbed aboard. The little dinghy rocked around a little. But Les soon had the oars in the rollicks, the rope untied and was rowing towards the pebbly beach on the right. A few minutes later Les crunched up alongside the wreck of the *Milton*. He jumped out and dragged the dinghy up onto the pebbles proud that he never got a drop of water on him.

Before he slung his backpack on, Les had a look at the old wreck. It was a forlorn sight rusting its life away against the rocks and it must have been an awful night when it got wrecked and the crew all drowned out in the middle of nowhere. Les had a look around and also surmised this was a beach in the making. Another ten thousand years or so and all the pebbles would be ground down to sand, the *Milton* would be gone and this would probably be a nice, safe little beach; full of yobbos drinking tinnies, wogs kicking soccer balls round and Asians stripping all the shellfish off the rocks. I don't think I'll be here to see it somehow. Les took a close up of the wreck then the camera started rewinding. He replaced the film with a spare he'd brought, hoisted his backpack over his shoulders and set off.

Before he reached the slope leading up from the bay, Les stopped to look at a clump of brown, volcanic rock. Stuck all over it, like raisins in a Christmas cake, were pebbles of all colours and sizes. Les was no geologist, but he figured give or take a million years, Virgin Island probably wasn't all that old compared to the mainland. Les got a photo then climbed a slope and looked around. Apart from the two mountains in the distance, it was all thick, scrubby, green dunes dotted with prickly pears. He found a trail and started walking.

Les was strolling along thinking how peaceful it all was — the only sound was the sea and the wind smoothing the top of the tussocks clinging to the ground. When suddenly the peace and quiet was shattered by the roar of a plane low overhead. Les looked up as an F-18 fighter from Williamtown airbase rattled across the sky before banking into the clouds. He watched the plane disappear over Mount Buladelah, sticking up like a pyramid on the mainland, and continued walking.

The island was fascinatingly beautiful, except there were no trees or birds. The only signs of life were the remains of a dead rabbit drying on the trail and countless mutton bird holes under the grass waiting for someone to step in and break their ankle. Scattered around the prickly pears were the purple fruits with the middles chewed out. I'll bet there's some happy birds flying around out there, smiled Les. A bit of prickly pear wine wouldn't go astray right now actually. Take a trip and don't even leave where you're standing. The trail veered off near an easy way down the rocks to the water. Les climbed down and found these beautiful rock pools and lagoons washing in and out with the tide. They were deep enough to stand or lie in and on a hot summer's day Les couldn't think of anything nicer than lying back in one on a banana chair, a delicious in one hand, a hot one in the other and a ghetto blaster playing your favourite music. The pools further away from the ocean were crystal clear and ringed with bulrushes and had that pungent, brackish smell about them. There were tiny caves in the cliffs and spread across the rocks was green, orange and yellow lichen, so bright it was almost luminescent. Les snapped off more photos. Virgin Island was unique and the further he went the more Norton liked it.

Les followed the rocks along, skirting more rock pools, then climbed a rise and found another trail. He followed it along for a while then stopped in his tracks. Beneath him were two of the most beautiful little bays Les had ever seen in his life. They were dead calm with turquoise water lapping against the white sand and looked like something out of the Greek Islands. There was one small runabout anchored in the nearest bay and dotted along the beach were half-a-dozen fishermen's huts and their dinghies. Sitting on a rock near the beach, drinking a tinnie, was a solitary fisherman. He didn't notice Les. So Les left him to his thoughts and his tinnie while he took some photos. He took one of the fisherman through the zoom lens then looked at his watch. By the time he got back to the boat it would be close to forty minutes.

Les put his camera away and started back to the beach. The dinghy was still sitting on the pebbles; Les pushed it in the water and rowed back out to the *Gainsborough*. He just had time to stow the dinghy back on board when two sets of bubbles broke the surface just off the stern. Brendon came up first and dropped a string shopping bag on the platform with six good-sized lobsters in it and ten abalone. Digger popped up alongside him. Les helped Digger on board first then gave Brendon a hand. Water dripping from their wetsuits, they hunched over the deck and took off their face masks and flippers.

'How was it?' asked Les.

'Oh! It was fantastic,' said Digger. 'You should have seen the fish. We even swum into a school of tuna. They were huge.'

'What about when that little octopus crawled up inside your BCD,' laughed Brendon.

'Yes.' Digger's eyes were sparkling. 'Then he started swimming round my face.'

'An octopus up your wetsuit,' Les gestured disfavourably. 'You can keep that thanks.'

'If only you'd had your camera, Brendon,' said Digger.

'Yeah, bugger it. It won't be ready till tomorrow afternoon.'

Les nodded to the shopping bag. 'I see you got yourself a nice feed while you were down there Brendon.'

'Yeah. But I only take what I need. I don't rape the place, like some of them.'

'Fair enough.'

'What did you do?' asked Digger, placing her scuba tank on the deck.

'I took the dinghy and went for a walk on the island,' replied Les.

'What did you think?' she asked.

'It's the grouse. There's a little bay over there looks like a poster in a Greek restaurant.'

'That's Vanessa Bay. It's beautiful,' said Digger.

'Are there rabbits on the island?' asked Les.

'Not many now,' said Brendon. 'They've poisoned most of them. They eat all the young trees.'

'All I saw was one dead one. And plenty of prickly pears. And mutton bird holes.'

'Those bloody things. I nearly broke my ankle in one last year.' Brendon got down to the bottom half of his wetsuit. 'Righto. What's for lunch? I'm starving.'

'Corned beef sandwiches and fruit salad,' said Digger. 'And I'll make a pot of tea.'

'I've got some OJ and two bars of chocolate,' offered Les.

'That might come in handy,' said Brendon.

Digger and her cousin exchanged a brief look. 'I'll start getting things ready,' she said.

'Can I give you a hand?' asked Les.

'No. You're our guest,' said Digger.

'Okay.'

Les talked to Brendon about the dive while he put the lobsters and abalone in a plastic drum then washed their gear and placed it back in the two baskets. Brendon said the water was clear, there were heaps of fish and the only sharks they saw were a few grey nurses in a cave and a lot of wobbegongs and Port Jacksons. Another F–18 rattled across the sky, then Digger called out from the cabin.

'Lunch is ready.'

'Righto,' answered Brendon. 'You hungry, Les?'

'Yeah. I am a bit.'

'That's good,' said Brendon.

They went into the cabin, where Digger still had the bottom half of her wetsuit on same as Brendon. Spread across the map table were two plates of sandwiches cut neatly into triangles, a pot of tea, milk, sugar and some tomatoes. Digger was already eating. Les placed his two Cherry Ripes and the orange juice on the map table then poured himself a mug of tea and one for Brendon. He added milk and sugar and picked up a sandwich. Being a bit peckish from the salt air and his walk on the island, Les popped most of the sandwich into his mouth at once and started chewing away. A second later, water started pouring out of his eyes. The next thing, it felt like his nasal passages were full of burning aircraft fuel and the top of his head was going to come off.

'Jesus Christ!' yelped Les. 'How much mustard did you put in these bloody sandwiches? Arrrraaggghhh!' Les spat the sandwich into a paper napkin and gulped down some tea.

Digger looked shocked. 'Les. That was a little uncalled for. Wasn't it?'

Les gasped like he was having an asthma attack and wiped his eyes and mouth with another paper napkin. 'Okay Digger,' he spluttered. 'If I took the Lord Jehovah's name in vain I'm sorry. But what did you put the mustard on with — a trowel?'

Digger looked most indignant. 'I spread a little on. That's all.'

Les turned to Brendon. He had that loopy smile on his face and was scraping mustard off a sandwich onto a paper napkin. 'What's the matter, Deacon?' he said. 'Don't you like my cousin's cooking?'

'No. It's great,' said Les, staring apprehensively at

the remaining sandwiches. 'I suppose you got sandwiches like this in the army.'

'All the time,' said Brendon. 'Especially when we were training for chemical warfare.'

'You're both just hard to please,' sniffed Digger. 'Besides. If you don't like them. Don't eat them.'

'Digger. The sandwiches are okay,' said Les. 'You just didn't have to heap all that industrial strength mustard on them. That's all.'

'I didn't,' repeated Digger.

'Of course you didn't, mate,' said Brendon.

Les got another sandwich and scraped off all the mustard the same as Brendon did, then added some sliced tomato. It still tasted ordinary. But at least this time it was palatable.

'Anyway, you'll like my fruit salad,' said Digger. 'It's got lamingtons in it.'

'I love a nice lamington,' said Les.

They finished the tea and sandwiches, then Digger served up the fruit salad. It was out of a tin and she'd added half a dozen cake shop lamingtons filled with mock cream and strawberry jam. After slopping around in the Tupperware container all morning, it looked like something Yogi Bear might have vomited up. Nevertheless, after the attack of the killer corned beef sandwiches, Les was able to get a bowl down without too much trouble.

'How was that?' smiled Digger.

'Very nice,' replied Les, swallowing a glass of orange juice. 'The only thing missing was some ice-cream.'

'I told you to fix the deep freeze,' Digger said to her cousin.

'That,' replied Brendon. 'Is my next priority.' He looked at his watch. 'Well Digger. We'd better make a move, if we're going to get another dive in.'

'I can clean up,' said Les.

Digger shook her head. 'No, leave it. I'll do it on the way back. You make sure you have a snorkel.'

'Okay,' said Les. 'You going to be forty minutes again?'

'Yeah. Same as last time,' said Brendon.

'I'll be here waiting for you.'

Les watched Brendon and Digger change tanks then get into the rest of their diving gear and go through all the safety checks before they shuffled back down to the hatch at the stern. Apart from a few clouds here and there, the sky was as blue as ever and the southerly still hadn't come up; if anything the nor'wester seemed to have eased off a little. Les didn't bother to take a photo. He just assured Brendon and Digger he'd be waiting there when they got back in forty minutes. There was a splash as they stepped off the stern, another flurry of flippers on the surface then they disappeared towards the bottom leaving Les on his own once more.

Les stared into the clear, blue ocean for a moment then looked around him. Well. This is it hero, he told himself. The moment of truth. I have to get in the water this time. Or else I'm nothing but a c-c-craven little c-c-coward. But try as he might, Les still couldn't rid the picture of sharks from his mind. Even now he could see that bronze whaler ripping Forbes Zaccariah's shoulder apart. Still, there's no mad hurry. Why rush these things, Les asked himself. Why not have a bar of chocolate before I plunge into the depths? Give me added strength. Les went into the cabin, picked up a Cherry Ripe from the map table and started gnawing on one end.

While he was summoning up every vestige of raw courage in him, Les had a look round the cabin. He nudged the solid Yale lock on the storage compartment. I wonder what Brendon's got in there? All his money. Les had a look at the barometer then got behind the ship's wheel and gave it a bit of a turn. The depth sounder looked like it was switched off. But the ship's compass was still on. What am I talking about, Les smiled to himself. You don't switch a compass on and off. Les gazed from the compass across to the wreck of the *Milton*. Moving around in the gentle nor'wester, the *Gainsborough* had settled almost parallel with the old ship. Les had another look at the compass then started thinking about something Brendon said earlier. What was it? The wreck of the *Milton* faced directly north, and you could line your compass up with it. Well either Brendon's compass was stuffed. Or the wreck was. What was left of the *Milton's* bow faced north-north-west. The hull faced north. But even if it was out by a degree or so, there was no way you'd use it for a mark or compare your compass to it. Les lined the compass and the wreck up again. Yep. For sure. Then Les realised what must have happened. When he was up on Tomaree Point during the earthquake, he saw the water shimmering around Virgin Island. And according to the news the epicentre was only a few kilometres away to the north. The earthquake must have cracked the *Milton* somewhere near the middle and moved it. Les took another bite of Cherry Ripe. I know what I'll do. I'll paddle the dinghy over to the wreck and take a quick look around. Digger said it's only shallow on this side and if I so much as see a goldfish, I can be out of the water that fast I won't even leave a ripple. Plus I can show those other two how smart I am. They never noticed the old wreck had moved and they've been out here a million times. Les got his bag from the cabin at the bow and took it out on deck. Everything in it was a bit damp and smelly. But it was all there. Including one of the mini scuba tanks he'd forgotten to give Eddie when they left Jimmy's Beach in a hurry. Les left it in the bottom of the bag and got into his wetsuit. He lowered the dinghy into the water, threw his bag in along with the oars, and after a few minutes rowing pulled the dinghy up on the same pebbly beach again.

The beach dropped away quickly and the split in the wreck's hull was about twenty metres out from shore. From where Les stood the tide appeared to be coming in and the split looked to be sitting in around five metres of water before the rest of the hull sloped down deeper into the bay. The split wasn't all that wide. Maybe half a metre or so where the earth tremor had twisted the hull before pushing it back together again and was more like a jagged bend than anything else. The sun was out, the ocean calm and on any other occasion Les would consider this a pleasant afternoon snorkel sucking. But today Norton's nerves were a little on edge and it wasn't very appealing at all. Oh well, he mused. What do Midnight Oil say in that song? It's better to die on your feet, than live on your knees. That's me baby. A hero to the end. Les cleaned his face mask, put his flippers on and plunged in.

The water was colder than in Port Stephens, but much, much clearer. Les stuck by the side of the wreck and swam out. Soon the pebbles gave way to grey volcanic rock and white boulders scattered across the bottom, however, despite the clarity of the water, everything still looked dark, shadowy and sinister. There was a lot more hull jammed against the rocks than Les expected because not having to cope with air and sun, metal doesn't so much rust underwater, it corrodes slowly. Les kicked leisurely along with the current, then started to notice all the fish. Bream, luderick, drummer, long toms, pike, whiting darting through schools of slimy mackerel and other smaller fish. But so far no sharks. Not even a slow moving wobbegong. Les got to the crack in the hull and floated on the surface slowly breathing into his snorkel. At the bottom was a hole where the ship must have split when it wedged itself into the volcanic rock. It was a good two metres in circumference going from the hull out across the bottom. Shit! That cave must be deep, thought Les. It's not just blue. It's pitch bloody black. Les looked

275

down at the hole for a few moments and thought he'd take a look. There might be a few lobsters round the edges. And I wouldn't mind a nice feed of bugs myself. Les took a couple of deep breaths in and out then dived down towards the hole in the *Milton's* hull. He was almost at the bottom, when the hole started to shake. There was a flurry of sand and pebbles and the hole took off like a drag racer and headed for the open sea.

'Aaaaarrrhhhhh. Shit!' Les howled into his snorkel and kicked for the surface in a flurry of terrified bubbles. His heart was pounding like a trip hammer and the big Queenslander was about two seconds away from filling his wetsuit when he reached the top. 'Jesus Christ!'

The hole was a huge black stingray. It had to be a metre thick and the sting at its tail was like a length of firehose. 'Fuck me dead,' gasped Les. That's all I bloody need. Les watched the edges of the stingray's white underbelly as it flapped off into the distance. Go on. Piss off you fat cunt of a thing. I hope a shark gets you. After a while Les settled down and started to laugh. Even though the stingray almost scared the life out him, it was fairly harmless and quite beautiful to watch in flight. And it was hard to tell who got the biggest fright. Les or the stingray. He stared down at where the shell grit and sand was still swirling around on the bottom, and suddenly noticed something. Where the stingray had been sitting against the hull, there was a hole. A triangular-shaped one a metre wide on the sides and across the seabed. Only it wasn't black. It was blue. Hello, thought Les. There might be some lobsters down there after all. Despite almost having a heart attack, he took another deep breath and dived down again.

The hole wasn't wide enough for your shoulders. But you could poke your face mask through. On the look out for wobbegongs and anything else, Les very gingerly gripped the metal at the edges and peered in. It was dark inside, but soon Norton's eyes got accustomed to the gloom. There was an underwater cave beneath the wreck and there was something in there squashed under the *Milton's* hull. It was grey and corroded and looked like another ship's boiler only bigger in diameter. From where he was lying, Les couldn't see the rest that clearly. But there seemed to be a rudder at this end and a length of cable running up from it. Les stayed down as long as he could then kicked back to the surface.

I wonder what the fuck that is, thought Les, as he trod water and got his breath back. It didn't look like part of the *Milton*. Maybe it was some of its cargo? His curiosity now getting the better of him, Les floated on the surface a moment longer then dived down and stared into the hole again.

This time Les could make out rivet heads in the metal. He twisted his head to the left and was starting to make out more of the shape at this end when something coming towards him made Les pull his head back from the hole. It was a moray eel, floating through the water like a fat, green ribbon. The eel had its mouth open and several spiked teeth stuck out in the gloomy blue of the cave like white sewing machine needles. This time however, Les didn't hit the panic button. After the monster black stingray, the eel was small potatoes. But keeping an eye on those evil-looking teeth, Les ran out of air before he got a further chance to check out whatever it was in the cave. Les kicked for the surface again and started sucking in air. I'll bust a lung at this rate, he puffed, before I find out what that is down there. Hang on. Upstairs for thinking. Downstairs for dancing. The little scuba tank. There's about five minutes air in one of those. If I've got the one I didn't use? Les turned and swam back to the beach. He crunched across the pebbles, got the tank from his bag and swam back out to the hole in the side of the *Milton*. He sucked on his snorkel for a few moments while he got his bearings, then stuck the little tank in his mouth and breathing slowly and steadily, dived down again.

The moray had gone and the little tank made things easier. Les held onto the sides of the hole and stared into the cave. Now he could see it was definitely a ship of some kind. There was a propeller at the back, with four rudders shaped like a cross in front of it, and a corroded docking ring. Norton's eyebrows knitted behind his face mask. He'd been on a vessel like this. A small object floating amongst the pebbles and shell grit near the edge of the hole caught his eye. It was a piece of faded cloth with something attached to it covered in green corrosion. Les picked it up and stuck it in the leg of his wetsuit just as the air in the tank abruptly cut out. However Les felt he'd seen all he needed to. He kicked for the surface, put his snorkel in his mouth and swam back to the beach.

Although his mind was elsewhere, the first thing Les noticed was that the southerly had arrived. It was only light so far, but enough to ripple the surface of the ocean and swing the *Gainsborough* round so it now faced the bay stern on. Shit! That was quick, thought Les. He put his snorkelling gear in his bag then pulled out the strange little object he'd poked under his wetsuit and had a look at it. The corrosion wasn't that thick. But there was still too much to tell what it was. Les put it in his bag then pushed the dinghy down to the water's edge and rowed back to the *Gainsborough*. Brendon and Digger had already got back from their dive when Les bumped up against the stern. Brendon was sitting on the gunwale rubbing his calf muscle and Digger was fiddling with her regulator. Les was on board and had the dinghy pulled up on deck almost before they got a chance to look up.

'You're back early,' said Les. 'What happened?'

'I got a cramp,' answered Brendon. 'And Digger's regulator started playing up.'

'I knew this was going to happen,' huffed Digger. 'I jolly well knew it.'

Brendon stopped rubbing his leg and did a couple of squats. 'Anyway. It's all fixed now.'

'So are you going to finish your dive?' asked Les.

Brendon looked around him. 'Not much use. The southerly's come up.'

'I see you got in the water,' said Digger. 'How was it?'

'It was good,' nodded Les. 'That's what I want to see you about. How much air have you got left in your tanks?'

Brendon and Digger exchanged looks. 'About fifteen, twenty minutes,' said Brendon.

'Okay. Come here, I want to show you something.' Les led them into the cabin and pointed to the compass. 'Didn't you tell me the *Milton* faced due north?' he said to Brendon.

'Yeah. That's right.'

'Well have a look at that.' Les pointed to the wreck lying off the stern, then to compass. He did it again for Digger's sake.

'Well I'll be blowed,' said Brendon. 'I never even noticed.'

'Goodness! Look at that,' exclaimed Digger.

'So you'd both agree. The bow of the *Milton* now faces north-north-west?' said Les.

'Yeah. For sure,' replied Brendon.

'Absolutely,' agreed Digger.

'Righto.' Les told them how he discovered the *Milton* had been moved by the earthquake. How he went for a dive round the wreck and got the shit scared out of him by the stingray. Then seeing the hole and having a look. He didn't mention using the little scuba tank. 'I'm telling you. There's something underneath the *Milton*.'

'Underneath the *Milton*?' Brendon looked sceptical. 'Like what?'

280

'I'm not sure,' replied Les. 'I couldn't hold my breath long enough. But there's definitely something there.'

'Les. We've dived and swum over that wreck a hundred times,' said Digger.

'Yes. Before it was hit by an earthquake,' said Les. 'Look. Why don't you go over and see for yourself. It's two minutes away. And you've got enough air left in your tanks.'

Brendon shook his head. 'I don't know.'

'Ohh shit!' said Les. 'What's fifteen minutes. Christ!'

Digger gave Les a double blink then looked at her cousin. 'Well. Seeing Deacon Les has put it so nicely. What do you think, Brendon?'

Brendon gave a non-committal shrug. 'Allright. Why not? Is your regulator working properly now?'

'Yes. I managed to fix it,' said Digger.

'Are you sure?'

'Yes. I'm sure Brendon. I'm not a blonde you know.'

'Okay. Let's get wet again.'

'I won't come with you,' said Les, ushering them back out on deck. 'I'll only get in the way. But I'll help you as best I can.'

Les gave them a hand to get back into their BCDs and five minutes later Brendon and Digger were in the water swimming towards the wreck. Not much else I can do now, thought Les. I may as well get changed. Les towelled off and got into his tracksuit. He had another look at whatever it was he had picked up near the wreck then put it in his pocket the way he found it. By the time he finished the last Cherry Ripe, the southerly had come up a little stronger and two streams of bubbles appeared off the stern. Les helped Brendon and Digger back on board. They took their face masks and hoods off and got out of their BCDs. Neither of them said anything. But they were exchanging very strange looks.

'Well?' said Les. 'What did you see?'

Digger shook her head. 'I don't want to say.'

'Why don't we go inside and get out of the wind,' said Brendon.

They picked up their towels and went inside the cabin. Les followed and closed the door behind them. Both Brendon and Digger looked totally mystified.

'Allright?' asked Les again. 'What's the verdict?'

Brendon shook his head. 'You go first, Digger.'

'Allright,' said Digger. 'I say it's a mini-submarine.'

'Yeah. It sure looks like it,' said Brendon.

'I knew I saw something under there,' said Les.

Brendon turned towards the wreck now lying off the *Gainsborough's* stern. 'But if it is? What's it doing there?'

Digger turned around also. 'Exactly,' she said. 'What?'

'Buggered if I know,' said Les. 'I'm just a tourist.'

Brendon and Digger were both staring at the wreck of the *Milton* completely bewildered. Les stepped across behind them as if he wanted to have a look also and quick as any dealer at the Kelly Club, palmed what he'd found in the water under the back of Brendon's wetsuit. He then leant back against the seat opposite the map table.

'Hey Brendon,' said Les. 'What's that in your wetsuit?'

'What?'

'There's something caught in your wetsuit.' Les pointed to where the top half of Brendon's wetsuit met the bottom half at the hip. 'Look.'

Brendon turned his head and noticed the piece of faded material. He pulled it out and looked at the corroded little object that was attached. 'How did that get there?'

'It must have got caught in your wetsuit when you were lying on the bottom looking into that hole,' said Les.

'What is it?' asked Digger.

'I don't know,' answered Brendon.

'Give me a look.' Digger took the object from Brendon and rolled it in her hand. 'It's a button,' she said.

'A button?' said Les.

'Yes,' nodded Digger. 'Wait a minute and I'll clean it up.'

Les shrugged a look at Brendon. Brendon shrugged the same look back at Les. Digger went down to the galley and got some steel wool and Brasso from a cupboard over the sink. Les and Brendon watched silently as her nimble fingers went to work. A few minutes later she came back up, polishing the object with a Chux. There was still some corrosion, nevertheless Digger had managed to bring up most of the shine.

'What did I tell you,' said Digger. 'It's a brass button.'

'Show me.' Digger handed Brendon the button. He held it between his fingers for a few moments then got a magnifying glass from a drawer in the map table. 'This is off a navy uniform,' he declared. 'Probably an officer's.'

'A navy uniform?' said Les. 'How can you tell?'

'Look.' Brendon moved the magnifying glass around and pointed out an anchor with a piece of rope round it engraved on the brass button.

'Hey. It is too,' said Les.

'It looks like an Australian navy button,' said Digger.

Brendon shook his head and stared at the brass button. 'No. It's not Australian. It's Japanese.'

'Japanese?' chorused Les and Digger.

'Yeah. Look at this.' Brendon pointed to one edge of the brass button beneath the anchor. There was the faint outline of a flower and tiny Japanese lettering.

'You're right, Brendon,' said Les. 'That's Japanese for sure.'

Brendon turned to his cousin. 'But what's ...?'

Digger waved her hands by her side. 'I wouldn't have a clue,' she said, shaking her head. 'It's a complete mystery, as far as I'm concerned.'

Les watched Brendon and Digger staring at the brass button still completely baffled. After a few moments the Sherlock Holmes came out in Norton and he felt it was time to take control.

'I don't believe you two,' said Les. 'It's almost biting you both on the arse. And you can't see the bleeding obvious.'

Brendon looked up from the magnifying glass. 'What are you talking about?' he said.

'When did the *Milton* go down?' asked Les.

'1942. I told you.'

'Yeah. But when in 1942?'

Brendon had to deliberate for a moment. 'June. Early June. The fifth I think. This huge storm came out of nowhere.'

'Okay,' said Les. 'Now what happened in Sydney Harbour in 1942? Come on Brendon. You're the military buff. And we've all done Australian history at school.'

'There was a Japanese mini-submarine attack,' cut in Digger. 'On the first of June.'

'Well done Digger,' said Les.

'That's right,' said Brendon. 'They missed the *Chicago* and sank a ferry. The *Kuttabul*. No. It wasn't a ferry. It was a depot ship. Nineteen ratings got killed.'

'Hallelujah!' said Les. 'I'm surrounded by genius.' He looked at Brendon. 'And how many mini-submarines were there Brendon?'

Brendon started to look like he was on *Sale Of The Century*. 'Three. There were three. I know this. A harbour patrol boat, the *Sea Mist*, reported seeing three mini-submarines in Chowder Bay. At 0500.'

'Hey Brendon. You know your oats,' said Les. 'And what happened to the three submarines?'

'They sank two,' said Brendon. 'The *M–27* and the *M–22*. One of the captain's names was Matsuo. I remember, because it sounds like the soup.'

Les turned to Digger. 'You're cousin is a military genius.' He turned back to Brendon. 'And what happened to the third submarine?'

'What happened to the third submarine? They hit it with depth charges. But they never found it.' Brendon paused for a second. 'It ... it got away.'

'It got away,' repeated Les. Les pointed to the wreck of the *Milton*. 'And that's what's over there I reckon. The one that got away.'

Brendon shook his head emphatically. 'No. No. It's too much of a coincidence. Besides. Submarines just don't go missing.'

'One did in 1942,' said Les.

'Wait on Brendon,' said Digger. 'Les could be right. They just found an old World War Two submarine near Seal Rocks. The *K–9*. Don't you read the papers Brendon?'

'Digger's right,' said Les. 'I saw that in the paper myself. There was a photo of two blokes probing the beach with metal pipes.'

Brendon shook his head. 'Yeah. But ...?'

'Hey. Picture this,' said Les. 'You're the captain of the third submarine. You've just been depth charged. Your periscope's stuffed, your steering's damaged and your radio's out. You head for the open sea trying to find the mother ship. Now, you said yourself there was a lot of Japanese activity round here during the war. And I know from my history lessons Japanese submarines used to hang around between Newcastle and Wollongong picking off the coastal shipping. So the captain aims for Newcastle, keeping as close to the shore as possible. He goes past Newcastle and crash lands on Virgin Island in one of those volcanic caves. And in 1942 this would have been pretty much a wilderness. Right?'

'Yeah. Pretty much,' agreed Brendon.

'A couple of days or so after the mini-submarine hits Virgin Island a storm comes up and the *Milton* lands on top of it sealing it into that volcanic rock. The crew probably committed suicide and it's been there ever since. And only for that earthquake, no one would have ever known. The final clue's that old brass button you're holding.' Les looked at Digger and Brendon. 'Well. What do you reckon?'

Digger turned to her cousin. 'Sounds pretty good to me Brendon.'

Brendon returned her gaze and turned the brass button over between his fingers, then slowly nodded his head. 'Yeah. I'll go along with it. There were a lot of Japanese ships around here during the war years.'

'I told you.' Les patted Brendon on the back. 'And the thing is. Mate. You discovered it.'

'Me? What about Digger?'

'Yes. Digger's half in the rort,' agreed Les. But you picked up the button off the Japanese uniform. So you take top billing.'

'Hey wait a minute, Les,' said Digger. 'What about you? You found it in the first place.'

Les shook his head. 'I found nothing. I was just snorkel sucking and I saw something in a hole. I didn't even know what it was. Remember? You two can take all the credit.' Les shook his head again. 'I don't want anything to do with it.'

Brendon looked a little suspiciously at Norton. 'Hang on a minute Les. If this is what we think it is. It's a pretty important, historical discovery. How come you don't want to be part of it?'

'How come? Allright Brendon,' said Les. 'I'll be honest with you. I defended your cousin's honour on Friday night. Did she tell you?'

'Actually she did,' said Brendon. 'I meant to thank you for that too.'

'They were really horrible men too,' said Digger.

'They weren't the best,' agreed Les. 'Anyway. I was having a cup of coffee this morning. And I overheard a couple of people talking. Evidently, one of the blokes got banged up pretty bad. And the cops are thinking of laying charges if they can find the person responsible.'

'Oowah!' exclaimed Digger.

'So if I've got a choice between getting my picture in the paper. And going in the nick, I'll settle for the less people know I've been up here the better.'

'Fair enough,' said Brendon. 'So me and Digger take joint discovery.'

'Yep. That's it,' said Les. 'The thing is though. Something like this is worth a fortune.'

'A fortune?' said Digger. 'How do you work that out?'

'Digger. This is the story of the decade.' Les turned to Brendon. 'If I were you Brendon. As soon as this southerly settles down I'd get straight back out here with an underwater camera and a pinch bar. Bring Digger with you, and get inside that cave and film everything. And don't tell a soul about it till you've finished. Then take out some sort of copyright, and sell the story. You'll make a killing.'

Brendon started to get a bit starry-eyed. 'Hey. You're right, Les.'

'I know I'm right,' said Les. 'So just do it Brendon. Okay?'

'I will. I will.' Brendon cocked an experienced eye towards the wind and the increasing clouds. 'In the meantime, we'd better make a move. Or we might not be going anywhere.'

'Yes. It is starting to look that way,' said Les.

'I'll pull the anchor up,' said Digger. 'Then I'm getting changed out of my wet gear.'

Brendon got behind the wheel and started the engine. 'I'll wait till we clear these reefs.'

'While you're doing that,' said Les, 'I'm going out on deck and get a few photos.'

Les left them to it and went back to the seat at the stern. He got his camera out of his backpack then knelt down and took several last photos of the old wreck and Virgin Island as they began to fade into the background. Brendon steered the *Gainsborough* expertly out of the bay and once they'd cleared the reefs and bombys it wasn't all that bad. Sailing into a wind is always better than running with one and the *Gainsborough* faced the southerly confidently. So it was more vibrations from hitting chop than pitching and rolling into the swells. Out from land, the seas hadn't picked up yet, and even though the grey clouds had thickened, every so often the sun would come out and turn the ocean blue again.

Les sat back against the stern and closed his eyes for a moment. It had been quite a day. He'd seen another part of Australia he never knew existed and finding that submarine couldn't have come at a better time. Digger and her cousin would be famous and they'd end up with some money out of it as well. It wasn't the end all and be all. But it would compensate a little for what Les had done to her father. So it appeared. All's well that was going to end well. And tomorrow he'd be back in Sydney. There'd be no more Digger. But. Sometimes you just can't have everything. Les was miles away when he opened his eyes and looked up to see Digger standing in front of him wearing her black tracksuit.

'Hey, Digger,' said Les. 'How are you? Hasn't it turned out a good day.'

'Yes,' said Digger. 'It's turned out an excellent day. Deacon Les.'

'Digger. You don't have to keep calling me Deacon Les all the time. Just plain Les'll do.'

'Okay. Les.'

'Thanks. Digger.'

Digger was looking directly down at him. The look in her eyes wasn't angelic and if anything, it had an edge to it. 'Les,' she said. 'Last night you said there were a couple of things you wanted to tell me.'

Oh shit, thought Les. Here we go. You can run. But you can't hide. Les dropped his gaze to the deck at his feet. 'Yeah. Yeah Digger. There was.'

Digger kept standing in front of him. Les couldn't quite bring himself to face her. It seemed like an age before she spoke. 'Stay there, Les,' she said. 'I'll be back in a minute.'

Les looked up to see Digger go into the cabin. She said something to her cousin. Brendon turned around towards Les as Digger bent down out of sight. A few moments later she stood up, then came out of the cabin holding an ex-Australian Army SLR with a full clip and brought the barrel up towards Les. Even though everything suddenly seemed to be happening in slow motion, Les quickly realised what was going on. They knew. Somehow he'd slipped up. He first realised it when they kept calling him Deacon Les all the time. How Digger found out he'd killed her father, Les didn't know. But he had a feeling he was going to find out. Before she shot him and they dumped his body overboard. The icing on the cake for them was finding the old submarine. Now with Les out the way, the discovery was their's for sure. Oddly enough, Les felt no fear. He was totally fatalistic towards what was about to happen and if anything he felt relieved. After what he'd done to her father.

It was pretty much all he deserved. He watched Digger point the SLR at him in a motioning fashion.

'Les. Move across to your left,' she said.

'My what?' asked Les

'Your left. Move over. Quick.'

Les did as Digger told him and shuffled across the back seat. Digger knelt down on the deck and rested the FN on top of the upturned dingy as she sighted up towards the starboard side of the stern. Les turned around to see what she was aiming at. A good two hundred and fifty metres away, between the *Gainsborough* and the coastline, was the baby dolphin they'd run over earlier swimming hard against the southerly. The pod must have been hanging around chasing the plentiful fish in the area and he'd got separated. Les could make out his little grey and white figure battling through the whitecaps trying to catch up. Circling the baby dolphin, was another shape, like a sleek indigo blue rocket with coal black eyes. Les knew a mako shark when he saw one, and this one was four metres long, its eyes fixed squarely on the injured baby dolphin. Digger steadied the SLR on top of the dinghy and allowed for the wind, the distance, the rocking of the boat, the shark's movement in the water as well as everything else and squeezed off five shots in less than three seconds.

'Crack, crack, crack! Crack, crack!'

The first three got the mako in the head. The second two got it in the tail. The mako leapt out of the water, there was a flash of its white underbelly as it splashed down again then it disappeared beneath the surface.

'You got him,' Brendon called out from the cabin.

'Yes,' Digger called back. She turned to Les. 'Nasty creature. I wasn't going to let him take that poor little baby. Mother nature or no mother nature.'

Les didn't know where he was. A few seconds ago he thought he was about to die. Now he was well and truly back in the land of the living. Somehow he managed to mumble, 'Where did you learn to shoot like that?'

'Brendon taught me,' replied Digger, picking up the shells. 'He was in the army, remember?'

'He did a bloody good job.'

Expertly, Digger cleared the rifle and removed the clip then took it back inside the cabin and stowed it in the compartment with the Yale lock. Les eased himself back into the seat absolutely speechless. All he could do was look up at the sky and nod a mental thankyou. Digger returned and sat down next to him. She put her hand on his thigh and looked directly at Norton.

'Les. Before you say anything, I'm going to tell you the truth about me. There's only one other person who knows this. Brendon. But I feel you should know too.'

'You do?'

Digger nodded. 'I'm telling you. Because I know you're a decent man Les. And because of the look on your face when I told you how my father died. It nearly broke my heart.'

'It did?'

Digger's green eyes went angelic again. 'Oh Les. You looked so sad. I've never seen anyone look so sad.'

'Well I was Digger,' said Les. 'I was grief-stricken.'

'And that meant a lot to me.' The edge suddenly returned to Digger's eyes. 'But before you get too upset about what happened to my father, Les. Bad and all as it was. My father was the meanest, evilest man ever to draw breath. I hated him.'

'You hated him?'

Digger nodded soberly. 'Forbes Zaccariah was a monster, Les. He put my mother in an early grave and robbed me and Brendon out of the estate. He got my young brother killed in a car accident. He stole thousands of dollars from where he worked.' The edge hardened in Digger's eyes. 'And when I was fifteen he tried to rape me.'

'Bloody hell!' said Les.

'So don't be too put out over the death of my father, Les.' Digger's eyes bored into Norton. 'That Thursday morning I bumped you in the paper shop, the reason I was a bit confused. Was because I was getting ready to go and shoot the bastard.'

'You were what!!?'

'Around lunchtime. I was lying in the sandhills at Jimmy's Beach holding a rifle with telescopic sights and a silencer fitted. Ready to put a bullet through his brain. And his friend's too. Only the sharks beat me too it.'

Les gave Digger a double, triple blink. 'Digger. This is unbelievable.'

'Believe it, Les,' she said. 'I was seconds away from pulling the trigger. I turned around to check out the wind and everything else for the last time. It wouldn't have been half a minute. And when I turned back they were gone.'

'Gone?' said Les.

'Yes. They both just disappeared. It was weird. The boat was still sitting where it was anchored. There was no one splashing in the water. It was as if the sea had swallowed them both up. The papers and everyone else said it was a shark pack. Well if it was. They must have sure worked fast. Then a big tiger shark came from out of nowhere. Bit the back of the boat and flipped it over. That was enough for me. I packed up the rifle and got out of there. Then when I heard it on the news I contacted the police. I think you know the rest.'

'Yeah.' Les suddenly reflected on the glint of light he saw in the sandhills when he was sitting in the runabout with Eddie looking through binoculars. That would have been Digger. 'I remember you saying to me last night, Digger. There was something odd about your father's death.'

'There was. But I like to think it was God's will. For saving me from having to do something terrible.'

'Having to do?' said Les.

Digger nodded. 'Brendon's going to need an operation on his eyes. And the only way we could raise the money would be if something happened to my father. Then we'd get what belongs to us from mum's estate.'

'What's wrong with your cousin's eyes?'

'He's developing these rare kind of cataracts and he'll go blind. The only person that can perform the operation is a doctor in America. And with plane fares and everything it'll cost us a fortune.'

Les turned to Brendon, standing behind the wheel in the cabin. 'The poor bastard.'

'We've been planning this for a long time, Les. Then when my father started hanging round with that crooked detective. Fishbyrne. We thought, why not kill both of them at once? And the police would think gangsters in Sydney did it.'

Les shook his head. 'Whatever made you think that Digger?'

'I'm not sure. We just did. But the sharks came along and saved us the trouble.'

'God bless those ... jolly sharks.'

'Exactly. They were a blessing.' The edge returned to Digger's eyes, harder than ever. 'Now I'm going to tell you something else Les. The other reason besides money, that I was prepared to do this terrible thing. When I said my father tried to rape me. We used to live in Maitland. Mum was away at her parents with my young brother. And I was in the house alone. When my father grabbed me, I didn't know what was going on. But I kicked him in the groin. Hard. And more than once. He had to go to the hospital. When he got back I was sitting in the backyard. As soon as he saw me. He started punching me in the head.'

'Nice father you had,' said Les.

'Yes. And this is the best part. You know what a *Monstera Deliciosa* plant is, Les?'

'Yeah. We used to have them growing back home in Queensland.'

'We had them in the backyard too,' said Digger. 'Because I'd kicked him, he couldn't do anything himself. So that's what he raped me with.'

'Oh shit!' grimaced Les.

'Besides the pain. I bled for a week. I had to tell the doctor I fell out of a tree. I mean. What was I going to say? My father raped me with a piece of fruit? I was a fifteen-year-old virgin. And he told me. If I said anything to mum he'd kill me and my brother.'

Les squeezed Digger's hand as the hardness in her eyes temporarily misted over. 'You poor bloody kid.'

'I can't have children, Les. Unless I have an operation first. But it made no difference. Because I've never let a man near me since that day.'

'What was that?' said Les.

'I've never had sex. Apart from Brendon and my boss, I've avoided men since I was fifteen. Remember my Aztec profile Les. The Wind. We circumvent obstacles. We prefer to evade the issue. Technically speaking Les. You took my virginity.'

Les was completely gobsmacked. 'Digger. This is the most incredible thing I've ever heard.'

'Incredible?' Digger tilted her head slightly. 'Les. As well as all the trauma in my life, can you imagine what I've been going through these last months? I'm a Christian. I believe in God. And I'm plotting to murder two men. Then somehow. And I honestly believe it was God's will, my whole life is suddenly turned around and I don't have to. Then I'm sitting on a park bench, praying. And you walk up to me. It was like God sent you along too.'

Les smiled at her. 'All I wanted was my two dollars back.'

'There was a lot more to it than that,' said Digger.

'Yeah. You're right.'

'Les. When my father got killed. As well as having the weight of the terrible, terrible thing I had to do lifted from my shoulders. It was like a huge mental weight being lifted off me as well. I can't explain it to you. But it was like I'd been set free or something. That Friday night in the club I was walking on air. I'd never been in there because that's where my father used to work. And all night it felt as if I was dancing on his grave. Along with my mother and my brother.'

'Right,' nodded Les. 'I thought you seemed a little strange at times.'

'And you made me laugh. You and that singer. You even fought those awful men over me. It was a wonderful night. And I thought, this is it. I'm free. No more evading the issue. So between you, and all that Scotch. I decided to have my first taste of sex.'

Les looked at Digger for a moment. 'It's funny. But I felt like I'd ... I mean, I didn't feel good about it.'

Digger smiled and touched Norton's cheek. 'I know you didn't. And that's another thing I like about you.'

'Hey. But hang on a second, Digger. That was Friday night. What about Saturday night?' said Les.

'Well. Like I just told you. I've had this bottled up inside me since I was fifteen. I'd heard about sex. And read about sex. And sixty-niners and doggies and things. And what was that other way we did it? With the pillow on the edge of the bed. And my ankles up round my ears.'

'That's allright, Digger. I think I get the picture,' said Les.

'So not only did you get me drunk and take my cherry, Deacon Les, you turned me into a mad, raving case as well.'

'Sorry Digger. I didn't mean to. Maybe if you dressed down a bit.'

'Hey. Don't worry about it, Les. It was great. And I'd had this coming out planned since I was fifteen. Dancing to that song with someone. The surroundings. I knew in my heart God would send someone along one day. And he did.'

'Maybe he did, Digger,' said Les. 'I'm not going to argue.'

'Plus I do like you,' said Digger. 'No. I love you, Les. You're sweet.'

'Thanks Digger. I . . . I guess I love you too.'

Digger reached across and kissed Les softly on the lips. 'So that's my story Les. I've laid it all on the line for you.'

'Yes. You certainly have, Digger. You certainly have.'

Digger smiled at Les. 'Now. You said there were a couple of things you wanted to tell me.'

'Tell you?'

Les looked into Digger's emerald-green eyes. Everything about her had fallen into place. But even though he and Eddie had inadvertently done Digger a huge favour. There was one thing she told him that sent a chill up Norton's spine. If Digger hadn't turned away just before he came up out of the water to grab Forbes Zaccariah. The bullet intended for Digger's father would have got Les. A few seconds either way and Les would have got his head blown off. Even if she'd missed, she would have seen what happened. What would she have done? Who knows? One thing for sure. He wouldn't be out on the ocean, sitting on her brother's boat looking into those beautiful, green eyes.

'Well Digger,' said Les. 'The first thing I have to tell you, is ... I'm not a deacon in a church.'

The moment Norton said that, the sun came out and caught the shine in Digger's hair, as she tossed her head back and laughed. 'Oh Les,' she said, giving him a gentle slap on the leg. 'I knew that.'

'You did?'

'Yes. When Brendon was in the army. He was stationed at Victoria Barracks for a while. You work at some club in Kings Cross. They thought it was a disco and tried to get in one night when they were drunk. And you told them to ... well you told them they couldn't come in. Brendon never forgets a face.'

Les smiled sheepishly. 'That sounds like the Kelly Club. Me and Billy Dunne.'

'Brendon told me on Saturday morning. That's why I was a little annoyed when you called round. I thought you might have been poking fun at me because of my religious beliefs. But you told me that before I said anything about myself. So I knew you weren't being snide. Even if you were lying.'

'It's just my weird sense of humour,' said Les. 'I'm sorry.'

'In fact after a while I thought it was quite funny. The MOB and all that. So I went along with it. I would have caught you out sooner or later.'

'Sooner or later,' nodded Les.

'But I knew your heart was in the right place,' said Digger. 'And you do think of other people besides yourself.'

'Thanks. But yes. That's me Digger,' confessed Norton. 'I'm no more than a half-baked heavy. Up here on holidays.'

'Who cares,' said Digger. 'I forgive you.'

'Yeah. Who gives a rat's.'

'Not me,' said Digger. 'That's for sure.' She smiled up at Les again. 'Now? What was the second thing you wanted to tell me?'

'The second thing?' Les looked Digger straight in the eyes. They had that angelic look mixed in with the emerald again and Les couldn't help but hesitate for a moment. 'The second thing. Digger. Is. You know when I told you I have to go back to Sydney tomorrow?'

'Yes.'

'Well. I don't have to go back till Wednesday.'

'Is that all?'

Les nodded sincerely. 'Look. I'm not quite sure how to put this Digger, but I started to fall for you.

And I thought. I'll bail out now before I get too involved. Before I get myself trapped. Then when you told me about your father. I knew I couldn't leave. I had to be here for you. Now it's too late. I am trapped. Till Wednesday. Maybe longer.' Les tossed in a bit of little boy lost. 'That's if you still want to see me, of course.'

'If I still want to see you? Oh you big softy, Les. Of course I still want to see you.' Digger's eyes were swimming. 'This is fantastic.'

'That's exactly what I reckon,' said Les. 'And I also reckon. Seeing as we got something to celebrate. And I don't have to get up in the morning. Why don't we all go out tonight and paint the town red?'

Digger put her arms around Norton's neck. 'Well, all I can say to that, Deacon Les. Is you bring the bucket sweetheart. I'll bring the brush.' Les wasn't sure whether to kiss her, say something in return, or what, when Digger pointed excitedly to something in the water. 'Les. Look,' she said.

Norton turned around to see what it was. Swimming near the stern were the mother dolphin and her baby. They'd come over to swim alongside the boat for a moment before they joined the rest of the pod. Les wasn't sure if it was the sun in his eyes, the glare from the water. Or the two tiny rainbows round the dolphins flukes, when they dived under the ocean for the last time. But he could have sworn the mother dolphin winked at them. Whether she did or not. Les definitely winked back at her.

A MESSAGE FROM THE AUTHOR

First up, I want to thank all the people who came to see me on the *Goodoo Goodoo* book tour. It was great to meet my readers again, say hello and sign all the books. I reckon I could write a book on just the people I met. I even met Mrs Les Norton. Mr Norton runs a service station near Geelong. I couldn't believe it. I took a stack of terrific photos. In fact, the photos were that good, Paul B. Kidd used some of them in an article for *Max* magazine and I'm going to put others on the web site. I have to. Especially me with those two laughing sisters in Adelaide. So thanks again to all of you for making a good tour even better.

Now, to all those people writing to the possum lady or clogging up the HarperCollins web site wanting to know about the CD. Well, it's finally done. It's called *Les Norton's King Hits* and it's out now on Festival Records. I have to tell you, there was a giant drama getting this CD together. The wrong track went on it and they all had to be recalled. Then something else and something else stuffed up. So I spat the dummy and wouldn't do any publicity. Which sent all the record company execs' stress levels into hyperspace. But I'm a superstar author. I'm allowed to #@%^*! 'em. Anyway, it's out there. There's still a spelling mistake on the CD. The track by Kevin Borich is supposed to be *Tell Me Why*, not Tell My Why. Nevertheless, I promise you, the CD hoots, honks, howls and hollers. Give it a listen at your favourite record shop and see what you think. If they haven't got it the possum lady will send it out to you for $29.95 including postage. My favourite track is Sleepy LaBeef's *Standing In The Need Of A Prayer*. But I've always been a sucker for honky-tonk piano.

We also got a talking book together: *You Wouldn't Be Dead For Quids* is now available on cassette. I read the first story, Terry Hannagan does the others. Is it any good? All I can say is I played it driving back to Terrigal in my ute and missed the Gosford turnoff I was that surprised. I was halfway to Newcastle before I realised where I was. As further proof, we got a letter from a teacher at Harvey Agricultural High School in WA which said, in parts: 'I purchased the Robert G. Barrett tape for my Year 11/12 reluctant readers. The student response has been excellent. I would be happy to receive any information about similar tapes/CDs.' So how about that? If your local bookshop hasn't got any, the possum lady can mail you these out too for $21.95. I know this sounds like a bit of a sales pitch, but we're only trying to help those who want them, and I honestly believe the CDs and talking books are pretty good value.

But hey! That's not all. We're now working on *The Les Norton Pretty Grouse Cookbook*. I couldn't get two fat ladies, but I found one lean, mean sheila up my way who is the ultimate kitchen Nazi. Wait till you taste Les Norton's Root Soup, Bundaberg Rum Mud Crab Boogie Cake or Grungle Lamb Rissoles. To quote Raymond Chandler, 'It'd make a bishop kick a hole in a stained-glass window.' That should be ready by next winter.

To all those people kind enough to write to me, I'm doing my best to reply. But there's a stack of letters there Emma George couldn't jump over. It just takes time. However, make sure you put your address on the letter as well as the envelope. The possum lady's just had the tattoos burnt off her knuckles and it all got infected. So between the bandages and when she gets the shakes the next day after a night on the plonk, she gets the envelopes mixed up. And if I don't have your address, you've got Buckley's of getting a reply. And I honestly do my best to answer your letters. Not only because I love to hear from my readers, but when I'm on tour and people come up and say they wrote to me then thank me for writing back, it's a nice feeling all round. Just be patient though.

Also, the possum lady said to say hello and there's heaps of T-shirts and caps and things available. We've even got black T-shirts available now. Especially for those rockers who bailed me up in Geelong. Just write to her at:

Psycho Possum Productions
PO Box 3348
Tamarama NSW 2026

Or look her up on the web site:

http://www.robertgbarrett.com.au

On another note, if you're ever up the Central Coast and you happen to make it down to Avoca Beach at the south end near the surf club, you'll see a brand new surfboat called *Les Norton*. Psycho Possum Productions, on behalf of myself, the possum lady and the people who buy my books, have shouted Avoca Surf Club a new surfboat. They're a good bunch of men and women who do an excellent job and they're very competitive as well. They do it all for nothing. So we decided to do our bit too. Say hello to the crew and the rest of the members. They're friendly folk and they'd love to meet you too. Bring your camera and get your photo taken next to the boat, you'd be lucky to find a more beautiful place to have your photo taken than Avoca Beach.

So that's about it for the time being. I hope you liked *The Wind and the Monkey*. Les and I will catch up with you in the next book. Thanks.

Robert G. Barrett

Available now

GOODOO GOODOO

Robert G. Barrett

Wolfman Les — Rock'n'Roll DJ.

Another good idea down the gurgler ...

What should have been a quick gig on a radio station followed by a whitewater rafting holiday in Cairns finishes up a mud-soaked four-wheel drive trip to Cooktown with Norton looking for two missing scuba divers! The army, the air force and half the Queensland water police couldn't find the two missing divers. So what chance does Les have?

Along the way Les meets a kooky little space cadet who spends her time chasing UFO's and predicting the future; man-eating crocodiles; heat and humidity; and strangers everywhere out for his blood. Then, in a place of indescribable beauty, he uncovers unimaginable terror ...

From FM radio to FN Queensland, *Goodoo Goodoo* is a roller-coaster ride of thrills and spills and shows once again why Robert G. Barrett is one of Australia's most popular contemporary authors.

ISBN: 0 7322 6737 4

MUD CRAB BOOGIE
Robert G. Barrett

Les caught the DJ's eye. 'Hey mate,' he said. 'If I give you ten bucks, will you play two songs for me?'

'Mate,' replied the DJ. 'For ten bucks, I'll play you Tiny Tim singing *A Pub With No Beer* in Vietnamese.'

Look out Wagga Wagga, Les Norton's in town and he feels like dancing.

Extreme Polo. The wildest game on water. That's what it said on TV. All Les had to do was drive down to Wagga Wagga for an old mate who owed him a favour, Neville (Nizegy) Nixon, and pick up the Murrumbidgee Mud Crabs. Then keep them at Coogee till they played the Sydney Sea Snakes in the grand final at Homebush Aquatic Centre. And naturally there would be a giant earn in it for him. Why not? thought Les, he had the week off from work.

Next thing, Norton was on his way to the Riverina to meet the locals, the lovelies and oogie, oogie, oogie — do the Mud Crab Boogie.

ISBN: 0 7322 5843 X

Available now

SO WHAT DO YOU RECKON?
Robert G. Barrett

There was a time when Robert G. Barrett was 'in his forties, out of gaol, out of work, had three books published, but was stone motherless broke'. Political correctness had him confused and he had no desire to be more literary, even if he was the author of books that had been described as 'the scatological nadir of the pile' and 'insidiously revolting ... pray God they don't get published overseas'.

Then, through a twist of fate and good fortune, along came *People* magazine, who signed Barrett to produce a weekly column focusing on Australian life and its heroes and villains. *So What Do You Reckon?* is a collection of the best of these columns. Many are outrageous and all are written in Barrett's highly popular and immediately recognisable style. Together they represent an often funny, always entertaining and uniquely telling assessment of modern-day Australia.

ISBN: 0 7322 5961 4

Available now

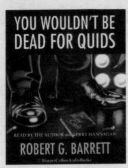

YOU WOULDN'T BE DEAD FOR QUIDS — Audio book
Read by Robert G. Barrett and Terry Hannagan

Robert G. Barrett's Les Norton novels have made him Australia's favourite contemporary author. Now, for the very first time, he reads a selection of stories from the book that started his phenomenal success ...

As far as fighting went, Les wasn't really a scientific fighter and for all he knew the Marquis of Queensberry could have been a hotel in Parramatta. Whenever Les went off it was anything goes ...

Look out Sydney — Les Norton has just hit town. *You Wouldn't Be Dead For Quids* is a series of adventures involving Les, a big, red-headed country boy from Queensland who is forced to move to the big smoke when things get a little hot for him in his home town.

Working as a bouncer at an illegal casino up at the Cross, Les gets to meet some of the fascinating characters who make up the seamier side of one of the most exciting cities in the world — gamblers, con men, bookies, bouncers, hookers and hitmen, who ply their respective trades from the golden sands of Bondi to the tainted gutters of Kings Cross ... on the wrong side of the law.

As raw as a greyhound's dinner, Les is nevertheless a top bloke — fond of a drink, loves a laugh and he's handy with his fists. And, just quietly, he's a bit of a ladies man, too.

2 tapes; abridged; approx. 3 hours listening.

ISBN: 0 7322 5272 5

Available now

Les Norton's King Hits

LES NORTON'S KING HITS

A word or two from Robert G. Barrett:

'If you're wondering about this CD or maybe thinking of buying it, please be advised Les is not a singer or a musician. He's a fictitious character in a series of books, and being the author, I can assure you Les Norton couldn't carry a note if it had handles. Les is lucky if he can talk in key, let alone sing, but he likes music and through the books he comes in contact with a lot of music. Not mainstream music or music you mostly hear on the radio, this is your classic stuff — rhythm and blues, reggae, rock ballads etc. Music that doesn't give you GBH of the earhole! So that's the story behind this compilation, a bunch of good songs that have appeared throughout my many books that are now featured on this CD, *Les Norton's King Hits*.

'Now to all those lovely people that read my books. Instead of the usual media push of "you've read the book, now see the movie", this is "you've read the book, now hear the music". These are some of the songs you talk to me about when I'm signing at book launches. For example, the Adam Brand song playing on a jukebox in a bar in Cooktown when Les had to fight the three mugs — it's here on the CD, plus many, many more. I call them "odd shaped" music that fits an occasion! I hope you enjoy the music as much as me and our old mate Les Norton, and after listening to this CD, maybe you'll agree that for a rough diamond, Les Norton hasn't got too bad a taste in music!'

© 1999 (this compilation) Festival Records Pty Ltd, Australia.